CAUGHT BETWEEN TWO
PAGANS

TREASURE OF THE RAVEN KING
book two

I0549788

C. WAYNE DAWSON

A Division of Y&R Enterprises, LLC
PO Box 2283
Lindale, TX 75771

Book design by Champagne Formats
Cover design by Simply Defined Art

Library of Congress Control Number Data
Dawson, C.Wayne
Caught Between Two Pagans/ C. Wayne, Dawson
Historical—Fiction.2. Military—Thriller—Fiction.
Fiction. | BISAC: FICTION / Historical.
LOC: 2017938943

ISBN: 978-1-940460-77-2

www.cwaynedawson.com

Books by C. Wayne Dawson

Treasure of the Raven King Series:

Vienna's Last Jihad (Prequel)
The Darkness That Could Be Felt (Book I)
Caught Between Two Pagans (Book II)

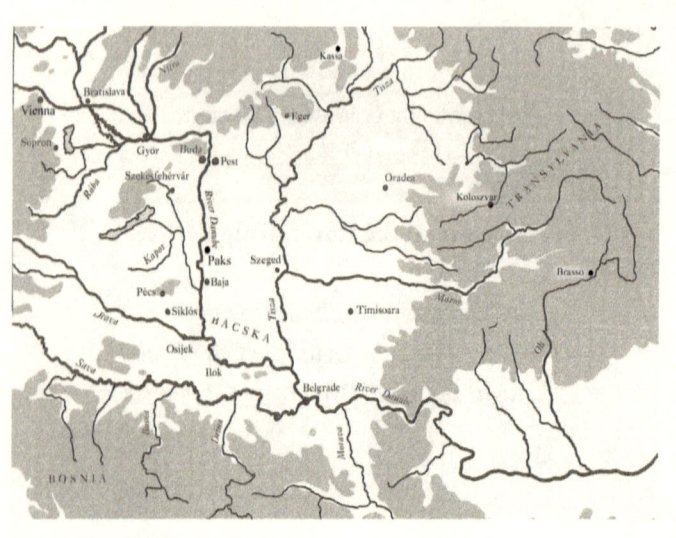

In 1684, Captain Mathis Zieglar and Sarah Oppenheimer, a brilliant Jewish temptress, are close to discovering the location of the Treasure of the Raven King. The documents they've uncovered will now empower them to free hundreds of hostages from Ottoman slavery. If they make the secret public, they will betray their emperor and country. Are they willing to risk everything to save others they've never met?

Caught Between Two Pagans begins where the last book in the series, *The Darkness That Could Be Felt,* ends. Mathis Zieglar is alone in the cell that once held Vlad Dracula. By feeling his way along the engravings in the wall, he pieces together clues concerning the location of the treasure. But in order to recover the secret, he must combine his knowledge with information held by Sarah Oppenheimer, a bewitching and brilliant beauty who keeps her own secrets.

Together, the two must brave the intrigues of the Church and travel through a country in the midst of a Catholic/Muslim war to obtain the treasure. As the inhabitants describe the conflict, they are "caught between two pagans."

Mathis and Sarah's last chance to rescue the hostages ends at a farm hiding an alchemist's laboratory and the secret it contains. A secret the sultan and the emperor would kill for.

CHAPTER ONE

September, 1526
Twenty-Five miles North of Buda, Hungary

Ezra Mendel looked nervously over his shoulder. There was no sign of anyone following him, but that didn't mean there wasn't. Only an hour ago, he had evaded a band of ragged deserters by slipping into the forest. The group must have been one of the few to escape the slaughter of the Hungarian army by the Turks. Such survivors could be counted on to vent their frustrations on Jews like himself.

He urged the donkeys pulling his little wagon forward, striking them with the end of a switch. One brayed in protest.

"Stop hitting, Ezra," his wife Rebecca pleaded. "Why are you in such a hurry? Visegrad will be there tomorrow."

"Take some herbal tea and relax." He ran his hand through his hair. "Remember the promise I made to Grandfather Jakob on his deathbed?"

"Yes, yes. You promised to leave a written record to

1

help your family find Matthias Corvinus's secret. But can't you just tell them where it is? *Oy*! Why all this extra effort?"

"Why must I repeat this, woman? There are too many rumors the Turks will exile Buda's Jews to Ottoman lands. If the Mendel family leaves Hungary, they'll forget everything in a generation. Our family's legacy is at stake."

Rebecca rolled her eyes. "Please, husband. People who memorize the entire *Torah* should remember the king's message is hidden inside the palace doors. It doesn't need to be written in stone."

Ezra waved the comment off like a circling wasp. "My grandfather could see the future like a prophet. He knew those doors could be removed from the palace and end up anywhere once the King passed away." He faced Rebecca, keeping a tight grip on the reins. "Think about it. Who knows how many years will pass before the Mendel family returns to Buda, if ever? Legends grow and change over the years. Important information must be written down, like in the *Torah*. The written word is everything."

"I don't like taking risks, Ezra. Let's go back to Buda, be with our family. And stop repeating 'think about it.' It's annoying."

"Some risks have to be taken." Ezra pointed his finger at her. "Like grandfather Jakob said, 'Whoever holds the Raven King's secret will become the sultan's master."

Rebecca dragged her hands down her cheeks. "So you think you'll become the sultan's master? That's what this is all about? I'm getting ill."

"Think about it. The *Mishneh Torah* is one of the greatest works of literature in Judaism, and this edition is especially valuable because of the secret code written inside it. If the Mendel family has something to remind them this book is inside the doors, all they have to do is keep track of where the doors are. Even if Sultan Suleiman removes our people like he will everything else in Buda. Then we wait for the right time to take them."

"I thought about it," Rebecca mocked. "You're playing with fire, Ezra. Don't vex a Turk, let alone the sultan."

The wagon cleared a bend in the road, and Ezra stopped the donkey. In the distance, a sharp mountain pierced the sky. Midway to its peak, a walled city nestled on a plateau and commanded the Danube rolling beneath it.

He raised both hands. "We're almost there, Rebecca!"

Rebecca's jaw hardened into stone. "Did you remember to bring your tools?"

Ezra reached back into a compartment behind their bench rummaging through their supplies. He raised his head to scan the area, wary that the bandits might return. "This is a shame and a disgrace. I *know* I packed them! Where are they?"

Rebecca gazed at his feet. She pursed her lips in a coy smirk and pointed to a box under his legs. "Try there, Master of the Sultan."

Ezra reached in and pulled out a package of wrapped linen swaddling hiding his chisel and hammer. "All right, then. This is all I need. This, and a few hours in the Tower of Solomon."

"And how do you think you'll get in there, Mr. Master?"

"Leave that to me." Ezra patted a bag attached to his belt. It jingled. "Just have to *schlep the gelt*."

"Bribing someone is your answer to everything."

He worked his finger up and down. "Watch your tone. Respect our family's sacred mission."

"But of course, Master of the Sultan."

Ezra rolled his eyes heavenward. "Forgive her, Grandfather Jakob. Your promise to the Raven King remains safe."

Friday, June 16, 1684. One hundred fifty-eight years later
Visegrad, Hungary

"Wake up, infidel.

Frigid water splashed in his face, pulling Mathis Zieglar from an uncomfortable sleep on the prison floor.

"You have work to do." Kamil sneered at him.

The man had thrown him into this dark prison cell and abandoned him only hours before, seemingly with the intent of letting him die.

Sprawled on the floor, Mathis wiped the water off his brow, and painfully twisted his head toward the door. His body throbbed in pain and ached from the cannon balls that had exploded close to his cell and knocked him into one of the walls. Piles of rubble and dirt littered his tiny cell, debris from the crumbling prison. His voice crackled. "Why did you lock me in here? All I did was ask to see the cell where Vlad Dracula had been held."

"Because the *Aga* ordered it. Now he commands your release so you can negotiate for us."

"Negotiate? With whom?"

"Your commander."

Kamil clinked a key into the door's lock. "On our way to see him, you'll tell me what you found in your cell. And the honor you promised it would bring me."

He helped Mathis to his feet and gave him a staff to

4

lean on. After a few wobbly steps, Mathis' head cleared. He spoke through clenched teeth. "All I can tell you…is I've found out… there's a treasure…hidden…in the royal palace of Buda. When you get me there…you'll hear the rest of the story."

Kamil took a torch from the stone wall and brought it close to Mathis' face. "I've risked my life to get you released. Tell me about this treasure and what Dracula's cell has to do with it."

Mathis hesitated. He couldn't reveal the book he was looking for, the *Mishneh Torah*, contained a hidden message proving the sultan was descended from a line of imposters. Disclosing that would insure the Mohammedans would never let him leave Visegrad alive. He had to buy enough time to escape with his neck intact. It was the only way he could get to the treasure and use it to bargain for the hundreds of Christian slaves held captive by the Muslims.

Mathis moaned and slumped against the wall. "I can't think straight. Need something to drink."

Kamil gripped Mathis by the throat and slammed him back against the wall. "Answer my questions, or I'll slit your neck and tell the commander you died of your injuries."

"All right," Mathis croaked. "Calm down. Let me sit a moment."

Kamil allowed him to slide to the floor. "Wait here, infidel. You're obviously too weak to talk." He put the torch back on the wall and disappeared.

Mathis realized he had to make it so no one could look inside Dracula's cell and read the code etched into the wall. Otherwise, the Mohammedans might put two and two together, locate the treasure in Buda and destroy it. Using his heel, he pushed away a heap of rubble. It would only be a matter of time before the bombardment resumed.

Stretching his leg out, he relaxed a minute despite the aches throbbing throughout his body—a result of the concussions that had blown him from one side of the jail to the other. The debris on the floor was exactly what he needed.

Grunting, he made a pile from the rubble and wrung water from his greatcoat over it. Soon, he had two handfuls of mud and gravel. Struggling to his feet, he grabbed the torch from its brace and walked back into the cell. He steadied himself against the wall. One hand felt the two sentences carved into the stone: "Read ye Bonfini's epigram and find the treasure's home. The writings of the sage are inside the hard substance that opens wide."

Fortunately, he had memorized the epigram that Bonfini, Corvinus's court historian, had inscribed over the door to the royal palace in Buda: "The hall with statues cast from bronze and doors proclaim the genius of Prince Corvinus. That Corvinus should perish, after gaining so many triumphs over the enemy, his virtue, bronze, marble and writings forbid."

Had he reached the right conclusion? Yes, of course he had. 'The hard substance that opens wide' must refer to the doors that stood at the entrance to the palace. The beautiful bronze doors whose panels were adorned with the labors of Hercules. Hercules, revered by the Greeks as a demi-god. The panels must contain the treasure, the copy of *The Mishneh Torah* that contained the secret message. He sighed. Now, all he had to do was to get past the Mohammedan army in Buda and extract the book from the doors. Perhaps God would first send a plague there and make his life easier.

Footsteps sounded outside the tower. Kamil.

Mathis quickly plugged the carvings with his makeshift paste of dirt and rubble, leaving only "The writings of the sage are inside the hard substance" exposed. The grungy mud blended with the grey stone and covered the etchings. It would be unlikely someone would detect the last part of the sentence reading 'that opens wide'. The fragment was critical, since it revealed to Mathis the treasure was in the palace's bronze doors.

He hobbled out to the hallway where Kamil had left him. Before resuming his position on the floor, Mathis put the torch back on the wall. He sat down just as his jailer emerged from the stairwell, holding a ceramic container in one hand and a stout candle in the other.

Kamil laid the candle on a pillar at the top of the stairs and handed him the flask. "Take this."

Something sweet and delicious trickled down his throat. He licked his lips. "Do I taste blackberry juice?"

Kamil gave a wry smile. "That and other things to stimulate your tongue. Now talk."

From his experience as an army interrogator, Mathis knew his best chance of keeping Kamil in the dark was to mix truth with error.

"There wasn't much to learn." Mathis pointed to Dracula's cell. "Putting together what I've read in there and from different sources, I think the book I'm looking for is in the palace in Buda. The sentence on the wall says the book is inside the hard substance in the palace."

Kamil snorted. "That says very little. There must be all kinds of 'hard substances' in the palace."

"True. But the other sources imply marble. The question is, how much of it survived Sultan Suleiman?"

Kamil took the flask back. "God's blessed caliph,

Suleiman the Lawgiver. You refer to when he occupied Buda over a century ago? I doubt if he left much of the material from the royal palace behind."

He reached inside a pouch strapped to his waist and pulled out another cup. He took the flask from Mathis and poured a drink for himself. "How will this precious secret bring me honor?" he mocked.

Mathis racked his mind for something to say, something that wouldn't give too much information away. "What if you discovered your enemies knew a secret that would put the sultan's life in jeopardy? What do you think would happen if you brought this knowledge to him in time to save his life? Imagine the reward."

Kamil sputtered disdainfully. "You must have drank wine inside that room. There is no such secret and you know it. Besides, why would I want to do business with a man that destroyed the profitable coffee trade Davudoff and I arranged? You've cost me a fortune."

Mathis didn't want to focus the conversation on how he recently helped break up the smuggling operation carried on by Kamil and his friend, Davudoff. Mathis had discovered the two of them smuggling fertile coffee beans out of the Ottoman empire, a capital crime, and trading them with people connected to the Holy Roman Emperor, Leopold I.

Mathis waved his hand. "No such secret? Would I have gone to all this trouble to risk my life for nothing?"

Kamil's eyes narrowed. "You have killed too many Muslims to hand over such information. Why do you want to help people you hate?"

"Because I made a vow to the people of my village I would rescue their women and children from bondage." Mathis raised his palms to calm Kamil. "After I've uncovered the proof, I'll trade the information to you for their freedom. You know the importance of fulfilling a vow, don't you?"

Kamil's eyes relaxed. "I understand you are obsessed with freeing slaves that belong to us. Nevertheless, I will give you the opportunity to prove your sincerity." He unsheathed his scimitar and raised the point under Mathis' chin. "Ample opportunity."

Kamil then pointed his sword toward the stairs. "Report to the *Aga*, now. He awaits us in the citadel that overlooks the city." He paused. "How much of this information is written on the cell walls?"

"Just 'The writings of the sage are inside the hard substance.'"

Kamil grabbed his candle. When he retreated into the cell, Mathis' heart hammered in his chest.

Attempting to disguise his fear, Mathis gave a wicked laugh. "What's the matter, Kamil, don't trust me?"

The cannons beneath the city boomed once again with a new bombardment. The walls shook and dirt fell from the ceiling.

Kamil muttered something, then raised his voice. "Let us go. We will have to discuss this further for it to make sense. Mind your tongue when we meet the *Aga*. Show him the proper respect due to one who holds your fate in his hands."

June, 1684, Twenty miles from Visegrad near the Southern banks of the Danube River.

The birds welcomed the morning light when Sarah

9

Oppenheimer heard a rustle outside her tent. Lacing her bodice as quickly as possible, she pushed the door flaps open. The dark eyes of a muscular, bearded man stopped her in her tracks.

"You have something that belongs to me." He pointed an angry finger at her. "I want it back."

"What are you talking about?" She turned, but he grabbed her wrist.

"Your cousin stole a *ferman* from Adam Mendel, then you helped yourself to a page sewn in the binding. I want that sheet."

Sarah squirmed in his grasp. The scent of blood on his coarse black tunic filled her with terror. "My cousin stole nothing! That proclamation from the sultan was sold to him."

"Take your hands off her." Simon Oppenheimer approached a few yards away, waving his hands. "I purchased the document for a fair price. It wasn't stolen."

The stranger swung Sarah around and held a blade at her throat. "Do you want to argue or save her life?"

Simon's face blanched and he held up pleading hands. "Please be calm. We mean you no harm. Why does this paper mean so much to you?"

Sarah sunk her nails into the man's arm. She screamed until he clamped her mouth shut.

When Simon stepped toward them, the man pressed the knife against Sarah's windpipe. "Come any closer, Oppenheimer, and I'll slit her throat!"

Sarah tasted salt from the man's palm. When one of his fingers moved over her mouth, she bit down hard. He yelped, and pulled his hand away.

"Simon, can you see his knife?"

"Barely."

The man tried to press his hand over her lips again but she swung her head up.

"Is the end square or pointed?"

Simon pushed his looking glasses closer to his eyes and squinted. "Square."

"Idiots!" The assailant growled. "Get back or I'll rip her neck open."

Sarah relaxed her grip on the assailant's arm and chuckled. "You have no intention of slitting my throat, *Mein Herr*. Why don't you take the *chalaf* from my neck and explain what's really going on?"

The man heaved exasperation and lowered his blade. "Why didn't I let a *goy* handle this? How did you know I was a Jew?"

"Because only a kosher butcher uses a square-edged knife, the *chalaf*." Sarah untangled herself from the stranger's arms. "And I tasted the salt on your finger used for curing meat. You're a Jew, like us."

Simon scowled and wagged his finger at the man. "What kind of a Jew are you? Why would you threaten to kill another Jew?"

The man hung his head. "I am as much a Jew as you. I was just trying to scare you into giving me the paper."

"So you were deceitful. Ach," Simon spat his disdain. "Have you never read the Torah? 'Ye shall not steal, neither deal falsely, neither lie one to another.'"

Still grasping the *chalaf*, the stranger flipped his free hand up. "Have you never read the Talmud? Lying is permitted if there is no other way to ensure peace. I did what I must to protect Jewish lives."

Sarah held up her hands and spread them apart.

11

"Enough, you two! Stop the disputing. You sound like a couple of rabbis."

She turned to the stranger. "Who are you, and why are you here?"

"My name is Nathan Mendel."

"Mendel!" Sarah gasped. "Are you related to the Adam Mendel that sold the *ferman* to my cousin, Simon? The descendant of Jakob Mendel, friend of Matthias Corvinus, the Raven King?"

"I am Adam's cousin. And yes, Jakob was our ancestor of honored memory." He raised the *chalaf* and waved it at Simon. "Adam had no business selling you that document. It belonged to the Mendel family."

Simon raised his shoulders. "How was I to know?"

"You had the *ferman* returned to a relative of mine, a man called Davudoff. But not before you ripped out a sheet from the binding and stole it."

Simon shook his head. "Why should we believe this message was meant for you, considering how you've already deceived us?"

Mendel ignored the challenge and continued. "You shared the paper's information with Mathis Zieglar, captain in the Habsburg army. Thanks to you, he figured out the meaning hidden inside the poem. He was last seen heading for Visegrad, where Vlad Dracula's old prison cell is. If Zieglar reads the information inscribed into the walls, and puts it together with the information from that poem, he'll know too much about the treasure of the Raven King, Matthias Corvinus. That will be bad for Judaism."

Simon stroked his beard but his voice trembled. "I did not knowingly steal anything. Threatening my cousin with a weapon is not the way to settle a matter."

Mendel swung the *chalaf* so wildly Sarah took three steps back. His face reddened and his voice cracked. "The parchment belongs to the Mendel family. Give it back, now!"

Alarmed voices rose from a few tents away. Sarah hoped it came from soldiers who'd come and arrest Mendel. Perhaps she could delay him so they could squeeze more facts from him. "There, there, *Herr* Mendel. I'm sure we can reach an accommodation. Give me a chance to unstrap a few bags and see if I can locate the paper you want."

She pulled her skirt up, kneeled on the ground, and rummaged fretfully through her baggage. "Where did I leave that paper? I know it's got to be here."

Mendel's eyes darted left and right as the voices grew nearer. "If you want to see your friend Zieglar alive again, you'll leave it on your person. Keep it ready to hand over when we come back. I guarantee the next man asking for it won't be a Jew, and he won't stop until you release it."

He slunk away, casting nervous glances in different directions. "Remember to keep it ready," he hissed before disappearing behind a row of tents.

Sarah's knees went weak. Despite the fact the knife was no longer at her throat, she began to shake. Simon made the unusual gesture of wrapping an arm around her shoulder. "There, there. The fool has left."

As the shock of the incident wore off, something else made Sarah's spine tingle. The last she had heard, Captain Zieglar had disappeared when a Muslim raiding party struck against his regiment days ago. She was relieved to learn he was still alive, but he was obviously in danger.

"Why so downcast, cousin?" Simon's fidgety voice had calmed somewhat.

Sarah's eyes seemed to burn in their sockets. "We… we can't let them kill Captain Zieglar, Simon. We'll have to give in to Mendel's demands." She had tried to deny her feelings for Mathis, a man outside her faith. But deep down, she knew she would walk barefoot over a road of broken glass to save him.

Simon dismissed her with a wave of his hand. "Have you forgotten how Zieglar went back on his promise to help us find the treasure? We owe him nothing."

"He apologized for misleading us. He didn't know how to explain he intended to use the treasure to rescue women and children from the Muslim slavers. He was afraid if he told us the truth he would endanger them. That doesn't make him evil."

"Hmpf! Our first duty is to preserve *tradition*. Finding the treasure will restore part of that *tradition*. Without *tradition* there can be no covenant. Without the covenant, there is no Israel."

Sarah persisted in a calm but determined voice. "*Tradition*, Cousin Simon? Like the *tradition* of mercy? 'What does the Lord require of thee, but to do justly, and to love mercy, and to walk humbly with thy God?' Is this not our *tradition*?"

Simon grew red in the face and sputtered. "It is not fitting that a woman should quote Scripture to a man!"

"I'm sorry, cousin. Shall we have a rabbi settle the matter, instead? Might we ask him if it is appropriate to help someone like Captain Zieglar? The man who saved your father's life when the Mohammedans attempted to assassinate him?"

"You will not surrender that paper to a man holding a knife to your throat."

"Far be it from me to propose such a thing." She allowed a smile. "However, I know you won't disregard the wishes of your father, Samuel, either. He commanded us to cooperate with the captain, didn't he? Surely he would expect you to save Captain Zieglar's life."

Simon's face ripened all the more. He looked skyward and groaned. "Blessed are you, Lord, our God, ruler of the universe who has not created me a woman."

Barely suppressing a laugh, Sarah ignored the dig. Whenever her cousin quoted that verse from the Talmud, it was a sign he was at his wit's end and she had won. But something nagged her about the conversation with Mendel. "Cousin, you remember how Captain Zieglar and I decoded the poem written on the paper?"

"Again with the bragging. Now I'll hear about how it was your discovery that some kind of writing in the Tower of Solomon will lead us to the treasure. What kind of treasure is the *Mishneh Torah* if Zieglar has no intention of turning it over? What good is such a discovery?"

She knew Simon was just blowing off steam. She folded her hands as she often did when she had something serious to say. "The fact that we're about to find such an important book means it's no longer lost–and that's important. But, there's something else we should talk about before we forget."

She smoothed the hair falling over her shoulders. "Doesn't it strike you as strange if Mendel already knew what the poem said he would risk his life to retrieve it? Are we missing something?"

Simon shrugged. "He probably didn't want someone

15

outside his family knowing about the secret."

"Hmmm. It's too late for that. Captain Zieglar *does* know the secret, and Mendel knows it. Something doesn't make sense. I want to take a second look at the paper."

CHAPTER TWO

South bank of the Danube, with General Halliweil's regiment

"I JUST DON'T TRUST THOSE REPORTS, GENERAL."

Sarah looked up and stopped stirring the bubbling pot. Instead of being a dragoon, she wished Mathis was a cavalryman and wore the *cuirass* similar to the officer's in front of her. An armored breastplate and back plate would keep Mathis safer in battle.

The officer waved his hand impatiently at Simon, who sat only feet away. "Stop worrying, *Herr* Oppenheimer. Reduce the supplies you're ordering. Count von Mercy scouts informed us there aren't more than eight thousand Mohammedans between here and Buda. Our army will march through the infidels as if we were on a Sunday stroll to church."

"Are you sure about this, General Halliweil?" Simon questioned. "Why would the Mohammedans leave such an important city like Buda so lightly defended?"

"Quite sure, *Herr* Oppenheimer. We must watch

expenses and cut back. Those are my orders."

The general strode to his horse held by a waiting escort. "*Auf Weidersehen*" he bade Simon as he mounted.

As they rode off, Sarah scowled at the general's boast to his men about not giving "any more *kreutzers* to that money-changer than necessary."

After Simon had related their encounter with Mendel to General Halliweil, Sarah took grim satisfaction the commander posted a guard near their tent. Never mind that the private only carried a small thrusting sword and appeared so emaciated, a strong wind would blow him back to Vienna. Yet, he was better than nothing.

Simon sat down on a log, opened a record book and shook his head. Sarah approached him. "You look troubled, cousin."

"Mmm." He didn't look up.

"By the way, I knitted the tears in a sergeant's uniform yesterday. He told me something interesting about Count von Mercy, the officer in charge of reconnaissance."

Simon raised a reluctant brow. "And "

"Our count has only been in the army two years. Not exactly a seasoned veteran."

"You find this interesting? The army has lost so many officers during last year's siege that half of them are now brand new."

She sat beside him. "True. So what do you believe—the report of an inexperienced officer, or your inner feeling that says something doesn't ring true? The army will surely face more Mohammedans than the general thinks. They need more supplies."

Simon slapped the book shut. "Can't you see this is a military matter, woman? Men's business."

"I understand, cousin." She rose. "Forgive me for intruding."

Simon grunted and reopened his book.

She turned to leave, then stopped. "Oh, I forgot. As a champion chess player, maybe you can answer a question."

He sighed. "What is it now?"

"If you began a game, with all your important pieces on the board, would you leave your king unguarded?"

Simon shook his head again. "You're as subtle as a trumpet. So, you agree with me the Mohammedans won't leave Buda guarded as lightly as the count would have us believe?"

Sarah smiled. "You have such a quick grasp of matters."

"Hmpf." He went inside his tent and returned with a quill and an inkwell. "Just like you to get me in trouble." He stared hard at Sarah. "Why should I risk offending General Halliweil? Because of your intuition?"

"Cousin, do you remember my friend from Heidelberg, Hans the fishmonger?"

"*Ja, ja*. What does a fishmonger have to do with a military matter?"

"Many times, my father Abraham said 'Sarah, no more fish for the week. The budget will not allow it.' But the family would go hungry without some." She ignored Simon's wry look of exasperation, and continued. "Of course, I wanted to honor my father, but Abraham ordered this when the price of fish was so low it was a sin not to buy. So this is what I did "

"Enough with the parables, *Fraulein* Aesop!"

"I told Hans to keep the fish alive in the water a few days by leaving them on a chain until I returned and paid him. That way, I always kept our family well fed and within

19

the weekly allowance. *And* I honored my father. Do you see something worthwhile in my story, Simon?"

"I am not going to contract with a fishmonger, Sarah."

She shook her head. "Simon, Simon. Order a fleet of supply barges to wait at the town ten leagues upstream so the general can't accuse you of overstocking food-stuffs. If your calculations are correct, and there are more Mohammedans about to attack us than General Halliweil suspects, you can call the barges to the front lines when needed. That would make you a hero."

Simon sat motionless, seemingly unable to speak. He put the quill down and reverted to his nervous habit of striking his little finger with the index finger of his opposite hand. "Remind me to never play chess with you, woman."

■ ■ ■

The *Aga* extended his ring finger toward Mathis.

"Kneel." Kamil pushed Mathis' shoulder down. His knees struck the stone floor and he winced.

Grimacing, the Austrian lifted the commander's be-jeweled ring and kissed it. "Your Excellency."

The *Aga* was a short and stocky man with a close-cut, dark beard. He struggled with Mathis' name. "I want you to ask the Habsburg commander for a cease fire…Z-Z-Zee-gar."

Mathis bowed his head. "It would give me pleasure, excellent *Aga*."

He expected to be ordered to rise, but instead the *Aga* continued. "What is your business with Dracula? He's been dead for well over a century. And what did you expect to find when you went in the tower?"

The pain in Mathis's knees reminded him he kneeled

20

on paving stones. "May I rise and answer your question?"

"Answer from where you are."

Perspiration formed on Mathis' temples, not just from the weight of his bruised body on a hard surface. "I am a former professor of Middle Eastern languages at the University of Vienna. Recently, I came across a message that said Dracula's cell contained a message leading to an ancient treasure."

"Continue, Z-Z-Zee-gar."

"Unfortunately, all I found in the cell was a sentence that read 'The writings of the sage are inside the hard substance '"

"He's not telling you everything, Excellent One."

Mathis snapped his head around. His jaw dropped as Kamil spoke.

"The treasure Zieglar speaks about is inside a hard substance found somewhere in Buda." He slapped the back of Mathis' head. "The infidel thought he could bribe me into silence."

Mathis noticed Kamil omitted the part about the marble inside the royal palace. But why did he even repeat part of what Mathis had told him? He was obviously trying to make himself look heroic at Mathis's expense. But it risked everything Mathis had shared with Kamil.

The *Aga* looked amused. "Indeed?"

"Yes. He said he would share a secret that would save the sultan's life."

"Treasure inside Buda, much of which has laid in ruins for over a century? An infidel who would save the Holy One's life?" First, the *Aga* broke into uncontrolled laughter, then Kamil. They pointed their fingers at one another and their bellies shook until they seemed to exhaust

21

themselves. Then one would snort again and trigger the other. Finally, the *Aga* regained his composure. "Where did you find this lunatic, Kamil? Should I have someone beat the soles of his feet, or just have him impaled?"

"Neither of those solutions will stop the Habsburgs from bombarding you." Scowling, Mathis rose to his feet and looked at the hint of sunrise on the horizon. "It will be daylight soon. You'd better let me carry out your message of surrender while you still have a garrison."

Someone pushed Mathis to his knees again. He skidded along the paving stones and almost fell over. His knee socks warmed from the friction.

The *Aga* looked on him with pity and contempt. "Or perhaps I should lock him back up and let him waste away."

Dressed in a towering *bork* bonnet, a janissary officer approached the commander and bowed. "Most Excellent *Aga*, the Christians are preparing their guns to resume their barrage."

The words had no sooner left his lips than a battery of cannon below the city battered the walls with a fiery salvo. A series of crashes erupted from the outer ramparts below, spraying debris in their direction. When the smoke cleared, rubble slid from two places in the masonry.

"Put that dog on his feet." The *Aga* raised his finger at Mathis. "Tell your leader he can fire at us all he wants, but in the end, he and his men will have to enter Visegrad and fight us man to man. If he doesn't want the streets to run with blood, he better negotiate."

Soldiers shouted desperate curses in Serbian as they scurried to their battle stations. Another barrage fell into the city and rained fragments on the *Aga* and Mathis. Smoke poured out of buildings.

"I'll need to carry a white flag to keep myself from getting shot." Mathis brushed himself off. "Have another one waved from the outer wall ramparts. I can't leave until the bombardment stops."

"You will do whatever the *Aga* commands." Kamil stormed toward Mathis with an opened hand, ready to slap him again. "And you will speak with respect."

The *Aga* waved him off. "Give the infidel his flag and a torch. Release him as soon as the sun rises."

Kamil accompanied Mathis to the gate. "If you want to keep your little filly alive, you'll help me find this so-called treasure," he whispered.

"Little filly?" Mathis frowned, confused at another turn-around in Kamil's interest in the treasure. "Who are you talking about?"

"You and I both know of your desire for the Oppenheimer woman."

"You're despicable," Mathis growled, thinking of his late wife's death. Then he smirked. "What would you know of a man's love for a woman? You're too busy longing for your friend, Davudoff."

"What do you know about my tastes?" Kamil raised a mocking brow. "You're too busy dreaming about senseless women."

Shortly after Ottoman soldiers raised a white flag from the city walls, the Habsburg artillerymen stopped the cannonade. Bruised and smarting, waving his white flag, Mathis hobbled down the mountain into a huge garden area where the Habsburg army had dug in.

He hailed a squad of musketeers loading their weapons behind an earthen redoubt. "My name is Captain Mathis Zieglar, and I must speak to Duke Charles of Lorraine."

"Not when you look like that." One of them pulled a cloth out of his back pocket, and handed it to Mathis. "Clean your face before the field marshal sees you."

Two of them escorted him downhill, past rows of brass cannon until they reached a small ridge. As the three of them approached the rise, four guards confronted them with swords drawn. "Halt, and identify yourselves."

Mathis reached inside his pocket until his thumb passed over a hard, smooth surface. He extracted a silver medallion and thought about the day his father, Martin had given it to him.

"Charles of Lorraine gave it to me after I saved his life," his father had told him proudly.

Mathis held the medallion high so the guards could see it in the torch light, then handed it to one of them. "Captain Mathis Zieglar of the Emperor's army. Give this to the field marshal. He'll remember me."

While his companions stood shoulder to shoulder with their swords pointed, the guard grasped the medallion, turned, and marched to a commanding figure on the ridge. The officer wore a tricorn hat sporting a tufted trim over an embroidered uniform. After the guard lifted Mathis' medallion, the officer smiled and waved to Mathis. "Captain Mathis Zieglar? Get yourself up here."

Mathis took the ridge in three long strides, retrieved his token from the guard, and saluted Field Marshal Charles of Lorraine.

"Mathis Zieglar, son of Martin." Lorraine stood back and shook his head. His formal but affable way was uncommon for a nobleman addressing a member of Mathis' class but due, no doubt, to their mutual history. "Your friend, Prince Savoy reported you missing, yesterday. Are you in good health?"

"Thank you, Excellency. I'll be all right when I recover from the cannon blasts ringing in my ears. But I could use some rest."

"Brother D'Aviano and I were concerned about you. We can't afford to lose an interpreter with your skills."

Mathis winced at the mention of Friar D'Aviano's name. He wished the emperor's advisor would never find him. The brother desired to know more about the treasure than Mathis wanted to reveal. In the light from a nearby bonfire, Mathis thought he saw a glint of understanding in Lorraine's eye.

"Fret not, Captain. No one likes having the emperor's eyes looking over his shoulder. I can arrange it so the good brother will not realize you have returned to service."

CHAPTER THREE

MATHIS TRIED TO FOCUS ON THE POSITIVE PART of what Lorraine had just said. D'Aviano didn't know he had been in Visegrad. The friar was one of the few people who knew from general sources that the treasure could be used against the sultan, even if he didn't know what the code inside the *Mishneh Torah* spelled out. D'Aviano had threatened to excommunicate Mathis unless he unraveled the mystery surrounding the location of the treasure.

"Solve it, and you will atone for your sins," D'Aviano had warned. "Fail, and you will lose everything."

D'Aviano must never know the treasure was inside the palace doors. Otherwise, the friar would turn the information over to the emperor's men.

Mathis repeated the *Aga*'s warning to Lorraine about promising a bloodbath if the Imperial army attacked. "They're trying to frighten us so we'll negotiate peace on their terms. But they aren't strong enough to hold us back if we storm their citadel. It would cost us stacks of bodies."

The field marshal stroked his chin. "Then we will convince them to surrender on our terms." A devilish smile inched across his face. "I am certain your visit inside the city will prove helpful in more ways than one. Begin by instructing our gunners to aim their weapons where they will be most effective. Then we will discuss another project I have in mind for you."

Something in the way Lorraine smiled and mentioned "another project" raised the hackles on Mathis' neck. His father had once told him the field marshal was a fair commander, though he demanded a great deal from his men. But this was no time to question what the emperor's field marshal had planned. "*Ja*, Excellency. I know where their storage facilities and batteries are."

"Good, Captain." The corners of Lorraine's mouth pulled up. "I'm gratified to know your university education has finally served a good purpose."

Lorraine's comment was loaded. Mathis rubbed his fingers over the medallion in his pocket. After Mathis' father spared Lorraine's life, the field marshal had gone a step further beyond rewarding Mathis' family with his seal as a sign of his patronage. Lorraine had also financed Mathis' education. He must have been disappointed when the Jesuits had sacked Mathis from his teaching position for refusing to renounce Copernicus' belief in a sun-centered universe.

Mathis ground his teeth. Was Lorraine telling Mathis he was proud of him as a captain, but pained because Lorraine had spent so much in vain on Mathis' education? Perhaps this was an implication of some ominous task he had in mind to test him as an officer?

Lorraine's smile relaxed. "Your limp tells me you could

use a little rest and food."

He turned to a nearby aide. "See that Captain Zieglar is fed. Bring him back here in a couple of hours."

"*Jawohl*, Excellency."

Mathis was escorted behind the front lines, and led to a sutler. After Mathis selected a side cut of beef—a rare treat—he added a cup of schnapps to his meal, and returned to his tent.

Despite the nearby thundering cannon, the ordeal drained the energy from Mathis's body, his eyelids grew heavy and he dozed off. His father's voice echoed in his dreams with the same paternal warning he made when he was still alive. "Mathis!" His father's finger wagged in his face. "You must always protect the women."

Mathis's dream drifted back to the incident that had sparked Martin's scolding. A lad of twelve, he stood paralyzed with fear and watched when Tartars attacked his mother and their family servant. His father intervened at the last moment, and had never forgiven his son's cowardice.

The dream turned darker and Mathis found himself imprisoned by a recurring vision. One that dogged him whether he slept or was awake. His father, mother, and Mary, their servant hovered over him and chanted in unison. "Protect the women, Mathis!"

Then another scene from a more recent incident materialized. Hundreds of angry men holding torches in the cold winter moonlight surrounded Mathis. Father Lebsafft, the priest who led them, stood on the mountain slope above, and seemed to inflate into a gigantic figure. He pointed a long finger that stabbed into Mathis' heart.

"Mathis Zieglar," Lebsafft's voice rumbled like rolling

thunder. "Speak to them!"

Mathis raised his hand over his head and the mob quieted. "People of this land, on the grave of my father Martin Zieglar, I swear I will find your women and bring them home."

The crowd cheered, the men's faces lit with hope.

But guilt rippled through Mathis' gut. *May God forgive my lying lips.* He had made a vow he couldn't possibly keep. In the end, he knew he would let the villagers down. No one man could dash into the bowels of the Ottoman Empire and bring back the hundreds of women and children the Mohammedans had abducted.

Unless, of course, Mathis found the treasure of the Raven King and proved the sultan was the descendant of an imposter. The mission would bet his life, and the lives of the hundreds of hostages on the shaky proposition he could extract the *Mishneh Torah* from the doors guarding the entrance to the palace in Buda. But Buda was in Mohammedan hands. Even if he were successful, he would have to communicate with the sultan's agents that he possessed the evidence, and pray he could achieve it before D'Aviano discovered it.

Mathis woke in a cold sweat. The straw beneath his clothes was moist. He fought for breath and his heart thumped against his ribcage. "I…I have to…protect the women."

■ ■ ■

Lorraine's aide arrived, and announced it was time for Mathis to begin his duties. After he rose and dressed himself, the soldier handed him a straight branch snapped off a tree. "Captain Zieglar, his Excellency suggests you use this to point out targets for our artillerymen."

Mathis saluted smartly, looked around, and walked toward three cannon positioned behind an earthen wall. He approached the artillery officer. "Good day, *Herr* Lieutenant. The field marshal has instructed me to identify good targets for you."

Mathis raised his stick and pointed to some drab stone-laid-in-clay buildings inside Visegrad's walls. "Behind there you'll find a Turkish gun. Happy hunting, gentlemen."

After Mathis visited each battery, the ground shook anew as the barrage resumed. Approaching the last one, he noticed a familiar face. An artillery officer crouched over a barrel turned his head in Mathis' direction. Then he stood in shock. "You're alive, *Hauptfeder*! By the saints, you're alive!"

Hauptfeder. The German word for mainspring. Few called Mathis by his nickname and Frederick Tannenberg was one of them. Mathis could never forget the day in his boyhood when he demonstrated before a dozen villagers his ability to leap, whirl completely around, and land a blow on his opponent. A local watchmaker standing near said Mathis reminded him of an uncoiling mainspring. Hence the label *Hauptfeder*.

More of a mountain than a man, Tannenberg rumbled up to Mathis and lifted him off his feet. "Prince Eugene told me you were looking for the treasure," he whispered in Mathis' ear. "Did you find it?"

"Set me down, Tannenberg." Mathis laughed, rubbing his friend's scalp. "All went well. I know where the 'merchandise' is buried."

Shots rang out from the mountainside above.

Musket barrels poked out of ramparts next to the Tower of Solomon. "Damn. That reminds me." He lifted up the branch. "Tannenberg, do you see that hexagonal tower up there?"

"*Ja.*"

"Would you mind lobbing a few balls into it?"

"Are you sure, *Hauptfeder*?" Tannenberg's voice lowered. "You said before you disappeared that place contained information about the treasure. Do you want to destroy the evidence? Lorraine might question why I selected it as a target."

"I want every trace of that information destroyed so no one can find it." Mathis walked up to the gun and patted the barrel. "Just tell Lorraine you responded to enemy snipers and shot at the tower next to them. Make sure you put a big hole in the southwest side."

Tannenberg shrugged. "*Jawohl, Herr* Captain."

Then Tannenberg returned to his crew. "Soldiers of the gun, ready the piece! Let's see if we've got the range from where we positioned it yesterday."

Mathis knew what was coming, so he jumped toward the city wall a few steps away from the cannon.

Moments later, Tannenberg's piece roared. Acrid, blinding smoke choked the air. A nine- pound cannon ball cracked against the wall next to the tower. Masonry fell like hail. Mathis looked through a telescope. He spotted men running out of the tower onto the wall exiting opposite of where the ball had hit. Mathis wasn't sure, but one may have worn a Tartar's bonnet.

Had Kamil returned to the cell and poked around, trying to find out what Mathis had been up to?

Mathis's spine tingled. The secret of the treasure's

31

location was at stake. He had to prevent Kamil or D'Aviano from discovering it. Mathis nervously rubbed the smooth contours of the watch inside his waistcoat, then pivoted and yelled at Tannenberg. "The sooner the better with the next round!"

Tannenberg barked orders, urging his men faster. Four of them lifted the cannon's trail, the hindmost part of the carriage. Then they moved the cannon to the left. One swabbed the barrel; another packed it with powder and cloth; a third rolled an iron ball down it's length. A gunner poured powder into the touch hole at the barrel base.

Then a soldier moved forward, stepping as gently as a doe. He inserted something resembling a carpenter's square into the barrel. Reading it, he guided the men into aiming the gun.

"What's the matter, *Hauptfeder*, never seen someone use an artillery quadrant before?" Tannenberg growled into Mathis' ear.

Mathis' jumped, not realizing his friend had drawn near. "I'm not looking at your quadrant. I'm looking at the person aiming the gun. Is that a *man*?"

Tannenberg grabbed him by his sleeve and pulled him away from the cannon. A soldier lit a wick and inserted it into the touch hole. The powder sparked, and the artillery-men covered their ears. Mathis and Tannenberg did the same. The weapon thundered, jerked backward and dug its trail into the earth.

The cannon ball hit its target. After the men repeated their exercises and sent two more rounds off, the southwest corner of the tower sagged. A fourth blast pulled the masonry down and a hole yawned wide, exposing the inside of Dracula's cell. All five men of the battery clapped their hands and cheered. Mathis wanted to hug Tannenberg and lift him up, but realized the damage it might do his own back.

Tannenberg took Mathis aside and whispered, "There's not a man in the regiment that can sight a cannon like that. So, don't go talking to others about my little secret."

"How can you keep a secret like that, Tannenberg?"

"It's permitted for a wife to accompany an officer to the front, no?"

"*Ja.*"

"So, in between battles, she is *Frau* Lang, the surgeon's wife." Mathis' friend smiled slyly. "But when there's a siege, she becomes Private Weber, the best artilleryman in the emperor's service."

"Are you insane, Tannenberg? If people find out about this, you'll be sent through the gauntlet or assigned latrine duty for the rest of the campaign."

"Oh, I don't know about that. There are some pretty well-placed officers who owe their lives to *Herr* Lang's healing expertise." Tannenberg reached inside his waistcoat and pulled something out. He opened his palm and displayed a small collection of sprouted coffee beans. "And when it comes to my protection, there are always these."

Mathis lifted his chin and scowled. "Now I know you're a lunatic, Tannenberg. If you think you can blackmail the emperor's people into keeping you safe just because you can embarrass him with those…you're mad."

"Am I? The emperor would do anything to hide the fact his officers trafficked women to the Muslims in exchange for these beans. Even if he were unaware of what was going on. And I have the evidence to prove his officers did just that."

"I wouldn't display those beans openly and dare the emperor's men to do something about them. Better keep them secret until you really need them."

Tannenberg waved his hand impatiently. "Do you have any idea how important these beans are? Transplanting them in the Americas could make a country rich. The emperor would die for them."

Mathis gripped Tannenberg's wrist. "You're the best friend I have, now that my wife is dead. The traffickers killed her when she came too close to the truth behind the coffee trade. It would destroy me if the emperor's people did the same to you. Don't put your neck on the block."

Tannenberg's face melted into sadness. "Magda was a beautiful woman—in every way. I've mourned her death for months." He took a deep breath. "Maybe you're right, brother. Maybe Private Lang can train one of our men. That would make it less risky for her and me."

Mathis looked Tannenberg in the eye and patted his upper arm.

The bombardment continued for the better part of the day until it opened two breaches in the wall. Lorraine summoned Mathis to his ridge, and pointed to the Imperial infantry in front of them, massing into two long columns. Their uniforms were barely visible in the darkness. "We're going to storm the breaches and take the outer wall. What are your recommendations?"

Mathis realized Lorraine wasn't asking his advice, but, like a commanding officer often did with his juniors, was testing Mathis's thinking. "Well, sir, I'd have the grenadiers go in first and create shock. Then I'd send in the *jaegers*— their sharpshooting will pick off enemy snipers. Finally, I'd pour in as many troops as fast as we could cram them in."

"All good advice, save one item. We need to hit the area around the breaches with exploding shells a minute before the charge."

"*Oy*." Mathis raised his hand to his head. "Thank you for the lesson, Excellency." Although he felt like slapping himself for overlooking the first item, Mathis realized Lorraine thought enough about Mathis to personally instruct him in siege tactics. He wondered where he had picked up "*Oy*" from. Could it have been Sarah Oppenheimer?

The cannons rained explosive shells on the walls. They burst over the ramparts with rib-rocking thunder. Smoke drifted downhill and stung Mathis' eyes.

Finally, the artillery bombardment stopped. Grenadiers rushed forward and tossed their hand bombs over the wall. Deafening bursts broke out. *Jaeger* marksmen followed. Crouching from behind fallen cement, they aimed their rifles. Fire flashed out the end of their barrels. With each new wave of attacks, the crescendo of the screams of the wounded rose.

Several grenadiers and *jaegers* fell to the ground as the Ottoman soldiers fought back. The Habsburg army stirred impatiently. Lorraine raised his hand and brought it swiftly down. Habsburg trumpets rent the air. Two columns of warriors surged forward like gigantic snakes, butting their heads through the wall. Soldiers yelled in one voice "The Lord began it, the Lord will bring it to an end!"

Soon, the entire army pushed through. Inside the walls, the noise of battle rose to an ear-splitting pitch. Bursts of fire scorched the sky amid the shrieks of the wounded. Metal, smoke, and gunpowder combined in one nose-piercing stench.

Eventually, the shots and shouting dwindled. The smoke pouring through the breaches thinned and a familiar figure appeared. Prince Eugene of Savoy, Mathis' commanding officer, walked toward Mathis and Lorraine. "*Bonjour, mes amis.* It appears we have sent the enemy packing up the hill toward the citadel."

Lorraine and the prince embraced, and spoke in half-French and half-German to one another. Mathis was glad his mother had kept her family's French alive in the house since it enabled him to follow their conversation. The gist of it was that they hoped to complete today's taking of the wall by progressing to the citadel above it tomorrow.

Looking at the prince, Mathis marveled in his presence. Only twenty years old—his own age—and the prince was in charge of a regiment. Diminutive and possessed of an overbite painful to look at, few would guess Eugene of Savoy to be such a warrior he had won the prized Order of the Golden Fleece during his first campaign. But Mathis' musings soon turned to anxiety.

The Duke's wry smile reappeared. "I will need a volunteer to parley with the *Aga*, convince him to lay down his arms."

Savoy glanced at Mathis and winked. "I know just the man for that."

Lorraine guffawed. "We will make good use of his training in the Turkish language."

Mathis moaned. Now he knew what Lorraine had in mind when he'd smiled and referred to his university education to finally serve a good purpose.

Mathis traversed the slope until he found a crate and climbed atop it. He raised his telescope. Through the flickering light, the last of the Ottoman soldiers had filed up the slope toward the citadel's top perch. Taking that fortress would be a hard nut to crack. "Uh…don't you think they might need a little softening up, first?"

"They have tasted defeat, that's enough." Lorraine's smile returned. He handed Mathis a sheet of paper. "In the morning, you will read this to the *Aga*. You may leave your valuables with my aide. Make sure you see a priest before leaving."

"Nothing to fret about, *mon ami*." Savoy chuckled, patting him on the cheek. "You'll be safer carrying a white flag than a musket like some of us did. We'll pray for you."

Mathis clenched his pocket watch.

CHAPTER FOUR

Twenty Miles South of Visegrad,
with General Halliweil's troops.

SARAH PEERED OVER HER COUSIN'S SHOULDER. "WHO are you writing to?"

Simon lifted his head, but did not turn around. "I'm ordering the supply boats to dock upriver and await my order to sail to the front lines. I hope you appreciate the expense and risk this involves."

She put a gentle hand on his shoulder. "Have I ever told you what wonderful penmanship you have?"

"No...never." Looking a little suspicious, he deposited his quill into an inkwell, scooted his stool halfway around, and faced her. "When a *mensch* conducts business for my father, Samuel Oppenheimer, he must know how to write."

"An important skill, Simon." Sarah walked to the opposite side of the table and sat. "By the way, I took the document Mendel wanted and wondered if the backside might be written in invisible ink, like the message we read about buried in the *Mishneh Torah*. So I held the paper up to the

38

candle." She pressed the curled document flat and pushed it across the table. "Look what I found."

Simon lifted his stool up and returned it to its former position. He read aloud from the paper. "Seek ye the labors of the god? Find the nest where the Raven King's egg hatched. Then descend into the salt." His face tensed like an irritable bear. "What does *this* mean? I already have too much to think about."

Sarah gazed intently at her hands folded in her lap. "We've figured out the meaning of the poem on the other side of the document. It told us Captain Zieglar would find the location of the *Mishneh Torah* once he figured out the puzzle inside Dracula's cell in Visegrad. When we next see Captain Zieglar, he can tell us more about this. Then we'll understand better."

"*If* we see him the next time. We need him like a *loch in kop*."

"Like a hole in the head? Don't be silly. Focus on the good inside him." She looked up. "I read one of the books Captain Zieglar had describing the doors inside the palace of Matthias Corvinus, the Raven King. Their panels were decorated with scenes of the labors of Hercules."

She caressed the top of one hand with the palm of the other. "This document says the doors, described as the 'labors of the god', or Hercules, ended up in salt near some kind of nest belonging to the Raven King. I have no idea what this means."

Simon threw up his hands. "If you share this with Captain Zieglar, he'll make sense of it and snatch the *Mishneh Torah* for himself."

"Or, like any good person, he'll appreciate our help and repay us in a way he is able." Sarah looked at her hands again and thought a moment. "This message was written on the reverse side of the document that promised to direct us to the *Mishneh Torah*. We need to figure out the connection between the *Mishneh Torah* and this second clue."

"Have you forgotten Mendel's threat? He's sending someone to take this paper from us."

"Thank you for reminding me." Sarah flashed the smile that disarmed every man she spoke to, even her cousin. She produced a blank slip of parchment and slid it across the table. "Let's give *Herr* Mendel what he wants."

Visegrad
Saturday, June 17, 1684

In the early morning hours, Mathis watched the Habsburg army pull their cannon through the outer walls of Visegrad and park them at the base of the precipice beneath the citadel. They included two powerful mortars, pieces that hurled balls hundreds of feet into the air and fell with pulverizing force. Shortly after daylight, the artillery opened fire and pounded the castle above. Fiery blazes raced over its ramparts. Soldiers inside screamed as the clothes on their backs burst into flames.

Lorraine signaled a cease fire, and deployed an aide to instruct Mathis to begin his mission. Glumly resigned to his task, Mathis approached the citadel's gate, once again holding a staff with a white flag tied at the end. Though the morning wind blew cool, his forehead broke out in a sweat. He had a feeling the Ottoman garrison would receive him even less congenially than the *Aga's* send off on Thursday.

Dante's epigram over the entrance of hell flashed through his mind as he climbed the steps. "Abandon all hope, you who enter here." His trepidation grew as sentries grabbed him at the entrance and threw chains over him.

Mathis summoned boldness from deep within. "What's this? You let me roam freely when I was in the city."

"Silence," snapped an officer with a thick mustache. He pointed down the slope to the city below, where his men fought yesterday. Mathis's gaze followed the direction of the officer's finger. A building was pummeled into gravel from Habsburg mortar rounds. The Serbians must have rightly assumed, since Mathis was in the city before the bombardment, he must have helped the Habsburg gunners locate the Ottoman weapon behind the building after his release. A cannon barrel and several human limbs protruded from the rubble.

Mathis's stomach churned; he clutched his throat and gagged.

The soldiers behind him stopped. Excited conversation broke out in Serbian. The officer ground dirt in Mathis' face, and cuffed him repeatedly up the side of his head.

Mathis wobbled where he stood and cursed. The soldiers wrapped a thick scarf over his eyes and jostled him forward. He wondered how much longer he had to live as he stumbled over debris. He fell several times, and tore his knees on knife-edged rocks. At last, the prodding stopped and someone removed Mathis' blindfold. He was in a courtyard where a retinue of janissary and Serbian officers surrounded the *Aga*.

"You are courageous to return." The *Aga's* menacing voice contradicted his calm façade as he extended his ring.

Mathis ground his teeth, bowed and kissed the signet.

41

"Thank you, Excellency."

The *Aga* said something stern to the officer who escorted Mathis. The man pulled a cloth out of his back pocket, wetted it with water from his canteen, and wiped Mathis' face.

"Thank you, again, Excellency." Mathis looked around. "May I ask what became of Kamil?"

"Your friend left without announcing his intentions. But you did not risk your life to inquire about a Tartar's health. Why are *you* here, Captain?"

Left without announcing his intentions? Had Kamil solved the riddle of Dracula's cell and ridden off to find the treasure himself? A knot twisted inside Mathis' stomach. There was nothing left for him to do but complete his assignment and stay alive.

He unfolded the paper and read Lorraine's statement. "'Greetings to the most august *Aga* commanding the Visegrad fortress. I, Field Marshal Lorraine, commend your bravery, but now order you to surrender. If you resist, I will show you no mercy and impale every man in your garrison. Your obedient servant, Charles of Lorraine.'"

The *Aga* shook with emotion, but chose his words carefully. "Thank you for the message, Captain. We will vacate Visegrad when we have his assurance my men and I can leave without fear of molestation."

So the *Aga* wanted to bargain. Mathis assumed he would have to carry the counter-offer down the steps to Lorraine. Conveying proposals between the two warring parties was tiresome and Mathis wished he could stay with the Habsburg army. He would have his ears boxed a lot less.

Kamil's absence also nagged him. Had Mathis'

agonized efforts to rescue the trafficked women and children come to nothing? Was his adversary one step ahead?

The *Aga* patted him softly on the head and smiled. "Don't worry about carrying my reply to your leader. We will send our own messenger. In the meantime, you will remain here as our honored guest."

'Honored guest,' indeed. It was an eloquent term for hostage, yet he didn't know why he deserved such a 'privilege.'

■ ■ ■

Kamil grinned as he gazed down the wooded slope into the valley. General Halliweil's army was strung out in long rows of white tents over an expanse of trampled greenery. The camp was picturesque, but vulnerable to attack. The foolish Habsburg commander didn't realize a strong Ottoman force of armored cavalry was less than an hour ahead of the imperial army, and about to pounce.

He glanced back and confirmed two deer carcasses—one on each mount—were still draped over each of the two spare pony's rear quarters. Good, everything was in place.

This was the day Kamil would turn the tables on Mathis Zieglar, the man who had killed Kamil's closest friend at the siege of Vienna and ruined Kamil's coffee smuggling network months later. Kamil would hit Mathis where it hurt most.

The wind rustled the leaves in the trees reassuringly. The sound masked Kamil's ghost-like moves from any potential nearby ears. He took care to keep himself inside the forest's edge. The last thing he wanted was to have one of the Habsburg's scouts spot him before he was ready.

Slowly, he worked his way down the valley behind

the Imperial army. He dismounted and motioned with a flat palm for the ponies to stay put. They froze motionless while he pulled clothes out of his saddlebag. They were trained to stay until he signaled them. Soon he donned knee socks, *lederhosen*, and a long-sleeved linen shirt.

Finally, he covered his shaven head with a broad brimmed hat. Looking both ways to make sure no Imperials were nearby, he moved stealthily to a pond that looked like it was used to water livestock. His reflection depicted that of an Austrian huntsman, just as planned.

He slipped his hand over the right side of his belt, and felt the cold iron of a dagger's handle. He smiled.

Mendel had told him Oppenheimer's tent was somewhere in the rear of the army, close to the baggage wagons and cooks. Kamil tied the ponies together, harness to tail, and led them forward.

Two sentries guarded the rear of Halliweil's army, at attention and hard-faced. When they drew their swords, Kamil grinned, pointed to the animal corpses on the backs of the ponies and called out in perfect German, "Something for this evening's dinner!"

One of the guards licked his lips, the other one waved him on. Walking between the rows of tents, Kamil spied one of them with a gold colored ring hanging over the door flap, an indicator the inhabitants were Jewish. He led the ponies to a stand of saplings, and motioned for them to wait. Oblivious to his presence, an armed guard slouched against a bale of hay, smoked a pipe while gazing into the sky. The pungent aroma of tobacco teased Kamil's nose.

Kamil walked to the backside of the tent undetected by the guard and slid his knife out of his waistband. Gingerly, he moved alongside the tent and crept behind the sentry.

Cupping one hand over the guard's mouth, Kamil pulled up the man's neck scarf and ran a knife across his throat. His victim bled out in a silent death embrace, and dropped to the ground.

Kamil unknotted his victim's scarf and cut it in two with his knife. He returned his bloody knife inside his belt to stoop and pick up a heavy rock. He crept up to the tent with the gold ring above the door, and listened.

Inside, Simon spoke with Sarah. The man backed through the tent flaps as he exited the tent. This was the infidel Kamil searched for. As Simon fully emerged, Kamil struck him hard over the head with the rock. He sagged backward into Kamil's arms. Kamil stuffed the scarf inside Simon's mouth, dragged him back and laid him on the ground.

"Simon?" Sarah pulled back the door flaps of the tent. Her eyes popped wide. "*Oy ge...ge...gevault!*"

Kamil held up his hand. "I am Kamil. Be quiet, or your friend dies."

Sarah's shaking hands reached inside her blouse. She pulled out a paper and held it out to him. "Here. Take this. This is what you want."

Kamil snatched it from her. He reached into a side pouch, pulled out a whistle and shrilled out a note. Seconds later, the two ponies trotted over.

Simon moaned and shifted on the dirt. Kamil stepped on his arm and pinned him to the ground. "Any noise and you both die."

With two sections of rope from his saddlebag, Kamil tied Sarah's and Simon's hands behind their backs. He kicked the fallen guard's bale of hay he'd used as a chair next to a pony. "Mount him, Simon." Sarah followed with another pony.

Kamil took the scarf from the dead guard and stuffed it into Sarah's mouth. "Hmm." He noticed her fulsome lips and beautiful auburn eyes. He could make special use of this hostage.

Kamil mounted his pony and grabbed the tethers of his hostage's ponies. He dug his heels into his animal's side. Together, the three mounts galloped past shouting sentries. Minutes later, riders behind him gave hot pursuit. He looked over his shoulder and laughed. The Imperials would run into the Ottoman army before they caught up to his ponies. The fools rode to their doom.

CHAPTER FIVE

SARAH'S HEART POUNDED, THE IMPERIAL RIDERS gained on them with every stride over the grassy plain. Kamil veered their ponies into a nearby forest. She nearly choked on the scarf wadded inside her mouth, for the woods teemed with mounted Tartar archers, with bows and arrows aimed at the ready. There was no escape for her and Simon.

Kamil brought the ponies to a stop. Sarah could barely make out the Imperial horsemen through the trees. They rode at a breakneck pace as the Tartars raised their bows. "*Thwannng.*" A chorus of bowstrings sang in unison. A cloud of arrows flew toward the pursuers. Five of the shafts sank into Imperial bodies, two of them fell off their horses. An officer raised his hand and the rescuers' charge ground to a halt. The survivors turned back and fled for their lives as the Tartars emerged from the woods and became the pursuers.

"I own the two of you, now." Kamil grinned at Sarah as he pulled the scarf out of her mouth. Her heart sank.

47

After extracting the scarf out of Simon's mouth, Kamil led him and Sarah to a small clearing where he unfolded the parchment Sarah had given him. He turned it over to the blank side, then scratched his chin. "Hmmm. Maybe you and Zieglar are not as clever as I thought. You didn't even search for a hidden message."

Two Tartars rode over, each with fur upper body wraps tied around their waists. Kamil asked them something, and one of them pointed to a kindling pile barely visible on the edge of the clearing. While the two Tartars guarded Simon and Sarah, Kamil dismounted and approached the kindling. Sarah saw the slightest wisp of smoke rise from a campfire's charred remains.

Kamil heaped a few dry leaves on the wood, and fanned it into flame. He held the parchment over the heat a moment, then flipped it over and held it up to the sunlight, shading the back with one hand. Peering closely, he read slowly and deliberately. "Matjaž sleeps in his cave by Mount Peca until the end of days. Then he will share his treasure with the valiant and ride out to drive away the Turk."

Playing along with the ruse, Simon fidgeted on his pony and moaned. "My Lord. They've discovered the secret! Now they know where it is."

"Hush, Simon!"

Kamil lowered the parchment and studied the bonfire in intense thought. "The front of this parchment contains a poem that led Mathis Zieglar to an important secret in Visegrad, where I left him yesterday. He said the information took him to Dracula's old cell inside the Tower of Solomon. There were etchings…etchings on the walls that spoke of a secret that threatened the sultan's life."

Kamil walked around to the rear of Simon's pony, and grabbed his coat. "What is this secret? Tell me now!"

Sarah twitched with disbelief. She assumed that Mendel, the man who had held the kosher knife to her throat days earlier, had told Kamil what the secret was before sending him for the parchment. But Kamil didn't seem to know the secret was the code contained in the ancient *Mishneh Torah* that proved the sultan was not an Ottoman, hence a fraud. She wouldn't be the one to enlighten him.

Beads of sweat formed on her brow. How could she appear to cooperate, but still keep Kamil in the dark about the details? More importantly, how could she and Simon survive? "Sir, please understand. When Captain Zieglar asked to read the poem, he told us it contained a message to help us recover our sacred literature from the East. No sooner had he finished reading it than he became scarce... and we have seen little of him since."

Kamil scowled as he approached Sarah. "You expect me to believe you know nothing about the message I just read? That you didn't know it was written in invisible ink?"

"*Ja, Mein Herr.*" She tried to control her trembling. She had to project sincerity in order to convince Kamil the invisible message was authentic. Still, it wasn't in her nature to lie, even if the *Talmud* justified it in a case like this. Her heart was heavy. "But, if you're kind to us, I know a few things that might be of help."

"Such as?"

"Sarah!" Simon barked. "Think about what you're saying."

Kamil pulled Simon halfway off his pony and pressed a dagger under his chin. "Mind your tongue, Jew. She's the only thing keeping you alive."

Kamil released Simon and glared at Sarah. "Finish what you were saying."

Sarah squirmed on her pony's back. "Is it kind to keep us tied up like this when we try to help you? Loosen our ropes and we can talk like friends. Friends who share with one another."

Friends?" Kamil snorted. "Your uncle finances the Habsburg army. You are the enemy of Islam."

"My uncle does not choose how to use his money," Sarah protested. "The emperor forces him to loan the army hundreds of florins each month, with only vague promises of repayment."

Encouraged by the hint of sympathy she thought she saw on Kamil's face, she continued. "And you *must* know, *Mein Herr*, the emperor hates our people so much, we're banned from Vienna – only four or five of us are permitted there."

Kamil nodded. "The Ottomans are the only protectors you have. The Jews are fools to live amongst the Christians."

"No, my friend, we are not fools. We are desperate to survive." She paused and caught her breath, hoping that Kamil wouldn't see through her. If he would only relent and loosen their bonds, it might signal his willingness to spare them. That was crucial, considering the Tartars had a reputation for extracting information from prisoners and killing them afterward. "I beg you, cut us loose if you want our help. We will reward your efforts."

Thinking she saw Kamil's expression soften even more, her heart lifted with a glimmer of hope. "A little something to eat would encourage us to talk."

Soon, Kamil, Simon and Sarah all sat on the ground near the smoking logs. The Tartar broke several chunks of mare's cheese off a kneaded ball and offered it to them. "Tell me what this message means, woman."

"Very well, then." Sarah took a small twig and drew three circles on the ground, still damp from a recent rain. "This is Austria, Slovenia and Hungary." She pointed to the smallest circle at the bottom of a larger one and to the left of the second large one. "You are familiar with the land of Slovenia, yes?"

Kamil cast a dubious glance. "I know of it. The region south of Austria, west of Hungary."

Good, he understands me. The Tartar seemed less patri-archal about listening to a woman than a Jew or Christian. "That's right. Slovenia is this little sliver that runs along Austria's southeast border."

She created a hole in the dirt midpoint along the line separating Slovenia from Austria. "This is where Mount Peca is. A traveling peddler I once knew told me Matjaž's cave is nearby. It has something to do with the legend of King Matthias Corvinus, the Raven King of Hungary."

Simon fidgeted like a robin wrestling with a worm that turned out to be a snake. "You don't know what you're say-ing, woman. Close your mouth."

Kamil pressed his knuckles against Simon's teeth. "Last warning. Shut up."

Sarah laughed to herself. Her cousin's supposed pro-tests were convincing.

"Kamil," Sarah said softly, "how do you know Nathan Mendel?"

Kamil stared at her blankly. "How do *you* know him?"

"A few days ago he held a knife to my throat, and de-manded I turn the parchment over to him or he would kill us. Then he claimed the next person to visit us wouldn't be

51

a Jew like himself, so we'd better be ready to surrender the document, or the threat he made on my life would come to pass."

"He spoke the truth."

Sarah's gave a nervous laugh. "*Ja*, he was truthful about that part. But not so much about his original threat to cut my throat with his *chalaf*, blessed be the Name of the Lord God."

"*Baruch hashem Adonai Elohim*," Simon repeated in Hebrew.

Noting Kamil's irritation, Sarah waved the topic away with her hand. "Whatever this document refers to has some relevance for the Mendel family. Why would that concern a Tartar like yourself? Has he explained its meaning to you?"

"Your Captain Zieglar mentioned the secret affects the safety of the sultan. I expect Mendel will disclose that in greater detail when I see him next."

Sarah tried to hide her curious pause at his remark. Either Nathan Mendel hid the original information from Kamil mentioning the labors of the god and descending into the salt, or Mendel wasn't aware of its existence. At this point, Sarah wasn't sure which explanation was more credible.

Kamil rose and paced around the clearing. Unlike Simon, he kept his thoughts to himself. Sarah leaned over to whisper in Simon's ear. "What did you think of my map in the dirt?"

Simon smirked. "Since when did you become an artist?"

"Since Nathan Mendel warned us a cranky visitor would come calling."

"You prepared all this?"

She shrugged one shoulder. "I try my best."

"Just like you dreamed up that message about Matthias Corvinus riding out of the cave."

"*Well*, I have to give credit to an old Slovenian legend for that. I read it in one of Captain Zieglar's books, and simply recorded it on a new document for Kamil's benefit."

"You are too clever, cousin." Simon tapped the inside of his finger again. "Let's hope Kamil doesn't retaliate when he finds out his trip to Slovenia is an exercise in futility."

"Pray I have bought us some time."

Sunday morning, June 18. Visegrad Citadel

Mathis stood and pushed his palms against the wall of his cell. Again. The irons attached to his legs clanked against the stone floor. Why had the *Aga* detained him? Surely he didn't think Lorraine would call off his attack because the Turk held Mathis hostage. More important, why had Kamil fled the city?

Sunlight flooded the room's entrance between the guards' opening, allowing an officer to enter. Mathis' heart rate spiked when he recognized the thick handlebar mustache that belonged to the man who had cuffed him yesterday. He drew back his hands to cushion the expected blow.

"Relax, *Nasara*. I bring you a message from Kamil the Tartar."

Mathis lowered his hands, but remained vigilant. "A message?"

The officer reached inside his caftan and handed a paper scrap to Mathis. In dark and barely legible ink he read,

53

"The writings of the sage are inside the hard substance that opens wide."

Mathis slammed his palm against the wall and cursed. Kamil had made it into Dracula's cell and figured out the code. No wonder he left Visegrad. The *Aga* must have delayed Mathis to give Kamil a head start.

The officer's mouth stretched into a malicious leer. "Kamil wanted you to know one other thing. Simon and Sarah Oppenheimer will remain his guests until he finds the doors of the Raven King. Stay out of his way if you want to see them alive again."

CHAPTER SIX

KAMIL'S NOTE DUMBFOUNDED MATHIS SO MUCH, HE barely noticed the Ottoman troops lining up to stack their weapons in the courtyard, and file out the citadel's entrance. He focused his attention on them, and overheard something about "the Christians gave us safe conduct to Buda." The siege was over and he had survived.

But he had also failed.

Kamil had pieced the puzzle together and would reach the treasure before him.

Suspicion crept up Mathis's spine like an angry centipede. What did Kamil mean Mathis should stay out of his way until he found the Raven King's doors? Mathis assumed the portals were inside Buda's royal palace, less than a day's ride from Visegrad. But it didn't make sense that Kamil would worry about Mathis catching up to him if the doors were such a short distance away. Were that true, Kamil would have little reason to take Sarah and Simon hostage for insurance against Mathis because they would get to Buda before he responded.

After one of the *Aga's* men released him from his bonds, Mathis sat on a bench outside his cell. A friendly hand on his shoulder interrupted his mutterings. "We have victory, Captain. Why your sadness?"

That horrible German syntax mangled by a Hungarian accent could only belong to one man. Mathis managed a broken smile as he lifted his head. "Endre?"

A rush of joy filled him to the brim. The kind only made by a bond that transcended kinship. "Endre Bakos! Brother! I haven't seen you since the siege of Vienna."

The two embraced until Mathis stood back. He looked Endre over from head to toe, noted his friend's uniform's striking combination of red, gold and green. "By St. Stephen, look at you in that regimental dress. Did Count Esterhazy promote you?"

Endre took a deep breath and his chest swelled inside the colorful lacing binding his topcoat together in the Hungarian fashion, which favored laced grommets over buttons. "*Ja*. I am first lieutenant. Promotions easier during war."

Mathis was thankful that Endre had come back into his life. The Hungarian hussar had saved Mathis on more than one occasion—not to mention Mathis's career—when Mathis was a new recruit and prone to impulsive decisions. He could never understand why Endre risked his neck for his comrade repeatedly, except to know Endre was fiercely loyal to his friends. It must be a matter of Magyar honor.

"So, brother. Why so glum when Turks surrender?"

Mathis explained his quest for the treasure, and how Simon and Sarah had helped him. "But now Kamil has them in his clutches. If he gets to the treasure before I do, hundreds of women and children will spend the rest of their lives as Mohammedan slaves. I don't know how to stop him."

Endre winced at the mention of Kamil's name. "That scum. Thought he learned lesson when you crush his leader's head last year during siege. Where is now?"

"After Kamil snatched Sarah and Simon from General Halliweil's camp, they rode off to who knows where."

Endre's eyes glowed like a blacksmith's forge. "Now General Halliweil dead. Army attacked by Turks yesterday. Finally drove them back, but heavy casualties."

Mathis gnashed his teeth and squeezed the medallion in his pocket until his fingers ached. "Kamil must have used the confusion of war to kidnap Simon and Sarah. He has at least a day's jump on me. All I know is that he's searching for Matthias Corvinus' bronze doors. They contain a secret that would overthrow the sultan."

Endre's lower lip pushed somberly over the upper one. "Heard reports of two Jews kidnapped just before enemy attacked. Why Muslim take them hostage?"

"To keep me from interfering with his quest for the treasure. Which doesn't make sense if the treasure is in Buda." Mathis sat and rested his forehead against one hand. "Unless Kamil knew the doors weren't there to begin with. Another thing he's accomplishing is to disrupt Simon's coordination of the supplies from Vienna."

Mathis shot up from his seat as if struck by lightning. He nearly forgot Dracula's cell. He prayed the code etched on the walls was illegible. Bad enough Kamil knew about it, Mathis couldn't afford for Brother D'Aviano to follow suit.

Mathis began to run, leaving Endre standing openmouthed. Realizing what he'd done, Mathis stopped and waved for his friend to follow. "Let's go, Endre. We must keep this disaster from getting worse."

Endre shrugged, then broke into a jog as he followed. "Whatever you say, brother."

Mathis bounded like a mountain goat down the steps leading from the citadel to the city. Climbing up from the opposite direction, soldiers cursed at Mathis for knocking some of them aside.

"Slow down," Endre shouted between pants. "You do more damage to army than Turks."

Mathis charged to the bottom of the stairs and raced for the Tower of Solomon. The gate to the cell was open. He flung it aside and made for the pile of rubble deposited in front of the gap that had once been a wall. By the time Endre caught up to him, Mathis was on his hands and knees, turning over stone shards to see if there was anything readable on the remains.

"Brother ... what are you...."

"No, doesn't look like there are any clues left." Mathis paused to wipe the sweat off his forehead. The creases smoothed on his forehead. "The cannon blast destroyed everything."

"Indeed, my son. Perhaps you can explain these clues. Start by accounting for your disappearance over the last several days."

As Endre slipped into the shadows, Mathis sensed, more than saw a wraith-like figure inside a friar's cowl that hovered over the top of the nearby stairs. Mathis' blood froze inside his veins. There was no mistaking the low rumble that sounded as if it came from the burning bush. D'Aviano had caught up to him.

Mathis slowly rose to his feet. The slivers of stone stuck

through his trousers pierced his knees like tiny spears, but were nothing compared to the oncoming torment from D'Aviano. He strained to make out the friar's face. "The peace of Christ be with you, Brother. I have many things to share with you."

Dracula's cell had an unearthly feel. Mathis's shadow choked off most of the daylight from the gap in the wall created by a cannonball from the earlier siege. Shafts of muted light illuminated dust clouds rose like swirling fire-flies. D'Aviano's voice from the opposite side of the room was like heaven thundering through a lifeless, dark body. "Share with me, or hide? You can only know the peace of Christ when you speak the truth, Captain Zieglar. Do you intend to tell the truth?"

"The truth is, I was abducted by the Tartars." Mathis' experience as an interrogator taught him how to block the friar's probing. His responses were short and offered as lit-tle information as possible. "Thank you for your prayers on my behalf."

"Hmpf." The friar cleared his throat impatiently. "And the Tartars decided to bring you to Visegrad, where Vlad Dracula's old cell is located. He was imprisoned here by the Raven King for twelve years, wasn't he?"

"You have studied the subject well, brother."

"Now I find you here, on your hands and knees, searching for clues. How is it the Tartars happened to bring you to the very place where the Raven King had his sum-mer palace, and you look in the rubble, which I assume has something to do with finding his treasure? Please disclose why you are doing this, if you value your eternal soul."

The threat of excommunication, again. Mathis didn't want the conversation to be a referendum on his faith. He was ill equipped for this fight, considering D'Aviano was not only the emperor's closest advisor, but also revered by many who considered him a candidate for sainthood. When someone that powerful recommended Mathis's excommunication, it happened.

D'Aviano had previously admonished Mathis he would suffer excommunication for releasing Kamil from captivity in Vienna. Saving an infidel under those circumstances was considered a betrayal of the faith. The friar didn't care the act had successfully rescued a hundred Christian women and children from the Mohammedan slave market. Were he excommunicated, Mathis would be cut off from society and his career ruined, unless he could produce the treasure for the emperor.

The stone spears in his legs dug deeper. "Yes, brother, I am looking for clues because I still don't know all the answers. But I can tell you what I concluded when a Tartar held me in custody."

D'Aviano's mouth skewed. "Did you tell him where the treasure is?"

"I tried to hide the engravings on the wall of the cell by plastering them with mud and debris. But the Tartar cleaned out the etchings and figured out part of a code."

"*Part* of the code?" D'Aviano's tone turned sarcastic. "What part does the Mohammedan know?"

"It pointed toward the treasure's location. Bear with me...my memory is a little cloudy. The bombardment knocked me around."

Mathis had learned to duck directly answering aggressive questions after his experience last year when he had been examined by a panel of Jesuits. He thought he had successfully defended Copernicus' doctrine that the Earth revolved around the sun, as opposed to the other way around. But rather than congratulating him, the clerics branded him a heretic and dismissed him from his teaching post at the University of Vienna. That ordeal made him cautious around clergymen, especially powerful ones.

His experience had taught him the inadvisability of brash honesty. On the other hand, lying to a Capuchin like D'Aviano invited trouble. How could he give the friar what he wanted without enabling D'Aviano to confiscate the treasure for the emperor, rather than use it to ransom the enslaved women and children? Perhaps by telling the parts of the truth that led nowhere….

Mathis approached D'Aviano. No longer blocking the hole in the wall behind him, his movement released a flood of sunlight. "Unfortunately, the cannonade destroyed the exact wording, so I cannot recall the precise reading. Something about the treasure of the Raven King being placed inside the hard substance within the royal palace."

D'Aviano stroked his flowing beard, and frowned. "We have known it was somewhere inside the palace ever since John Corvinus, the Raven King's son, wrote a letter to the pope from his deathbed. Well over a hundred years ago. The only thing you have added is the treasure is inside some kind of hard substance. Is that what you consider a clue?"

"Yes, when you consider the engraving's context." Mathis's traced an imaginary sentence in mid air. "The inscription read something like 'the treasure is in the hard substance….'"

"Then the clue you spoke of would complete the sentence and tell us *where* the treasure is, or possibly *what* it is."

61

"*Ja.*" Mathis pointed to the debris near his feet. "But there's nothing here. The Tartar that held me captive must have pieced together the rest, considering his haste to leave Visegrad before the siege ended."

"There are a disturbing number of coincidences here, Captain." D'Aviano clicked his tongue. "Was it not your friend, Captain Tannenberg, whose cannon punched a hole into the side of the tower? How fortunate for you it destroyed the evidence you claim to be rummaging through. So we have no choice but to take your word for what the engravings said."

"Ahem." Endre cleared his throat from the shadows.

Startled, D'Aviano motioned Endre into the light. "Who are you, hussar?"

"Endre Bakos, of Count Esterhazy's regiment."

D'Aviano's eyes traveled from Endre's boots to the thick, cylindrical hat. "Obviously a Hungarian. Are you Catholic or Protestant?"

"I am Christian."

The friar's nostrils flared, his lip curled. "Don't be insolent."

Boots scraping over stone steps interrupted D'Aviano's interrogation and none too soon for Mathis. "Brother D'Aviano?" An Italian accent echoed. "It is I, Count Marsigli."

Mathis had heard that name when he taught at the university. Count Luigi Ferdinando Marsigli was a noted soldier, engineer, diplomat and geographer from Bologna. Now, here he was, dressed in a nobleman's tailored greatcoat and sporting a flowing wig, walking toward the cell's door.

Marsigli's almond-shaped head was accentuated by a high, peaked forehead. A long, thin nose stretched beneath it. He was light skinned, clean shaven, and had lips that bunched together as if he had wooden teeth. Not the sort of features Mathis associated with the darker, southern Italians he was more familiar with. Like many of his countrymen, including D'Aviano, Marsigli ended his sentences by adding an "-ah" to a word ending with a consonant. His syntax grated on Mathis' Austrian ears.

"At last, you've arrived!" D'Aviano exulted. "My prayers have been answered. Has Our Lady aided your recovery from imprisonment and escape from the Turks?"

"*Si*, good brother! There were times I thought the Turks would never let me see another Christmas. But your prayers shortened that trial and the illness I suffered in Venice."

"The blessed Virgin rewards the faithful." D'Aviano smiled and pointed to Mathis. "This is the man I wrote you about. You will oversee him until you find the treasure of the Raven King."

Mathis groaned inwardly. Although he had temporarily dodged D'Aviano's interrogation, Marsigli would be one more supervisor watching over his shoulder and questioning his every move. How would Mathis ever find the treasure and rescue the hostages?

While D'Aviano and the count chatted about his journey from Italy to Visegrad, Mathis walked over to Endre. "Soon as possible, find Captain Tannenberg—he's attached to the artillery," he whispered. "Tell him to search the Mohammedan headquarters, and make sure nothing looks like a message etched into stone. If there is, tell him to destroy it."

"So be it."

"And…find out where Kamil took Sarah and Simon Oppenheimer. They are critical to finding the treasure."

CHAPTER SEVEN

158 years earlier. Buda, September 1526.

"IF YOU VALUE YOUR LIFE, BE CAREFUL WITH THE statue." A supervisor cursed and threatened fifteen men who strained against a hoist that lowered a bronze statue of the Greek god, Hercules onto a barge. A turbaned man with a flowing white beard stood nearby on a platform, a stern expression on his face. The men lowered the figure into a cradle of straw in the center of the barge.

The vessel rose and fell as the Danube lapped against its sides. The statue came to rest, and the barge sagged heavily, creating waves of its own. A team of sailors strapped the bronze figure into the cradle.

The supervisor approached the turbaned man and bowed. "Excellent One, we have completed packing the statues of Apollo, Diana and Hercules. All that remains is to dismantle the bronze doors to the palace and load them on another barge. Very soon you will see all of Matthias Corvinus' bronze treasures in Constantinople."

Pagli Ibrahim *Pasha* stared blankly. "I will hold you

accountable if the panels are damaged. If your barge separates from mine, I will give you three days after we arrive in Belgrade to catch up. Arrive late, I will have your head."

"I understand, Excellent One."

Ibrahim walked down the dock and rubbed his hands in satisfaction. Events had gone spectacularly well for him. Who would have ever guessed that a boy once captured by pirates and sold as a slave to the Turks would someday rise and become the second most powerful man in the Ottoman Empire the Grand Vizier? His string of successes had continued until a month ago, when the Ottoman troops he commanded had wiped out the entire Hungarian army at the battle of Mohacs. Twenty-thousand Christians had perished in the space of an hour. Then Buda fell, the capital of Hungary and the home of the deceased Raven King, Matthias Corvinus.

Ibrahim walked up stairs that took him from the dock to the ground above it. His eyes traveled up a steep road that climbed toward Buda's royal palace on the city heights. Bare-backed laborers staggered down the grade, sweating as they carried pallets of looted material destined for other barges.

Ibrahim's thoughts returned inward. His honed powers of persuasion convinced Sultan Suleiman that Ibrahim should commandeer Corvinus' beautiful bronze statues. He couldn't wait to see the likenesses of these pagan gods raised inside Constantinople's ancient racetrack, the Hippodrome. Then, every morning he could wake up inside his palace, built on the edge of the famous site, and look on the glorious reminders of his Grecian past. So what if it provoked the ire of pious Muslims? His parents would be overjoyed to see their ancient culture revived.

65

Ibrahim snickered. The Muslim religious authorities, the *ulema* could feast on their bile. He had no more use for them than the scheming Orthodox priests who had oppressed his people for centuries.

Other grand viziers would consider sacrificing their children before snubbing the *ulema*. But not Ibrahim. Had not Suleiman promised that as long as he reigned, Ibrahim, his boyhood friend, would never be executed? The prospect of parading the pagan statues in front of those who had forced Islam down his throat almost made him levitate.

■ ■ ■

"Nooo." Standing beside her husband Ezra, Rebecca Mendel ground her teeth and moaned. A line of Mohammedan soldiers brandished spears in front of her, and pushed the angry onlookers back. At the top of the royal palace's marble stairs, brawny workmen swung their mallets against wedges, the loud pangs dislodging pins from the hinges. The polished bronze doors vibrated with each blow. Two angled timber trusses cushioned with heavy felt stood in front of the doors to break their fall.

Ezra trembled. Rebecca sensed he might be even more distraught than her. She forced herself to lay a comforting hand on him.

The gesture seemed to surprise Ezra, for he switched his gaze from the drama unfolding in front of them to Rebecca. She sensed his curiosity as her mother's words from yesterday echoed in her ears. "You must be nicer to Ezra. This is a man who provides well for you and our entire community."

"But mother." Rebecca had waved her hands in

frustration. "It's like I'm raising a little boy. When will this scatter-brain grow up? And so help me God, if he says 'think about it' one more time…."

Her mother gave a gentle laugh. "First mend yourself, and then mend others. Ezra swings to extremes now and then, but when all is finished, he is a true *mensch*."

"Mother, Ezra doesn't think things through, he *acts* – and always makes poor decisions. We'll never have money, like Uncle Joshua."

Her mother grew silent, her stare pierced through her daughter's words. "Do you remember when Ezra's parents came down with the bloody flux?"

"Yes, of course."

"Did you know who nursed them back to health?"

Rebecca shrugged. "Ezra?"

"Yes, Ezra. His sisters complained of the inconvenience and did nothing. But he took care of his parents until they were well again."

She sighed. "Well…I admit, he *is* giving."

"There isn't a man on Earth with a bigger heart." Her mother's smile returned. "That's why your father and I arranged your marriage. He's cleverer than you think."

Since then, Rebecca made an effort to be less critical of her husband, despite her inclinations. As she stood next to him, a young woman sobbed a few feet away and leaned her head on the shoulder of a lanky man. Her black, braided hair fell past her shoulders over a purple vest that laced up the front.

The man struggled—and failed—to hold back the tears streaming down his cheeks. The hilt of a sword protruded out of his full-length cape overlaid by a bulky fur wrap. Rebecca wondered how someone with his warrior's bearing had escaped the slaughter at Mohacs.

Rebecca approached the woman, and tried to keep her voice from quavering. "Take courage, woman. Christians are not the only ones mourning today. Matthias Corvinus was...a friend to the Jews...as well."

The woman looked at her with gratitude, but her husband snapped his head around toward her. The skin around his nose bunched together like a vicious dog about to bite. Hatred poured from his pupils. "Mourning accomplishes nothing with the Mohammedans. Only action."

He spoke with a distinctive Transylvanian accent. The two were probably *hajdus*, cattle drivers. Rebecca was trying to think of something comforting to say when the warrior grabbed his wife by the arm, turned on his heel, and dragged her over to four men dressed similarly as he.

A deafening *crash* made Ezra jump back. Despite the precautions taken by the workmen, one of the gates slid off its hinges and struck the truss. Ezra gripped his forehead and broke away from Rebecca. A team of muscular laborers rushed to the fallen door and pushed it up, while her husband climbed a nearby tree.

"Thank the Lord our God," He called down to his wife. "The panels are undamaged."

Rebecca nodded indulgently, then looked to see what had become of the warrior and his wife. The group had grown to a dozen men. Their fuming expressions and loud voices matched the angry fingers they pointed at the scene. They were planning something. She had to find out what.

The group dispersed and went down a street where there were few janissaries. Following them at a distance, she went a hundred yards until she remembered Ezra. She stopped and turned to see him shimmying down the tree.

She waved her hand, and he waved back. Was that a quizzical look on his face or an angry one? There was no time to find out. She continued following the *hajdus*, ducking behind bystanders whenever anyone glanced over their shoulder.

At last they turned into an alley. Rebecca arrived at the beginning of the lane in time to see a door close a hundred feet away. What were they planning?

She moved quietly until she reached the portal, and pressed her ear to a crack between its wooden staves.

"They've shipped the statues out and started tearing down the palace doors," a voice boomed. "We can't let them get away with this!"

"Hear! Hear!" a chorus of voices rang out. They shouted in unison "Stop the pagans. Stop the pagans, now!"

A cold chill raced down Rebecca's spine, as the *hajdus* grew more aggressive. She crept away from the alley, her heart a little faster than she wanted to admit. When she met the street and stopped, she poked one eye around the corner. Not far from where the original crowd had gathered, janissaries assembled shouldering muskets. An officer pointed in her direction. She turned and nearly barreled into Ezra.

"What in God's name are you doing, wife?"

"Ezra, shush," she whispered, pressing her finger to her lips. "People are stirred up over the Turks hauling down the palace doors. Something is about to happen."

"Stirred up? I'm stirred up, too. But there's nothing I can do about it. Neither can they."

"If I have information that concerns the doors, don't you want to hear it?"

"I suppose."

69

"Follow me. I think some people are plotting a rebellion."

Rebecca led Ezra down the alley. When they reached the door, she pointed to it. "The locals are planning something. We'd better let them know the Turks are on their way."

Ezra nodded. He pounded on the wood surface with the side of his fist. "Open up. The janissaries are coming."

The door flew open and nearly knocked him over. Two burly *hajdus* grabbed him by his robe and yanked him inside. Two others manhandled Rebecca beside him. They pinned the two intruders against a wall while a small crowd surrounded them. "Who are you? What do you want?"

"I am Ezra Mendel, grandson of Jakob Mendel, the Jewish Prefect appointed by King Matthias Corvinus." A murmur of recognition rippled through the onlookers.

Ezra wriggled to lift a hand free and pointed it at the crowd. "You will all die in a few minutes if you stay here. Janissaries are coming."

"What janissaries?" the man with the booming voice asked.

Rebecca lifted her voice. "The ones marching from the palace. Don't you people post lookouts?"

Just then, the door opened again and a girl entered, hands lifted high. "Brothers. At least thirty janissaries are marching down the street."

Everyone's eyes widened. "Quickly," the man with the booming voice urged. "To the cellar."

More than twenty people moved like packed cattle toward a trap door. One by one, they disappeared into the dark below. Finally, Ezra and Rebecca were the only ones left in the room.

"Come, Ezra." With that, Rebecca lifted her skirt with one hand, held on to the side of the opening, and her feet found a ladder's rung. She descended to the bottom and the door slammed over her.

Her heart froze. "Ezra? Are you there?"

CHAPTER EIGHT

Mohammedan Occupied Hungary
June, 1684

SARAH'S THIGHS NEVER FELT SO SORE BEFORE. Several days riding in a Tartar saddle smaller and with less padding than a German one wearied her bones. Humming several chants she remembered from her favorite cantor distracted her from her aches. It warmed her heart to reminisce on the temple vocalist's ability to shift from the deepest bass until he rose to baritone, tenor and even alto. It relieved her mind from her seemingly hopeless situation, and Simon's *kvetching*.

"*Oy* this is torment," he grumped. "Why don't you just send a note to my father and have him ransom us out of this misery? The Spanish torture my people, too," he complained. "But it's usually over with in a few days. *Do you hear me? Only days!* Why does a Tartar treat a Jew worse than the Christian Inquisition? I swear by everything holy, you people make hell look like paradise."

Kamil remained silent during Simon's jeremiads until

72

he finally lost patience and exploded. "Shut up, you whining dog! Or I'll cast you into the Danube."

Simon became quiet. After a period, he would recite one of the psalms or something from the Talmud. Then he would quote from the book of Job, comparing it to his own travails. That is, until Kamil barked a final warning. "Shut up, or I'll circumcise your lips from your mouth. Then the rabbis can write a new book about your troubles, wretched *dhimmi*."

Sarah grew determined to find the *brokhe*, the blessing in their situation. She waited until Kamil took one of his rare breaks to water the ponies at a stream. "Excuse me, Kamil," she called out cheerfully to him. "Do you mind if we take a moment to wash? We'll refresh ourselves and make better riding companions."

Kamil jerked his head toward the water, and grunted his assent.

Sarah unraveled the braids wound around the side of her head and tied them into a knot in the back. Holding her breath, she kneeled on the bank and immersed her head into the cool running brook. When she pulled up her dripping hair, she jumped. Simon stood a foot away, extending a towel to her. She took it. "Thank you, Simon."

He looked down, ever so serious. "We need to help one another."

His unusually agreeable mood stunned her. Was she hallucinating? She dried herself off, wringing the extra water from her hair, and walked over to Kamil, whose pony lowered its head to graze. "Give me your water skin, and I'll fill it."

"Mind your own affairs." There was no mistaking the distrust in his voice. Or the tension in his jaw.

73

Sarah smiled and walked back to her pony. Humming, she grabbed a water skin hanging from the saddle, and immersed it in the stream.

"*Ssst.*" Kamil sucked through his teeth. Glancing sideways, she saw him fingering inside his mouth. A long time passed while he dug until he finally stopped, looking annoyed. He soon repeated "*Ssst.*"

"Simon, do you still keep that Basque toothpick?"

"And what if I do? That is mine."

"Yes, it is. But if you act kind toward our captor, he may be nicer to us."

"Be nice to the slaver that kidnapped us? Am I hearing you correctly?"

"Please indulge me, cousin. Do it for me."

Simon mumbled his misgivings, but reached inside his waist pouch and fished out the pick. "Here, then. Take it."

"Thank you."

Kamil dismounted, kneeled, and searched the underbrush. He tried pulling his lips open with two fingers and picking his teeth with a thin branch from a bush, but nothing seemed to work.

"I hate to see you suffer." Sarah walked closer to Kamil. "This is a toothpick made of whalebone. My cousin hopes it will bring you relief."

Out of desperation or only to quicken things along, Kamil snatched the thin piece of bone, dipped it in the stream, and wiped it off on the hide wrapped around his waist. Sarah assumed he wanted to eliminate any poison she might have coated it with. He inserted the bone between his lips and worked it in and out. Soon, he spat a sliver of something out his mouth. His jaw relaxed.

Sarah stood before him patiently. "I am so happy the

bone helped you. Perhaps we can return it to Simon, and he can share it with you when you need it."

"Or perhaps I will keep it."

"However God touches your heart." Sarah turned on her heel and went back to her pony.

■ ■ ■

Count Marsigli's eyes flashed mischievously as he held out his hand. "Dr. Mathis Zieglar, a pleasure. Except for what is said about you by the Jesuits and other good Catholics."

Mathis's hand went limp in Marsigli's clasp. "I am friends with everyone who studies the sciences with an honest heart."

"Then San Petronio Basilica in Bologna is where you should come. Signore Cassini and I have explored the planets there with the order's blessing." Marsigli squeezed Mathis' hand hard. "Perhaps, they allow heretics there."

"Then you would enjoy the University of Vienna, where your associations account for more than your intellect."

"That is enough." D'Aviano wagged his finger. "The two of you are on a sacred mission, not a joust."

The count bowed. "Of course, beloved brother."

Mathis bowed also. "Yes, good brother. I will suffer *any* indignity to fulfill my responsibilities."

D'Aviano waved dismissively at Endre. "This is a private matter. Be gone."

Endre glanced at Mathis, then disappeared down the stairs. D'Aviano came up to Mathis and the count. "I charge you both to cooperate in finding the treasure."

D'Aviano walked past them and leaned against the wall next to the gap created by the bombardment. Looking out, he pulled back his cowl, unbuttoned the top of his robe, and mopped his brow with his long sleeve. "You must figure out where to concentrate your search before Buda falls. You have to find the treasure before the looters."

"The treasure. Hmm." The count fingered his shoulder-length wig. "The letter you sent arrived in poor condition. Remind me what John Corvinus, the son of the Raven King, said about the treasure."

"You didn't understand my letter?" D'Aviano's nose twitched. "I will repeat myself, then. When John Corvinus lay on his deathbed, he said 'the treasure of the Raven King is in the palace. Just read the words there of the father of ten children, the children of Hungary, born in Basel.'"

"How strange a riddle." The count's brow furrowed. "Basel is in Switzerland. Yet the father whoever the father is has 'children of Hungary', born in Switzerland.' My head whirls in such language, little sense is made by it."

Mathis did his best to stifle the smile growing inside. It gave him satisfaction to see his opponents confused, especially concerning something he had unraveled days ago.

D'Aviano's eyes scanned him intently.

"You know what those words mean, don't you, Captain?"

"Which? The twisted ones of Count Marsigli, or those of John Corvinus? If the latter, I can only guess they must refer to the same thing I read on the wall over there…until it was destroyed."

D'Aviano ignored Mathis' barb, and looked toward the ceiling. "'The treasure is in the hard substance….' This tells me the treasure may be found in the palace *and* inside a hard substance."

The friar brightened and whirled around, his long

76

sleeves flying as he pointed at Mathis. "You still have those books I gave you, Captain?"

Icy fingers squeezed Mathis throat. Those books had helped him piece together the conundrum. "Um…I should…*ja*."

"Turn them over immediately to Count Marsigli. Share everything you've read with him. Enlighten him to where you are in the investigation."

"*Jawohl.*"

Damn D'Aviano. Mathis had to stop the count from reading the dark green leather-bound volume that contained an illustration of Buda's palace entrance. Otherwise the count would see Bonfini's epigram over the palace's entrance. If Marsigli figured out its meaning, it would lead him closer to deducing the hidden treasure inside the bronze doors was the *Mishneh Torah*.

"I will leave you two to work this out." D'Aviano breezed past them, and strode down the stairs.

"Come," the count gestured toward the gap in the wall. "I will show you my tent. Bring me the books in an hour."

Mathis released a slow breath. His most pressing concern was to find Simon and Sarah. But first, he had to blunt D'Aviano's delving. An hour was plenty of time.

CHAPTER NINE

Near Lake Balaton, in Habsburg Occupied Hungary.
Late June, 1684

KAMIL TRAIPSED HIS CAPTIVES FROM THEIR CAMP, into the mountainous region overlooking the marshes of Lake Balaton in Southwestern Hungary. Forests of bulrushes grew to the height of a man beneath them. Looking west, Sarah shielded her eyes from the sun. The swamp melted into the horizon. It seemed endless.

As their horses threaded their way through the trees, Sarah sniffed. The pleasant fragrance of vineyards filled the air. She noticed the sun dip below the marsh. "Can we stop for the evening?"

Kamil halted his pony and looked around. He pointed to the grade above them to a rock shelf with an outcrop hanging above it. "We will camp over there."

They dismounted a few minutes later on a ledge whose surface was half moss, half blackened rock. Kamil wrapped a chain around their chests and bound them to a nearby tree half-blanketed with green mold.

"Is this necessary?" Simon's face reddened. "You usually wait until we're ready to go to sleep before tying us up."

"Open your mouth," Kamil commanded Simon as he wadded up a section of scarf into a ball. Kamil forced the fabric into his captive's mouth, then held it in place with twine tied around Simon's head over his lips. Kamil did the same with Sarah. He restrained their arms and hands with a light chain, and their legs with heavier ones.

"I'm going to get provisions." Mounting his horse, Kamil looked over his shoulder and laughed. "Don't wander off."

After Kamil left, Sarah bowed her head and lifted the chain wrapped around her chest. Next, she used her tongue to force the scarf outside her mouth, and then finally rubbed the twine against the chains until it broke free. She urged Simon to do the same, and soon they breathed fresh air without a sweaty scarf in their mouth, though their chains were still firmly fastened.

"Why did you tell me to push the scarf inside the twine, Sarah?"

"So that your lips wouldn't bleed when you rubbed the chain against them. We don't want Kamil to return and realize we've found a way out of our restraints."

"*Ja*, good thought." Simon's tone was mildly approving.

"You did well this afternoon, Simon. You repeated your lines of holy writ quietly to avoid angering Kamil."

Simon mumbled something that sounded grateful. Then his voice turned serious. "What are we going to do when we get to Mount Peca, and Kamil finds nothing in this cave? He won't hesitate to kill us, you know."

"I know, cousin. We have to escape and bring the code's explanation to Captain Zieglar. I believe we can do it."

"Zieglar! That man again." Simon threw up his hands. "The man who betrayed us."

"No, Simon. He's the man who will help us. I have felt his goodness."

Finding their chains impossible to loosen, they decided to re-insert their gags before Kamil returned. They clenched the twine in their teeth.

When afternoon shadows spread across their camp, Kamil returned and released them. His saddlebags bulged with vegetables, and dead chickens dangled over his pony's side. "We eat."

Sarah eyed the bundle of kindling under the saddle bags. Such a rare indulgence was risky because Kamil had mentioned they were in an area contested by the Habsburgs and Mohammedans, and patrolled by roving bands from both armies. He had avoided campfires up to this point, she assumed, to avoid detection from pursuers.

The Tartar climbed behind an embankment above the trail and disappeared inside a cave hidden behind it that went deep inside the hill. Sarah followed him, a light breeze wafted from the entrance into the bowels of a small cavern. Building a fire inside this cave made it less likely to alert a patrol.

The three of them sat on boulders, and feasted on chicken, bread and wine. Kamil kept his sword ready on his hip.

Simon wrinkled his brow. "Isn't it against the law for a Muslim to drink wine?"

The corners of Kamil's mouth quirked up. "Isn't against Jewish law to eat food that is not kosher? And yet here you are."

Sarah chuckled. "And here we are."

All three of them laughed together. It seemed to break the tension that had bound them to one another as tight as the twine Kamil had used to gag Simon and Sarah.

"You know, Kamil," Sarah said in between bites of her bread, "I am not sure what you hope to accomplish by bringing us here."

Kamil's smile arced beneath his drooped mustache. "Several things. Simon is a prize of war, one for which his father Samuel will pay handsomely. *Your* father will feel the same about you."

"Yes, I'm sure that would earn you a small sum. But are those your only reasons?"

The Tartar lifted a brow. "You think well, for a woman. Yes, there is more: as long as you are in my custody, Mathis Zieglar will stay out of my way."

Simon and Sarah glanced at one another. Simon shook his head. "You misunderstand our relationship with Captain Zieglar. We don't work with or for him."

Kamil's eyes twinkled. "That may be true of *you*, *Herr* Oppenheimer. But I am no fool. I see the way your cousin's face changes every time I mention Zieglar. Even he cannot not be blind to her beauty."

"Now see here," Simon sputtered. "She is a Jew, and will only marry a Jew."

"So you say." Kamil opened his mouth and wagged his tongue. "But someday, if you live to see it, Zieglar will say to you 'and yet, here we are!'"

Sarah clamped her jaw hard to keep from spitting out her food and laughing out loud.

Simon turned his back on Kamil, and muttered angrily to himself.

Sarah changed the conversation to keep Simon from

having a stroke. "I understand why you have...ah...shall we say...taken us into custody. But what do you hope to gain by finding the contents of the cave in Mount Peca?"

Kamil's face lost all expression A chill passed through the air between them. "You think you know me, don't you? The 'wild Tartar' from the steppes, who only knows how to steal and kill. That is all you know of my people."

"Well, you speak German quite well, and also read." Sarah smiled. "So, you know more than just how to steal and kill."

Kamil's face relaxed. "Yes. I attended *madrassas* and other schools for years in Constantinople. This Tartar knows music, theology, and languages. But when necessary, I kill like any warrior."

"You have sides I've never seen. But what does this have to do with the treasure in Mount Peca?"

"You wouldn't ask if you knew how things were for the Nogay Tartars. Ever since Genghis Khan, we've made our living by war, trade, and slavery. But now, our traditions are in danger."

Sarah's brows arched high. "Your people want to turn away from slave trading?"

"Your people have a saying." Kamil paused to stoke the embers of the fire. "'The handwriting is on the wall'. It has taken the English and Portuguese only a few decades to steal the same number of slaves out of Africa as the Muslims did over centuries. The Christians will soon surpass us."

Sarah shook her head, confused. "I don't understand the connection. You want the treasure because you're worried about European competition for the slave trade?"

"It's not just the slave trade. The Dutch and English

82

also broke the sultan's trade monopoly on goods from the East. If we don't stop them, the Christians will overwhelm us."

"You must refer to Christian Europe discovering a new route to India, instead of purchasing goods through the sultan. But, I still don't see what all this—"

Kamil threw the stick angrily into the fire, sending a shower of sparks into the air. "Yes, your precious Christian friends found a way to go around Africa and bypass us, thanks to the Portuguese. We have to copy the Europeans the way they've learned from us. We have to restore our old trade, and rely less on slavery."

Even though Sarah was still confused over why Kamil was intent on finding the treasure, she was impressed. He had a sophisticated understanding of the world. Due to her family's involvement in foreign trade, Sarah knew about Christian Europe's success in cracking the Ottoman trade monopoly. But she never expected to hear its implications discussed by a "savage" Tartar.

Kamil found a longer stick with which to stoke the fire, and his voice calmed. "The Muslims have excelled in commerce in the past, and they must return to it. The Prophet—Peace Be Upon Him—was a merchant, just as the Jews have learned to prosper from the same thing. We must take back our leadership in trade, or we will perish."

Sarah tilted her head to one side. "I understand. But how will finding the treasure help the Tartars accomplish that?"

Kamil snickered. "You are so persistent. I will say that, my friend Davudoff and I made a good profit exporting coffee beans to Vienna. The way things were going, we could have stopped the slaving expeditions altogether, where we lost too many men. That is, until your Captain Zieglar interfered and ruined our plans."

Simon turned around. "Perhaps we can work out something mutually profitable in your trading strategy."

Kamil wiped the wine from his mustache. "Never. Your friend Zieglar knows too much about my illegal activities, and hangs it over my head like a sword. If I refuse to do his bidding, he will report my coffee smuggling to the sultan."

Sarah could contain herself no longer. "Kamil, are you saying you want the Tartars to give up the slave trade?"

Kamil grunted angrily. "First, I have to find the treasure Zieglar seeks, so I can hold it over *his* head. That is why you two are so valuable. I will use you to force Zieglar to keep his mouth shut. Then I can return to the coffee trade."

Simon and Sarah shared a glance. Her stunned expression mirrored in his eyes. Clearing her throat broke the connection. "Captain Zieglar only wants to rescue his people from your slave market. If you help him, he'll leave you alone."

"*Only*, you say? *Only*? You have no idea of the fortune it would take to ransom the hundreds of slaves he wants. Zieglar is mad, and he has no money."

"That's what you misunderstand, Kamil. The treasure contains such a powerful secret, he believes the sultan will release the abducted women and children."

Kamil put his foot on a boulder, and rested an elbow on his knee. Reluctance dripped off him in a torrent. "My people are so poor, they starve and die from lack of shelter. If this secret is so valuable, I must use it to help them."

■ ■ ■

Mathis scoured through crates in his reserved tent, desperate to find the book he needed before the regiment relocated to Visegrad. And before his meeting with Marsigli. Beneath a dozen bound journals and extra blankets, he found the book he needed. He held it up to the candlelight with one hand and grasped a razor's handle with the other. With any luck, he could pick the binding apart, remove the page he wanted, and re-glue it without leaving a trace. D'Aviano would have to look elsewhere for clues, and Mathis could search for the Oppenheimers.

The flap to the tent entrance rustled. "Coming in, Captain Zieglar."

Mathis froze.

D'Aviano.

He hadn't anticipated the friar's arrival for another half hour. Mathis dropped the razor to the ground, and kicked it under his cot as the friar drew back the canvas. He grasped the book behind folded arms.

"Thought it best to drop by and refresh myself on your progress." D'Aviano's smile was too cunning. The brother's early arrival was not accidental.

The flaps parted again, and Count Marsigli entered. Instantly, he grimaced. "Such a dark place. Perhaps we can move things outside?"

Flabbergasted, Mathis nodded numbly and the party removed themselves to a table prepared outside the row of tents. D'Aviano tarried a moment and was the last of the three to leave the tent.

Three ravens hopped around several flasks of wine and helped themselves to a plate of cheese. D'Aviano and the count waved frantically at the birds in a flutter of feather. Mathis enjoyed their frenzy. It was obvious the men had

85

planned to surprise him, but the birds had turned the tables on them.

Much to Mathis' annoyance, the count yanked the book out of his arms. As Marsigli laid it down on the table and spread the pages apart, he repeated D'Aviano's words, "The treasure of the Raven King is in the palace. Just read the words there of the father of ten children, the children of Hungary, born in Basel."

Finally, he came to the picture of the palace entrance. "Well, Brother, somewhere here is where the promised words must be, as John Corvinus said, 'in the palace.'"

D'Aviano fit a pair of spectacles over his nose and hunched over the page. He traced the illustration with a delicate finger. "'The father of ten children...ten children.'"

The count's eyebrows lifted, and he pointed to the arch over the entrance. "Look there. Aren't those words written by Antonio Bonfini? Once again, I am thinking of his written works. He was the author of *Rerum Hungaricum Decades*."

Mathis stiffened. The count was much too close to solving the puzzle.

D'Aviano ran his fingers quickly through his beard. "*Si, si*! Did you find out more about Bonfini?"

Marsigli looked down, said something in Italian, then disappeared behind a tent.

"What did he say?" Mathis shook his head in frustration. The two Italians seemed to talk to each other, and ignore him. "Where did he go?"

"Calm yourself." D'Aviano said absent-mindedly. "He will be back."

Mathis lifted a skeptical brow. "Perhaps when he returns he will favor us with something in German or Latin so we both can understand him."

D'Aviano peered out at Mathis through narrowed eyes. "Patience. The count is brilliant, even if a little eccentric."

Marsigli returned, holding an open book and talking under his breath as he walked. "As I thought, as I thought." He stopped in front of D'Aviano and lifted his head. "Now it is so obvious. *Rerum Hungaricum Decades* was a history of Hungary, written in ten volumes and published in Basel."

Mathis's neck hairs prickled. The count still directed his comments exclusively to D'Aviano. It was as if the nobleman considered himself on too high a level to address Mathis.

D'Aviano walked over and put his hand on Mathis' arm. "I see you are distressed, young Captain. Are you not happy with what we have found? The ten volumes of the history must be the ten children of Hungary. Can you not see it?"

Mathis' heart pounded. He might as well be a man forced to recite his sins before execution. "*Ja*," he said through tight lips, "the interpretation is possible. The ten children of Hungary, born in Basel."

D'Aviano's smile spread across his face as he read Bonfini's words from the illustration. "'The hall with statues cast from bronze and doors proclaim the genius of Prince Corvinus. That Corvinus should perish, after gaining so many triumphs over the enemy, his virtue, bronze, marble and writings forbid.'"

He turned. His eyes seemed to drink Mathis in. "You know what Bonfini's words mean, don't you, my son? Your posture tells me everything. You want to unburden yourself to us."

"Well...ah...." Mathis's breath caught in his chest, the sinews in his neck tightened like a crossbow's string. Damn D'Aviano, and damn his interrogations. The cleric was like a cat that had cornered a mouse, and now teased Mathis for the pleasure of it. "I think I need a cup of wine."

D'Aviano's brows arched, his smile melted and his eyes hardened. He raised his hand, clutching the straight razor Mathis had kicked under the cot. "Tell us what you know, or I'll call in the inquisitors. They'll pull it out of you."

Mathis' breath came in short, choked bursts. D'Aviano spoke of torture. The inquisitors would break his bones and pull his limbs out of joint. They wouldn't stop until Mathis talked. The longer Mathis resisted, the more painful and permanent the damage. He would never be able-bodied again. His life and career would be over.

CHAPTER TEN

"WHAT DO YOU WANT FROM ME, BROTHER?" Mathis threw up his hands. "You can't expect me to know what the missing words were on that wall. They weren't in the rubble."

The friar kept his tone even, and eerily calm. "You duck my questions, and you color your answers. You do everything but tell the truth. When did you turn into a deceiver, Mathis Zieglar?"

D'Aviano's words struck home and unleashed Mathis' shame. Inwardly, he couldn't deny the assessment was true, but he told himself his deception served a higher purpose.

D'Aviano's snapped his fingers. Guards seemingly appeared out of nowhere. They bound Mathis in chains. D'Aviano's face was granite-like. "You're not fooling anyone, my son. You can explain everything to the inquisitors."

Mathis was led up the hill inside the gates, and taken to a tiny house undamaged from the bombardment. An iron ring had been screwed into a rafter. He groaned inwardly. His tormentors intended to suspend him with a rope, a *strappado*.

His hands would be manacled behind his back and the rope attached and threaded through the eyelet. Then he would be suspended above the floor until his arms were yanked from their sockets.

D'Aviano's face softened into pity. "Would you like me to hear your confession before I leave? It might strengthen you in your hour of need."

Mathis shook his head bitterly. "I have nothing to confess."

"I don't understand you." D'Aviano's sigh sounded mournful. "Somewhere deep inside, you changed from an honest, God-fearing man into a liar. When did it happen, my son? What blackened your heart?"

A mixture of fury and fear welled up so strongly inside, Mathis could contain himself no longer. "You want to know when I changed from being straightforward, Brother? Do you want to hear what makes me choose my words so carefully?"

D'Aviano's eyes brightened. "Go on."

"When I found out the church values loyalty to itself over the suffering of ordinary people."

D'Aviano blinked. "What?"

"I am more concerned about saving innocent women and children, than making the church supreme in Hungary."

The friar shook his head. "Your words make no sense whatsoever."

"What's more important, Brother? Getting back the thousands of people taken from our lands, and thrown into slavery? Or conducting another crusade against Islam so we can plant the cross in another country? Which is more important?"

D'Aviano looked bewildered at Mathis' challenge. "There is no way for us to rescue the victims of slavery. God has willed them lost to us."

Mathis swallowed back the disgust in his throat. "You know I have rescued a hundred already. Why not trust me to figure out how to save thousands?"

D'Aviano cast his gaze to the floor. "You must be purged from the devil whom controls your tongue. The Inquisition is the only way to purify you. May God have mercy on your soul." He made the sign of the cross, turned on his heel and left.

Mathis shuffled inside the small one room house containing no furniture save a wash basin mounted on a stand. He was grateful for the solitude. The fear of impending torture brought him to the breaking point, and he almost confessed information that would have destroyed the secrecy behind his motives. He needed to rest, regain his composure and prepare for the ordeal ahead.

As he walked over to a bed of straw in a corner, the door clicked behind him. He heard a crossbar slide against the outside. A small opening in the wall admitted narrow light over his bed. He shrugged in his chains and sat down.

Hours passed in silence until one guard opened the door, and another brought him a wooden tray with a plate of cheese and a wine flask. "Brother D'Aviano says you probably won't mind the beak marks left by the ravens."

"It's not the ravens I mind. It's the bite of the snake."

■ ■ ■

Tannenberg held a candle shoulder height, and turned over stone chunks with a stick. Dozens of such fragments

91

were strewn across the floor of the *Aga's* headquarters.

"Found anything yet?"

Amused at her attempt to keep her voice low and manly, Tannenberg cast a glance over his shoulder at Private Weber. "Nothing but rubble from our guns. You?"

"Maybe. Come look."

Three stone fragments were aligned side by side. Weber glanced at him. "Can you read Latin, Captain?"

"Uh-huh." Tannenberg bent down and rearranged three chunks. "'The writings of the sage...are inside the hard substance...that opens wide.'"

He stood up and rubbed both hands together. "I knew I could count on your eagle vision, Private."

He pulled out a mallet and chisel from the bag on the floor. "Let's see if we can use your eyesight to make something to entertain Brother D'Aviano."

Private Weber frowned. "You're not asking me to lie, are you, Captain?"

"Lie?" Tannenberg laughed from his belly. "Of course not. Not any more than when I tell people you're a man."

Weber held out her hand reluctantly and took the tools from Tannenberg. "May God forgive us."

■ ■ ■

On a farm a few miles outside of Brasso, Transylvania.

Endre trudged up the hill toward the white-washed cottage with a thatched roof. Yes, this was the place his mother had described. He congratulated himself on having received permission from Count Eszterhazy to leave his unit during the siege. The count's initial stern demeanor had melted into warmth once Endre mentioned his goal was to rescue

Simon Oppenheimer—and restore the flow of supplies to the half-starved Habsburg troops.

"We'll have a prayer recited at mass for your success," the count added as Endre headed for his horse.

Endre rode away from the Habsburg camp to the north, to the roads of Upper Hungary, safe from the Turks.

After a day's traveling, and his horse's gait slowed to a crawl, he came to a fork in the road where he encountered a merchant driving a wagon loaded with goods. "Hail, stranger. Which of these roads will take me to the forests of Transylvania?"

The man halted the mule pulling his cart. He pointed to the left. "That will take you east over miles of mountains and plains. A day and a half's ride will take you to the Transylvanian border."

"Thank you, sir."

Endre pulled off the road and dismounted from his horse. He shed his regimental uniform, put it in a canvas bag and buried it beneath a tree. A quick glance at his map's legend reminded him that Transylvania was a partially autonomous state, but a vassal of the Ottomans. He would not receive a warm reception if he wore dress that identified him as part of the Habsburg army, a power that had persecuted many of the region's Protestant inhabitants.

"Time to slip into something more traditionally Hungarian," he said half-aloud. He stepped into tight, peach-colored trousers that extended just below the knee. Then he put on two Turkish-style boots: each had lower halves tailored to the shape of his foot; the tops were made of a separate, broad sheet of leather that wound around his calves.

Next, he slipped into a mauve, light linen coat that fell

to his thighs. Then he draped a heavy, long-sleeved coat over the ensemble. As he tightened the laces around grommets on the garment's front, he smiled. He could never figure out why his friend Mathis and other Germans like him preferred buttoned coats.

With a broad sash fastened around his linen coat, and a long-handled hammer tucked inside, Endre finalized his transformation. He hung a curved saber from his belt against his left thigh. Finally, he attached a canteen and a circular powder canister to the sash, and fit a round hat over his head. Three tall feathers rose prominently behind an opening in the cap's upturned brim above his forehead.

Feeling a chill, he reached into a saddlebag and pulled out a shaggy lamb's wool overcoat and fit his arms inside. "Well now, if I've done this right, I should look like a Transylvanian *hajdu*."

Endre went to his horse, fit his toe into the stirrup and mounted. It was time to traverse the Transylvanian border and complete the first leg of his mission.

After crossing the frontier, he traveled southeast several days until he reached the village of Brasso. He recalled the tales he'd heard hundreds of times over a military campfire about the area's significance. It was close to the site where, more than two hundred years before, Vlad Dracula had impaled thousands of Saxons.

He rode near the city, nestled inside a ring of mountains. Its outer and inner walls and the gate were two stories high, ornate and well guarded.

Endre hesitated. Should he go in and seek shelter for the night? He shook his head, and turned his horse away. Better not to expose himself to the Brasso constabulary and raise questions about the purpose of his travel. He decided to travel a few miles more and lodge in a small inn a short distance outside the city.

The next morning, he found his way to a whitewashed, thatch-roofed home not far from Brasso. As he dismounted and tied his horse to a tree, Endre called out, "Anyone home? Endre Bakos, here."

Pigeons cooing led him behind the home to an octagonal birdhouse perched high on a pole. Three more birdhouses rose behind it, one of them boasting two stories. Several empty casks were strewn around the area next to a well-worn trail that looked made by the wheel of a barrow. He looked back at the birdhouses. "Dovecotes," he mumbled, then hesitated. Why were there so few bird droppings on the ground?

Seeing no one, Endre noticed the outline of the long side of a barn within a stand of pines a few hundred feet behind the house. The scent of turpentine filled his nose. Wind running through the boughs whispered caution. Following the path toward the building, he pushed back needle-bearing branches.

"Hello?"

The path disappeared. His foot stepped into a void, and he plummeted. He grabbed a cleft in a nearby boulder with one hand. It broke his fall and kept him from tumbling into a pit. He planted his other palm above the rim. Pushing himself backwards, he sat on level ground.

Endre shook his head and focused. Twenty feet below, at the bottom of a sharply dug moat, foot-high iron spikes jutted out from the mud and dirt. A few feet away from where he stood, a boar skeleton lay skewered on several of them.

It could have been him, had it not been for the rock to

which he clung. His heart raced, and his mother's words returned to him. "The descendants of Orban owe our family much, but you will expose yourself to great danger if you ask their help."

Endre shuddered. *Great danger, indeed.* His nerves calmed and he felt strangely serene. Despite his close call, somewhere inside his soul he felt everything happened as it should. There was no stopping now; too many people relied on him. He had to find the descendants of Orban, no matter what the cost. But how could he span the trench?

He surveyed his surroundings, and let the cool air on his cheeks calm him. A bridge to his left spanned the channel, but a solid gate with a heavy padlock blocked the path. There was no easy way through that.

A thick tangle of thorns to the left of the bridge convinced him not to explore the area to find another way to cross the moat. To the right of the abyss he would have to fight his way through pines growing close together to avoid the precipice. It looked more promising.

He pushed through the branches, lowering his head to avoid the stinging needles that snapped back in his face. The firm soil under his feet became knife-edged rock that threatened to trip him as he stumbled on. After making his way along a parallel path to the moat, he found himself blocked by a new valley, one deeper than the moat. It ran into the trench at a right angle. He was about to curse his luck when he looked along the edge of the moat to his left and saw a single plank conveniently stretching over it.

Whoever had put the beam there had made it difficult to find. No seeable path led to it. The row of iron teeth at the bottom of the moat had followed him right to the juncture of the valley. He hesitated. Should he try to walk over the beckoning slab?

Something told Endre to test the situation first. He traced his steps back to the dovecotes where the empty barrels sat. A shovel stained white from being used to pick up the pigeon droppings leaned against the cottage. He used it to fill a barrel with soil. Cradling it in his arms and unable to shield himself from the pine needles whipping into his face, he made the torturous trip back to the single plank.

Gingerly, he placed one foot on the slab. It creaked. He carefully placed the barrel on the plank and shoved it with a stick to the beam's midsection. The plank sagged, then splintered into pieces into the pit below. A trap. Someone had gone to great lengths to isolate the barn from intruders.

Endre made his way back to the bridge. He had to find a way past the smooth door that stood on the near side of the moat, blocking his path to the bridge. The door rose between two posts connected by heavy cables to two others on the far side of the trench. Thinner cables hung from the heavier ones and supported a walkway.

Endre studied the posts on the other side. How could he climb over the abyss without ending up like the skewered boar? He untied a rope hanging from his horse's saddle, and fashioned a loop on both ends. After several attempts, he landed a loop over the post.

He summoned his mare and guided her against the smooth door. He halted it and stood upright in the saddle. With the second loop in one hand, he crouched low, and sprang up with all his might.

It was just enough to propel his hands to the top of the beam on the near side. Endre gripped it tight and slipped the rope over the post. Good. The rope now spanned the moat and hung parallel to the bridge.

He grabbed the line with both fists, and whispered a prayer. Hanging on for dear life, Endre advanced hand-over-hand until he was part way over the abyss. Pressure tore at the sinews beneath his arm and made him grunt.

He stopped and held on with both hands. He rocked his legs away from the bridge then back again repeatedly until the momentum landed him on the walkway. Releasing the rope, he grasped the bridge's vertical cables to keep from falling backward.

He heaved a sigh of triumph. He had found his way past the door blocking the entrance to the bridge, and could walk to the other side.

CHAPTER ELEVEN

Visegrad

A SHAFT OF DAYLIGHT SHONE THROUGH THE narrow window, and woke Mathis from his stupor. The prospect of appearing before the Inquisition stole any possibility of restful sleep. Yet, the memory of something happening last night gave him a glimmer of hope.

Fingers had tapped against the bars of the window, and a throaty whisper filtered through the darkness. "Don't give up, *Hauptfeder*. Remember one thing and you'll be safe."

"Tannenberg? Is that you? You shouldn't be here. If they see you they'll come after you like they went for me."

"Listen closely, *Hauptfeder*. There's no time to explain. No matter what you see me do tomorrow, keep quiet and shut up. It's for the best."

Then he was gone.

Mathis dozed off before re-awakening. Thinking again of what had happened earlier, he dipped his face in a wash basin. Had he dreamed of Tannenberg's visit? Or was the message real? What did his friend have in store for him on the day of his execution?

■ ■ ■

The door opened and a sergeant walked into Mathis' room. He stopped and clicked his heels. "Prepare to face the tribunal, Captain Zieglar."

Mathis stood and brushed the straw from his coat. "What are the charges, Sergeant?"

"Treason and heresy, Captain. Civil magistrates have arrived to hear your case."

Mathis wasn't surprised. Handling charges of violation of the faith were not something a military court was designed for. "I'm flattered I should warrant such attention."

He departed his room, surrounded by four guards. He had no sooner walked into the sunlight than D'Aviano approached, his right palm extended above his head. "In the name of all that is holy and that of your emperor, think of what you are doing, Mathis Zieglar. Think of your salvation and the good of your country. Think of everything you have fought for and all the good you have accomplished ...."

D'Aviano's homily was interrupted by a high-pitched squeal. Mathis and the friar turned their gaze toward the source of the raucous grinding emanating from down the road. Tannenberg sported an expansive grin as he wheeled a barrow filled with jagged blocks. Private Weber nervously trailed behind him.

"This might answer the questions you have for Captain Zieglar." Tannenberg chuckled. "Fresh from the *Aga's* quarters."

Remembering his friend's warning of the night before,

Mathis stifled a scream of protest in his throat. Tannenberg was about to reveal the location of the treasure of the Raven King. How could he betray him like this?

Tannenberg took the stone pieces and laid them side-by-side on a table next to the house, the smooth side of each chunk facing up revealing the etchings. He read each one as he fit the fragments together. "The writings of the sage…are inside the hard substance that…." Tannenberg paused, raised his voice, and pointed dramatically at the final block. "Adorns the arch in the library."

D'Aviano frowned and raised his hand again as majestically as a statue of Augustus Caesar. But before he could pronounce condemnation, Tannenberg boomed. "Captain Zieglar's memory returned last night, and he told me where to find the missing pieces of the code. He asked me to bring this to you as an expression of his willingness to cooperate with you in finding the treasure."

D'Aviano's hand dropped. He looked as if he were chewing his lips. He walked up to the stone blocks, breathing like an annoyed bull.

Tannenberg's face lit up. "You'll see that the jagged edges of the stones fit together, Brother. As they did before someone carved them out of Dracula's cell."

"*Ja, ja.* It all appears in order."

Mathis wiped the sweat off his forehead. "Then I am a free man?"

"*Ja, ja,*" the priest muttered. "You are free."

Mathis scanned the people collected around them. Private Weber had faded away. The group parted and Count Marsigli appeared with a smug face. "How fortunate that before the trial begins, you remember the information. Let us hope your memory as quickly returns when

101

you command men."

Mathis sniffed. "Let us hope you speak proper German when you command men."

D'Aviano folded his arms and stood back from their verbal skirmishing. He turned to Tannenberg. "Tell me something, Captain Tannenberg. Where is that aide of yours whom seems to follow you around the camp?"

Tannenberg stood motionless. "Brother?"

Mathis knew from Tannenberg's unusually stiff response that his friend hid his feelings. His lies had saved Mathis's life.

"You know…Private…Private…."

A guard cleared his throat. "Private Weber, Brother?"

"Ah, *ja*. Private Weber." D'Aviano's lips curled into a smile, and he addressed one of the guards. "Have his commanding officer investigate how long it's been since the private's last confession."

"*Jawohl*, Brother."

D'Aviano's was sniffing for something with a persistence rivaling a bloodhound's.

■ ■ ■

After crossing the bridge, Endre approached the barn, remembering his mother's warning, "You will expose yourself to great danger if you ask their help."

Looking around for signs of trouble, he called out. "Hello?"

Only bleating of sheep answered, which grew louder as he neared a weathered structure.

"Hello?"

Endre circled the building until he stood a short distance from the entrance where several of the wooly

102

creatures grazed. Something seemed out of sorts, but he couldn't tell what. Suddenly, one of the "sheep" ran and lunged at him with gnashing teeth. The animal sunk its teeth into Endre's arm and pulled him to the ground. Endre's thick jacket and undercoat kept him from serious injury, but the bite drew blood. He kicked himself free and rolled away, the monster straining at the end of its chain.

He was now face to face with a growling Komondor. Heavy cords of hair hung from its coat and shook as the dog barked. Komondors held a reputation for blending in with a flock of sheep, only to surprise and destroy a marauding bear. He counted himself lucky to have escaped the worst of its bite.

Reaching into a satchel he pulled out a chunk of meat. He waved it a few inches from the creature's nose, and tossed it against the barn. The dog glanced in the direction of the morsel, but continued to stand his ground, snarling.

"Damn, dog. That meat's good enough to make me run after it."

Leaving the animals, Endre scouted along the edge of the moat until he found a long, sturdy branch on the ground. Assuming the owner of the animal was somewhere near, he wanted to avoid killing it with his sword. But he had to use the limb to get past it and see what was in the barn. Then he'd find the people who could help him locate Sarah and Simon Oppenheimer.

When he returned to the barn, the hound had deserted the entrance and sniffed the ground for the meat. Endre summoned his courage and made for the opening with every ounce of his energy. The dog broke off its search and attacked. Endre snagged the dog's collar with the branch and pinned the animal against the barn.

Endre dropped the branch and ran. The dog caught up to him and sunk its teeth into his calf. Pivoting, he swung his fist into the beast's eye. The jaws released. He bolted into the barn out of the dog's reach.

As his excitement subsided, the pain in Endre's leg sent tears down his cheeks. He wiped the moisture away and he sniffed. A strong manure stench poured out of the barn, yet there were no animal sounds inside. His curiosity rose as his eyes adjusted to the dim light.

Ignoring the dog barking furiously behind him, Endre caught his breath and looked around. His nose directed him to the left wall. Beneath a hayloft, open barrels reeked noxiously. Could this be what had happened to the pigeon waste?

He caught the glint of a flame out of the corner of his eye. In the barn's right hand corner, a fire glowed through an arched opening of a brick furnace with a conical dome.

A metallic, gourd-like container rested on a stand a foot away from the furnace's flame. The rounded bottom of the "gourd" sat closest to the furnace; its neck pointed upward away from the heat, and connected to a tube leading to a barrel on the ground.

This was the workshop of an alchemist. But where was the master?

"Why do you intrude?" a woman's voice challenged behind him.

Endre instinctively grabbed the haft of his sword and wheeled. A short distance away, a striking-looking woman stood deathly still. Her graying brown hair was pulled back. Despite her maturity, she had fresh skin and naturally red lips. When she turned her head and gazed to his right, he noticed her bun was largely covered by a brocaded coif. *She is either married or widowed.*

Though inside a barn, she was dressed formally in the style common to many Transylvanian women. Her white, fluffy ruffle adorned her neck over a dark brown vest bound with ties over a long-sleeved white blouse. A brown, matching velvet skirt showed behind a lacy apron.

"Why do you intrude?" This time her voice rang with annoyance.

Though he had never set eyes on her before, there was something familiar about her, something he couldn't explain. Then he remembered to give the response his mother had told him. "My name is Endre Bakos, in the service of Count Esterhazy. I am looking for the descendants of Orban."

Endre noticed two flasks attached to either side of her belt. She lifted her eyes to Endre's and let her fingers fall around the flask on her right. "Which descendant of Orban do you seek, Endre Bakos?"

Endre swallowed, he sensed danger in that container. His response could very well determine the fate of the Habsburg army, not to mention his own life. He thought hard and chose his words carefully. "The matriarch descendant of Orban, the man whose cannon brought down the walls of Constantinople."

Endre's mother had raised him since his youth on the story of Orban, the Transylvanian caster of bronze who had offered his services to the Ottoman sultan. The Muslims had used Orban's twenty-seven-foot gun to smash the walls of the city, previously considered impregnable for centuries.

Orban's descendants had followed in his footsteps, and were rumored to have improved his skills in ways that some suspected derived from the black arts. The fact the descendants of Orban were led by a woman deepened that suspicion, though few dared disturb the family's peace.

The woman's hands gripped tighter around the canister. "What is your request?"

"I need to send a message throughout Hungary, Matriarch of Orban."

A faint smile formed on her lips. "You want to use one of my pigeons to take a message somewhere?"

Endre reached into his purse and pulled out a bag of coins. "Yes, my lady, but not just one bird. Every one you can spare. Send a message to every corner of Hungary. We are looking for two Jews who've been kidnapped by a Tartar. So far as I know, they could be anywhere. Whoever returns them will earn a ransom from Samuel Oppenheimer, the Habsburg emperor's chief financier."

"A ransom, you say." She lifted her face to the loft above her. "Family, can you hear me?"

Footsteps fell in the loft above Endre. He looked up, and saw two young men and three girls of varying age. The men held crossbows, the women, flasks. "Yes Constanta," one of the men answered. "We hear you."

"Do not harm this man." Her smile broadened. "Make him welcome."

■ ■ ■

Sarah couldn't remember when she had ever seen so much rain. Kamil had refused to venture out of the cave for a week and left her and Simon bound during most of the time. On several occasions, armed men passed by on the trail below them, undaunted by the downpour, their eyes fixed on the ground, voices low.

After they passed by on one occasion, Sarah whispered to Kamil. "Are they looking for us?"

At first, Kamil wouldn't answer. Finally, after her third questioning, he smirked. "They know someone has raided their farms. They're looking for hoof prints in the mud."

She nodded. "I suppose that's why we haven't left the cave for so long."

On the eighth day, the sun spread its warmth sufficiently, and the mud dried enough for them to leave the cave. They rode away from Lake Balaton westward toward Mount Peca, where Kamil hoped to find the treasure of the Raven King.

As they rode past a farm, a towering structure arrested Sarah's attention. A long wooden post rose seven feet high and forked at the top. A pole swung on an axle between the arms of the fork. A rope dangled off the end of the pole and was tied to a bucket. The bucket hung over a well.

Kamil turned his head to the lofty structure, his face tensed.

Sarah could contain her curiosity no longer. "What is it?"

Simon smiled widely. "A *shadoof*, dear girl. Hungarians use them to lift water from one place and dump it in another. Originated from the Arabs. It's used for irrigation."

They continued on to the next farm and rode past another *shadoof*. This time, Kamil spat out a Tartar curse.

Sarah shifted in her saddle and shrugged. "What's wrong?" she whispered to Simon.

"Hmm." Simon looked perplexed. "I've heard the Hungarians often send messages to one another by the way they position the arm and bucket. The two we've seen had their poles at a right angle to the ground, and their buckets dangled above the well."

They rode further and saw a third, then a fourth *sha-doof*, all standing the same way. Hurling invectives, Kamil looked repeatedly over his shoulder.

An eerie chorus echoed in the distance. "Cattle horns," Simon whispered. "The Hungarians play them to communicate to one another. They're close."

Kamil urged his pony forward, and the three accelerated into a breakneck gallop. They careened over a ridge, only to face four horsemen waving axes and swords. Kamil's party veered to the south, only to run into another group of pursuers. He doubled back east and bought some distance. But five armed men blocked their path.

Kamil stopped. He pulled out a long knife and looked toward Simon, who held up his hands. "Don't kill us."

Leaning over his mount's tail, Kamil severed the rope binding Simon's pony to his. His face contorted in anger. "Believe me, we'll meet again."

With that, Kamil rode over to the side of Simon's mount, and slapped it, sending the animal off. Then he repeated the same to Sarah's pony, which took off in the opposite direction. The intercepting horsemen split up and steered toward the hostages. The last Sarah saw of Kamil was his back, streaking through the gap that opened between their pursuers.

Men dressed in tall, feathered hats and long coats pulled up alongside her. They hemmed her in and slowed her pony to a walk. A rider took her reins and brought the animal to a halt.

"Sarah Oppenheimer?" he asked in broken German.

She patted beneath her lower neck to get her breath. "*Ja*, I am Sarah."

Another rider pulled in front of her and announced authoritatively, "You are now in our custody, Sarah Oppenheimer. All will be well if you stay with us."

The others joined them with Simon in tow, who doffed his cap and looked incredulous. "How did you know where to find us, good sirs?"

"Birds tell us many things," a man spoke with a leader's voice.

"Especially when it comes to finding someone who brings us ransom money," another chimed in, triggering laughter from the others.

CHAPTER TWELVE

Pest, Downriver from Visegrad
Mid July

STILL USING THE TARTAR PONY KAMIL GAVE HIM BEFORE the siege of Visegrad, Mathis waited in line to cross the bridge over the Danube from Pest to Buda. The bridge was rickety, a makeshift structure made of boards laid over small boats. Horsemen cautiously led their mounts across it as it bobbed on the river's flow. Mathis felt it an apt symbol of his career, questionably stable and in danger of oblivion.

Only three stood in front of him waiting to take his turn when someone cried "Captain Zieglar. Captain Mathis Zieglar. Message for Captain Mathis Zieglar."

Annoyed that he might have to fall out of line and lose his place, Mathis turned to a Hungarian in traditional dress standing outside the line waving a folded paper. Mathis led his pony out of the queue over to the messenger. "What is it?"

"Here, *Herr* Captain. I will stand and wait for your response."

Mathis unfolded the paper and read a message written

in broken German.

Mein Herr, We bear good news for you. Simon and Sarah Oppenheimer are rescued from Tartar. Please arrange for 200 ducats for Simon and 50 ducats for Sarah for freedom.

Mathis couldn't suppress a cry of joy: Sarah was safe. When other in line gave him a stare, he regained his military reserve. Yet he amused himself with the thought that were it up to him, he would reverse the payments, or even pay the Hungarians to keep Simon. "That is more money than I have available, but, if you give me a few days, I'll get the money from Vienna and pay you."

The man's face lit up at mention of the city. "Vienna? Perhaps we can send a messenger there and save you the trouble."

Mathis shook his head. Although the man and his companions had probably saved Sarah and Simon's life, he was a brigand. It was common for bandits in Royal Hungary—that part of the country ostensibly under Habsburg control—to seize rich Jews and hold them for ransom. If the people who held Sarah and Simon found out they were related to Samuel Oppenheimer—a man of considerable means—they might re-think the ransom amount. "Come back here tomorrow and I'll figure out a solution."

Later that day, Mathis's regiment made camp in preparation to lay siege to Buda. He took the brief repose as an opportunity to seek out Endre's cousin, Vadasz Bakos. Mathis found him in a stable brushing a horse.

Making sure no one saw them, Mathis walked over and patted Vadasz on the side of his shoulder. "Endre did it, he saved Sarah Oppenheimer. I just got a message from some Magyars who asked a ransom for her."

Vadasz waved his hand in a happy circle. "Praise God our Father. How much they ask?"

When Mathis related the information and how he had deflected the Magyar's offer to go directly to Vienna, Vadasz agreed. "Good idea. Must not know how important man is Simon Oppenheimer. If their messenger goes Vienna, will ask twice price."

Vadasz put two fingers to his lips and blew out a shrill whistle. "My people know how bargain with ransom bandits. Let me send message to family, they bring back your friends quicker." He smiled. "That way you not court-martialed for desertion."

Once again, Mathis owed the Bakos family a debt of gratitude.

■ ■ ■

Mathis' commander, Prince Eugene of Savoy, visited him the next day with his lips pressed together in irony. "Congratulations, Captain, Brother D'Aviano has recommended you be restored to your command. You are now assigned to the front lines."

At first, Mathis's chest swelled with a sense of vindication. Before long, however, he found himself huddling in terror at the bottom of a trench, his face plastered against freshly dug dirt. Arrows and musket balls whizzed above him.

Shortly after he arrived in his new assignment, an Ottoman musket ball ripped through the man next to him, another comrade was spiked by arrows.

Hefting picks and shovels, his regiment clawed

through the Earth, inching ever closer to Buda's walls where it hoped to blast a breach.

Mathis thought of his friend, Tannenberg with a twinge of resentment. Tannenberg could sit next to his cannon in the rear position lobbing shells at the enemy from a distance. Mathis, on the other hand, had to muck in the mud and stay vigilant for a Mohammedan attack. There were times he wished the scum would come after him just to relieve the tension.

There was one advantage to his new assignment. D'Aviano was so engrossed in overseeing the siege that he had little time to goad Mathis into searching for more information on the treasure.

Fortunately, Marsigli's arrival to Buda was delayed. When he did appear, he was consumed with meetings with Lorraine and the other generals, leaving him little time to insult Mathis. Now that his antagonists thought they knew the location of the treasure, they might forget about him. On the other hand, it was entirely possible Marsigli and D'Aviano were snakes who would strike again when they discovered the treasure was not where they expected.

Despite his miserable situation in the front lines, Mathis counted another blessing when standing guard the first afternoon.

"Who brought all these damned Italians into our army?" a voice grumbled behind him. Mathis turned and came face to face with Count Ernst Rudiger von Starhemberg, the dour former commander of the Vienna garrison during the siege there the year before. Starhemberg walked with a limp and sported an angry mustache.

Mathis had stopped an assassination attempt against

him during the Vienna siege of 1683. He suspected Starhemberg had recommended Mathis' promotion to Captain.

Starhemberg continued his rant. "*Brother* Marco D'Aviano, *Count* Luigi Fernando Marsigli—good God, where did all these spaghetti-eaters come from? Some military version of a tavern?"

Mathis couldn't understand Starhemberg's prejudice against Italians. His first impulse was to blurt out "What about our greatest general, Raimondo Montecuccoli?" but stopped himself. Starhemberg might turn out to be just the ally he needed. Even though Mathis didn't share Starhemberg's prejudice, he could use it to his advantage.

Mathis stroked his chin. "I have often thought about the ties both of these men had to the Republic of Venice— D'Aviano is a Venetian, and Marsigli once assisted the Republic's envoy to the sultan."

Starhemberg threw his hands up. "Damned spaghetti-eaters, they ignored our pleas when the Mohammedans surrounded Vienna, trying to kill us all," Starhemberg snarled. "They stabbed us in the back, and now they want to look like they're our best friends. I don't trust any of them."

He ended his fulminations by grumbling, "I didn't know about their Venice connection, it certainly explains a lot, the traitors."

As a military interrogator Mathis had learned how to manipulate conversation, something that would have repelled him when he taught at the university. Even though Starhemberg's prejudice amused him, it gave Mathis an opportunity to gain an ally. "Both these men have attempted to ruin my career and turn me over to the Inquisition. I would be in your debt if you hear of any future intentions they have toward me."

For a fleeting second, Starhemberg's face froze in shock. "Inquisition? You—a war hero? No! Trust me, Captain, I will do everything I can to help you. Don't worry about that imbecile, Marsigli. He actually told Lorraine that Buda will fall in ten days."

A cannon burst exploded in front of their trench, the shock wave knocked them over. Mud and debris rained down on their heads. Dazed, they struggled to stand and brush the dirt off their clothes. Starhemberg steadied himself against the side of the ditch and caught his breath. "Ten days, indeed! I told Field Marshal Lorraine we weren't prepared for this siege. This was asking for trouble. But would he listen? No! Not with those crazy Italians whispering in his ear. They won't be satisfied until they bring us all to ruin. We can't let them do that."

An arrow flew close to Starhemberg's shoulder, and he dropped below the trench top. Sitting in the relative safety of the dirt ditch, he pointed to the men scrambling before him. They all reached for the muskets the cannon ball had knocked out of their fingers. "Hmpf. Look at those scarecrows."

They looked so thin and drawn Mathis wondered how they could bear the weight of their arms.

Starhemberg continued his new rant. "Do you see how poorly fed and ill equipped they are? Where is our supply line?"

Mathis tried to inject a note of optimism. "Simon Oppenheimer oversees supply transport, sir. But he was captured and released by the Tartars. Perhaps the situation will return to normal when he comes back to us in a few weeks."

"Weeks? We need him today."

Starhemberg left to check on the rest of his men. Mathis breathed a sigh of relief that the man was on his side. He needed every ally he could get. Despite instigating Starhemberg's anger, Mathis bore no grudge against Italians, just the two who had tried to persecute him. He hoped Starhemberg would serve as a fresh source of intelligence on what D'Aviano and Lorraine were planning.

The next day, Starhemberg summoned Mathis to his tent. He found Starhemberg bent over a small table, flanked by an aide and another soldier. The commander lifted his head. "Join us, Captain Zieglar."

Mathis looked at a map with the word "Buda" emblazoned beside an asymmetrical paisley-shaped outline of the citadel, the fortress of Buda. Buda's lower town stood to the north of the citadel. The Danube snaked to the left alongside the city. Across the river, slightly to the south of Buda, was the walled city of Pest.

"There." Starhemberg thrust his finger to the north and west of the fortress. "Have Captain Tannenberg position our artillery in these locations. Tell him also to evaluate the southern heights."

"*Jawohl.*" The private saluted, then left.

Mathis let his glance follow Private Weber as "he" departed. "Captain Tannenberg's assistant?" he asked, amused.

"*Ja.*" Starhemberg frowned. "He doesn't cut much of a figure as a man, but he's got a supernatural eye that would shame an eagle." He sighed. "Look closer at this drawing." He pursed his lips, his stare returned to the map. "Our friend Count Marsigli has filled in some of the details based on his imprisonment by the Turks there ten months

116

ago. I command the infantry, Charles of Lorraine heads the cavalry."

Starhemberg's finger traced a line southeast of Buda. "This is where the Turks could send in their cavalry and lift our siege. Go to the Duke and tell him I need horsemen in this gap."

Mathis was about to say he was honored to carry the message when he remembered the last person to do so was Private Weber, a male impersonator. He decided to utter a simple "*Ja*, Count."

When Mathis had searched out Lorraine's tent, the sentries gave him permission to enter. He found himself in the presence of the Duke, Mathis's commander Prince Eugene of Savoy, and Marsigli. The intensity of their discussion appeared to absorb their attention so deeply none of them noticed Mathis.

"Our goal above all others is getting into the royal palace." Marsigli waved his hands dramatically. "It is the emperor's wish."

Lorraine nodded, but his eyes conveyed annoyance. "*Ja*, Count, that is something you and Brother D'Aviano have emphasized repeatedly. I am devoted to the emperor's service, as are you. So I am sure you will want to share with me why the palace is such a priority."

"I can only tell you a treasure is in the library, one I cannot disclose. A treasure that will complete the conquest of Hungary in total. You must give me soldiers and laborers to me so I can search for it."

Mathis couldn't suppress smirking over Marsigli's awkward German.

Lorraine nodded affably. "Of course. You will be given what you need as soon as our troops breach the citadel."

"*Grazie.*" Marsigli bowed deeply and turned to leave. He seemed startled when he came face-to-face with Mathis, but his eyes soon hardened to steel. "And please remember the request of what Brother D'Aviano asks concerning certain escorts."

"*Ja*, I will remember," Lorraine said, resignation in his voice.

Marsigli pushed past Mathis, making no further acknowledgement of his presence.

As Savoy exhaled a long breath of exasperation, Lorraine returned Mathis' salute. "Welcome, Captain. I am sorry you had to witness that."

"Please clarify, Excellency."

Savoy's face turned grave. "After we penetrate Buda's defenses, Brother D'Aviano has asked that you refrain from accompanying Count Marsigli when he searches the royal palace."

"But…Brother D'Aviano would have no idea where to look had it not been for me."

"A soldier must obey his emperor's advisor." Lorraine's voice was firm, but not unkind.

Humiliation burned hot in Mathis's face. Although he had formerly resented D'Aviano and Marsigli looking over his shoulder, now he realized he was being cut off from knowing what they were doing to find the treasure. He had to use Starhemberg and other sources of information to keep one step ahead of his adversaries. He prayed the doors containing the *Mishneh Torah* were no longer in the palace, and that he could find them before D'Aviano came after him again. But first, Mathis had to survive the battlefield.

CHAPTER THIRTEEN

Buda, September 1526.
A hundred and fifty-eight years earlier

"Ezra, what's going on?" Rebecca stared up the ladder toward the room she had just left. The fear in her heart dwindled a bit, when her husband reopened the hatch he had just closed. An edge of daylight shone above her husband's dark form. *So he will not abandon me after all.*

"Shhh."

Angry Turkish voices rang out above them.

She grabbed a candle perched on a small ledge by the ladder. "Ezra," she hissed, "for God's sake. EZRA!"

But he didn't stir. Finally, her husband whispered. "Pass up that candle, quickly."

The candle's flame lit up Ezra's terrified eyes as she handed it to him. Beads of sweat on his forehead glistened in the light. Then the candle light flickered, and Ezra bolted the trap door shut behind him. Seconds later, someone pounded on the planks over their heads. Ezra scurried down the ladder. "Let's get out of here before they find a way to pry it open."

A musket ball shot through the lid above them underscored the point.

Rebecca took the candle out of Ezra's hands and found a dark tunnel carved out of the earth leading from the base of the ladder. "Why did you take so long to come down the ladder?"

"I wanted to hear what the Turks said about the people we're following. They intend to kill them."

"Was it worth risking our lives?"

The passageway guided them several hundred feet until ending in a small chamber, where several *hajdus* took turns climbing up another ladder. Two men stopped them, one thrusting his hand flat against Ezra's chest. "What do you two want?"

Ezra trembled with indignation. "We came to warn you about the sultan's men. The least you can do is to show us some respect."

The man snarled. "We only respect Christians."

"Please remember who we are," Rebecca pleaded. "Matthias Corvinus turned to Ezra's grandfather in friendship. First Jakob Mendel, then the rest our family has honored the legacy of the Raven King. We have many secrets to share concerning Matthias Corvinus."

"Let them go," the man with a strong voice commanded. "I will speak to them when we reach top side.

The two men reluctantly backed off. Soon, everyone had ascended the ladder and assembled inside a small courtyard.

"I am Istvan." Ezra and Rebecca faced a robust, clean shaven man in a shaggy sheepskin that draped from his neck to his knees. "How do I know you are who you say you are?"

Ezra reached inside his tunic and pulled out a signet, holding it up to make the detail visible. There, in gleaming silver shone the image of a raven with a ring around his beak. The Corvinus court seal.

Istvan took the medallion and bit on it. "Seems to be the real thing. But Matthias Corvinus is dead. Why do you care about him now?"

Ezra shifted from one foot to another. "Sir, I know a secret that will give whoever possesses it the power to make the sultan obey his wishes. Whether or not you take this gift depends on whether you can wrest the doors away from the Mohammedans. Are you willing to try?"

Istvan threw back his head, laughter peeled from him like thunder. "Am I strong enough to take on the horde that just butchered the entire Magyar army? Are you mad, man?"

Frightened by Istvan's reaction, Rebecca drew back and gripped Ezra's wrist.

"Relax, good woman," Ezra released Rebecca's hand, and patted it for extra measure. "Look here, Istvan, aren't you ashamed your country has lost the doors of the palace to the Turks? Do you want them to become Mohammedan trophies?"

Rebecca gawked at Ezra. She couldn't believe this bold-speaking man was her husband.

Istvan, too, looked bewildered by Ezra's assertiveness. "No, we hate the idea. But how can we stop it? By throwing ourselves on the Janissary's swords? They have won."

"Won? Only if you lie down and die. Think about this: you and your men drive cattle across the Danube to market, yes?"

Istvan looked dubious. "What difference does that make?"

Ezra's raised his hands above his head. "We can stop the barge carrying the palace doors the same way you transport cattle."

Istvan eyed him suspiciously. "I have no idea what you are talking about."

Ezra pressed his finger against the man's chest. "Am I so hard to understand? In the right hands, a needle can be a spear. Think of how you can use a ferry boat to your advantage."

Istvan's jaw muscles flexed. "Why do you help us?"

Ezra grinned. "My family took an oath to protect the Corvinus treasure. I am the heir of that pledge."

■ ■ ■

The supervisor in charge of loading the palace doors onto the barge shivered. Even though ahead of schedule, Pagli Ibrahim *Pasha's* threat of punishment should they arrive late in Belgrade sent chills up and down the overseer's spine.

There would be barely enough daylight to finish the job. Just in case, he had the docks lined with enough torches to light up the river like noonday. Three hundred armed soldiers stood ready to deal severely with anyone who might interfere. Extra laborers stood ready to pitch in should there be any complications. The supervisor was not one to leave things to chance.

The wagons' axles squealed in the distance. The doors would be here shortly. Small boats filled with soldiers rowed or sailed past the dock.

"Hmmm." He fidgeted with a string of worry beads in his waist pouch. He couldn't wait to leave Buda. He was convinced the sullen people there gave him the evil eye, the grim revenge of a conquered people.

■ ■ ■

Two days later, the fully loaded barge glided down the Danube toward the village of Paks. The supervisor paced the deck, gripping his worry beads until his fingers ached. A crosswind had sent unexpected waves over the side of the over-burdened craft, and forced the crew to dock in a small inlet where they wasted valuable time bailing water.

While they put in for maintenance, soldiers in small boats navigated beside the barge's two armed galleys. Excited babbling broke out amongst the crew, and the sentry ships pulled away.

"Where are you going?" the supervisor called out to the closest ship's pilot.

"Just ahead is a town filled with women who've lost their husbands. The fruit is ready to fall into our lap. We must get there before the army does."

"Turn around now, or I'll have your heads."

"No one has bothered you up to now. You're safe. We'll catch up to you after we've had our fun."

"You'll be dead men after I get to Belgrade." He squeezed his beads. He was convinced more than ever he suffered from the evil eye. But in the end, the supervisor consoled himself with the knowledge he could no more control the soldiers than the sultan during the days of looting after Buda fell. He waved away the thought. His barge could sail faster with fewer boats.

Speed plagued him most because the barge had run

123

behind schedule. After the ship was sufficiently dried out, they headed for Paks. Rather than dock at the village for the evening, the supervisor decided to sail all night. The risk was great, since the Ottomans weren't familiar with this stretch of the Danube, and the boat drifted out of sight of the army, but what did that matter? The troops would be of little help. Those fools thought of nothing but burning and looting. Besides, after the Battle of Mohacs, the Hungarian army was no more. He convinced himself there would be no threat from enemy forces.

As the sun set, a few fires in the nearby village flickered, struggling to emit light amongst the battered ruins. A lookout lifted his voice in alarm. The supervisor rolled his eyes and walked over to him. "What's wrong now, Abdullah?"

The lookout pointed downriver to two ferry boats departing from shore. "Look there, Excellency. They are about to block our path."

The supervisor squinted. Each craft was flat and about half the length of the barge. A few cattle were tied to their sides. "Hmph. Just cattle ferries, that's all. If they get too close, we'll knock them out of the way."

Minutes later, another cry went up from the front of the barge. "Excellency. Two more ferries are leaving from the opposite bank. Looks like they're joining the other two."

Swearing an oath and fisting his beads, the supervisor stalked to the back of his ship. A small galley approached from the rear, powered by a wind-filled sail. Nine rowers on either side splashed their oars in unison. They would overtake his barge in minutes.

The lookout shouted. Abdullah pointed excitedly to

the far bank of the Danube where even more ferry boats pushed off from shore, all headed on a collision course with them. But instead of cattle filling the crafts, they brimmed with armed men.

The supervisor scanned his vessel's deck. A half dozen men manned the operations, only five of them armed. He looked back at the four ferries, now joined and forming a solid line in front of his barge. They were close enough to see bowmen balanced between the cattle.

If he veered his slow-moving craft sharp enough to avoid the ferries, he would run into another cluster of small boats joining the fray. Out-maneuvering the swarm was impossible They were trapped. Soon, three ferries pulled alongside his barge, lashed themselves securely in place, and two dozen men wearing *hajdu* clothing poured onto his deck.

As soon as the barge's guards bared their swords, they were cut down by the intruders' arrows. Only the supervisor and two unarmed crewmen were spared. He huddled in the back of his ship, shaking like a leaf, his scimitar sheathed.

A small man with a black beard, not dressed like the *hajdus*, motioned to the others to stay back. He approached the supervisor with a smile. "My name is Ezra Mendel. If you hand over your weapon, these men will spare your life."

The supervisor cast his eyes down. "My life is worth nothing. If you save me, the Grand Vezir will surely behead me."

Ezra's smile broadened. "Then your chances will be better if you come with us."

"And where do you think you'll be safe from the

sultan's army?"

Ezra dismissed the question with a wave of his hand. "In a place you would never imagine."

One of the more burly *hajdus* stood behind Ezra giving orders to the others. He turned to the men, raised his hands, and they cheered their victory. When their merriment died down, he approached the supervisor and extended his palm. "Surrender your scimitar now."

Reluctantly, the supervisor unsheathed his weapon, turned the haft toward the Hungarian and offered it to him. "May Allah be merciful."

CHAPTER FOURTEEN

Constanta's Farm

DESPITE ENDRE'S PROTESTS, TWO YOUNG MEN brought heated buckets of water inside and drew a bath for him. They would have helped him out of his overcoat had he not stopped them. Afterward, two of the young women knocked on the door and entered, arms filled with dressings and hands grasping bags of ointment for his wounds. They wore colorfully beaded hairpieces, coronets, from which their hair fell in long braids over their shoulders, covered by brightly colored lace strips. He looked them over appreciatively, knowing their hair styles identified them as maidens. An indefinable feeling of being at home settled over him again, though he had never been here before.

The women brought him to a larger cabin where the men served him cabbage, fresh bread, and a newly slaughtered chicken. When his belly was full, a woman poured him sweet wine.

Endre wiped his lips with a cloth, and rubbed his

stomach. "You treat me as an honored guest."

One of the maidens with large, dramatic eyes reminiscent of the matriarch Endre had encountered in the barn smiled modestly. "Constanta wants you to rest before you see her again. There is much to discuss."

The combination of bath, food and wine soon made his eyelids heavy, and he nodded off. He woke the next morning with his head resting on a pillow scented with mint, lemon, and lavender. The rich, heavenly aromas filled his lungs, and his head cleared. He hadn't enjoyed such a delicious sleep in years, if ever.

The maiden with remarkable eyes brought him a steaming beverage in a cup that tasted faintly of licorice. Alert and braced for the day, he was only too happy to follow when she beckoned. "Come. Constanta wishes you to see the results of her alchemy."

After his experience of yesterday's attempts to find a way to cross the moat, Endre wondered how the farm and its surroundings were situated. He was glad, therefore, to follow the girl behind the barn and up a steep hill that gave him a birds' eye view of the surrounding countryside. As they climbed to the top, he glanced around and saw the moat he had crossed yesterday nearly encircled the farm. The gulch that intersected the moat surrounded the rest of the "island." The portion rising above the gulch stood on such a sheer elevation, it made scaling it from the depth below a hopeless task. The farm was completely insulated from the outside world.

As the two neared the crest, a tower with a platform at the top, like a ship's crow's nest, rose from the bluff's summit. "Watch your step," the maiden cautioned as the path became stone stairs leading over a rim of rock crowning the summit's top. The steps led over the rim and descended into something like a volcanic cone, though Endre couldn't tell if the formation was natural or hollowed out of the bluff by hands. After stepping inside the clay colored cone, they were next to the tower. A ladder went up the side of the tower and to the crow's nest.

The girl stopped at the base of the tower and pointed up. "Climb there."

Endre frowned. Heights unsettled him. "I'd rather not."

The girl giggled, then covered her mouth. "Constanta says you must meet her there."

It wasn't that far, he told himself. Only twenty feet or so. He closed his eyes and grabbed the rung. After he'd climbed a few steps, he heard a sound and opened his eyes.

Midway down the bluff, on a ledge off to the side, a brass cannon sat ominously aimed at the sky. Constanta's steely voice rang above him. "Get up here, Endre Bakos. Duty demands your presence."

The treetops below his feet and the sheer drop of the nearby gulch launched Endre's heart into his throat. His palms filled with sweat as he grasped the ladder for dear life. He clamped his eyes shut and called out in a hoarse voice. "I'm coming. I'm coming."

By sheer force of will, he climbed until he reached the crow's nest. Constanta peered over the side through a telescope. "*Ptah*. Damned boars. We'll see how long they feed on my crops."

She handed him the spyglass and pointed toward a plowed plot of land. Grabbing the edge of the rails with one hand, Endre looked in the direction she indicated, but his heart only rose higher in his throat. He persisted focusing until he fixed on several dark and hairy objects. The wind wafted from their direction and carried a chorus of grunts on the breeze. Those were four wild boars rooting in Constanta's garden.

"Move the cannon ten degrees west," she commanded two men and two women standing beside the gun. They adjusted the piece as directed. "Cannon in position," one of them shouted.

"Fire when ready."

"Cannon is lit."

Flame and smoke belched out of the barrel, and a ball whistled straight up into the air. Seconds later, the cannon ball descended and exploded over the scene below, and a billowing smoke cloud rolled over the farm. Mad squealing broke out, but Endre could see nothing. The noise ceased. The smoke was so thick he sank to his knees, coughing. The area reeked of rotten garlic and something metallic.

The smoke poured out so copiously it seemed to never end, longer than Endre had ever witnessed from a single shot. It was as if an entire powder magazine had ignited.

"Here. Take this." Constanta reached through the smoke and handed Endre a wet cloth. He plastered it across his face and waited for the smoke to abate.

Finally, the smoldering cloud cleared. But not before Endre hacked violently and tears streamed down his face. "What in the name of God have you done?"

Constanta took another cloth and wiped herself off. "Just giving you a demonstration, young Bakos. A *small* demonstration."

"A demonstration of what?" he demanded, rising to his feet. "Witchcraft?"

Constanta laughed until her throat rasped and she coughed. "Now you sound like those fools who don't know the difference between alchemy and devil worship." She removed a small handkerchief from within her sleeve and daintily patted her lips. "This has nothing to do with witchcraft. Do you remember seeing the furnace inside the barn heating something that looked like an upside-down gourd?"

"Yes. It looked like a metal container." Endre put his hand to his head and concentrated. So much had transpired since yesterday. "It tapered into a spout that connected to a barrel. What was that?"

"That 'metal container,' as you call it, is an alchemist's retort. We use it to boil things, in this case, the pigeon droppings you saw in the barrels. As long as we keep the baked remains from reaching the air, this process produces something its inventor called phosphorus."

Constanta spread her hands. "And when it meets the open air, boom! You saw what happens."

Endre shook his head in disbelief. "Pigeon droppings? Phosphorus? Why have I never heard of this before?"

She smiled. "Because it has been a closely guarded secret for fifteen years, ever since Hennig Brand of Hamburg discovered it. But he sold the secret to a number of individuals who were not as fastidious in their secrecy as was he. Before my husband died a few years ago, he obtained the formula."

She held up her left hand, and spread her fingers. "You can count the number of people who know about this on one hand." She tapped his chest. "Now you are one of them."

Endre's head swam, trying to take it all in. Finally, he put one of his thoughts to words. "How will you use such a weapon...I mean...what do you need it for? And what do you do with the canisters you carry on your hip?"

Constanta straightened her lace apron and cleared her throat. "Well, more immediately, we keep the cannon and the canisters available to defend this farm. Those flasks containing phosphorus are very effective grenades. For the longer term, the use of these armaments will depend on the fate of our beloved Transylvania. Most of the time, the Turks have left us alone and allowed us to keep our way of life. But we may not always count on their benevolence."

Endre's heart sunk—he knew what she meant. Ever since the Turks had snatched most of Hungary nearly a hundred and fifty years ago, they had allowed Transylvania to remain semi-independent, but under their authority.

However, the Habsburg army he served had retained a narrow corridor stretching along parts of northern and western Hungary. If they succeeded in conquering Buda from the Turks, it would only be a matter of time before they moved east and set their sights on Transylvania. Judging from the way the Catholic Habsburgs had ruled their slice of Hungary in the past, the consensus among his Hungarian comrades was Transylvania could expect severe curtailment of its religious freedoms and persecution of its Protestant churches.

Constanta turned to fully face Endre, and her expression softened. "Your father had Protestant leanings, even though he enlisted with the Habsburgs. Has it been hard for you to serve in their army?"

Endre stiffened. "It is not safe to discuss religion where I come from."

A wisp of a smile crossed Constanta's lips. "Of course."

She turned to the ladder and looked down before descending. Endre supposed she went first to insure her modesty. "Come," she bid him before her head disappeared through the platform's deck.

Before following her, Endre squinted over the railing. Four boar corpses lay prostrate on the ground, flames licking their carcasses. "God have mercy."

CHAPTER FIFTEEN

THE HOT JULY SUN COOKED MATHIS INSIDE HIS woolen greatcoat, sending droplets of sweat down his forehead. His horse bowed its head and munched grass. As uncomfortable as his situation was, he was thankful for where he stood, even if the nearby artillery blasts shook his eardrums despite the stuffed wadding in them. At least his regiment was ordered away from Buda, and he felt safer, if only until the Turkish cavalry descended on them.

He remembered the bitter experience of two days before, when he served alongside the infantry. His regiment's objective was to occupy and defend the city of Buda beneath the Turk's citadel. Ultimately, the Habsburg army's goal was to advance through the city up to the heights above where the Turkish garrison dug in.

Through day and night, the soldiers desperately defended a series of smoking heaps that had once been homes against Turkish counterattacks. In one nasty encounter, two men fighting next to him fell in bloody heaps, and he had escaped death by shooting one Turk with his pistol and wounding another with his saber. An arrow had grazed his neck, but he barely noticed the prickling pain. Death was all around him. He began to long for the time when D'Aviano had relieved him of his command and made him a non-combatant.

But no matter how much ground his unit captured and no matter how close they inched to the heights above them, when they least expected it—usually at night—the Muslims would descend from the citadel, howling and screaming, to push the Habsburg Imperial army back. Then day would break and the Habsburg army would claw its way back, striving to regain what they had lost the night before. Sometimes they succeeded, and other times, the Turks would stay. Through it all, like a vulture of doom, the citadel loomed on the hill, ready to swoop down and carry the Austrians into their graves.

Then the order came: all mounted units were to assemble to the southeast of Buda. The Turkish cavalry, known as the *spahis*, were massing in the area, and they were expected to strike shortly. Mathis mounted his horse, grateful for the opportunity to leave the vicious house-to-house combat behind.

His thoughts were interrupted by shouts of alarm and trumpet blasts all around him. The thunder of horse's hooves rumbled in the distance. He looked to the southern horizon, where a crescent-shaped line of warriors approached. Mathis's unit, mounted dragoons armed with carbines and lacking body armor, lay on the extreme right flank of the army, organized into three rows. He rode in the middle of the second row. To his left, men on foot hurried as fast as they could into square formations consisting of six rows and six ranks of thirty-six men. The front squares were manned by pikemen, soldiers who wielded fourteen-foot spears to keep the enemy at bay, while musketeers in the squares behind them reloaded after firing.

As the Mohammedans approached, only two squares of pikemen were in position to protect six squares of musketeers. The exposed musketeers were easy targets for the Muslim *spahis* unless the cavalry and dragoons intercepted them and stalled them long enough for more pikemen to assemble. Where were those men?

The snaps of firing muskets sounded in the distance behind Mathis. He turned in his saddle, and witnessed smoke rising from the direction of Buda. The citadel defenders must have taken advantage of the distraction to launch a counter-attack against the besieging Habsburg troops. A trickle of pikemen ran toward Mathis's position post-haste from that direction, but not enough to provide sufficient cover to the four unprotected squares of musketeers.

Mathis took out his spyglass and focused on the rear of the Imperial troops, A man on a horse—possibly a messenger—rode to the rear, where the commander, Charles of Lorraine, waited on horseback with his bodyguards. Soon, two squares of musketeers disassembled and trotted toward Buda escorted by one cavalry regiment. That left two unprotected musketeer formations.

One of the horsemen next to Lorraine broke away and rode to the row of dragoons in front of Mathis, where he spoke to Eugene of Savoy. Mathis had no idea what was happening, but he guessed another band of Muslims had attacked the Imperial army somewhere in the rear. That would explain why the Imperial force on the battlefield lacked the necessary pikemen, and why two squares of musketeers were yanked from the front lines during an enemy attack and sent elsewhere.

Soon, the regimental trumpet sounded for the dragoons to make a slow advance. Mathis slid his spyglass back into its satchel. Savoy did not draw his sword, and the rest of the regiment kept theirs sheathed.

Another regiment of dragoons from the Habsburg left wing advanced toward the enemy on a parallel path. Soon, heavy cavalry, helmeted riders who wore thick, leather buff coats, under a *cuirass* breastplate, rode up between the two dragoon units. Only one regiment of *cuirassiers*, rather than the customary two, would accompany the dragoons. Could they hold the Mohammedans back long enough for the rest of the infantry to get into position?

The enemy was much closer now. Tartars and *spahis* joined together, their riders outnumbering the mounted Imperials. Trembling, Mathis gripped the stock of his carbine for reassurance. Maybe leaving the Buda occupation forces was not such a blessing after all.

The Mohammedan lines stopped short, just out of range. A single rider rode to the middle ground between the two armies. The only neutral territory meant for parley. Mathis pulled out and focused his spyglass. His pulse raced. It was Kamil.

Savoy dispatched a messenger to the Tartar, who soon turned and rode back to Savoy. After conferring with his commander a moment, the messenger rode to Mathis. "His Excellency requests your presence."

Mathis galloped forward and halted before the prince. A wry expression creased Savoy's forehead. "Captain Zieglar, the Tartar wishes to speak with you. Stall him as long as possible. The lives of our musketeers depend on you."

Mathis nodded, but couldn't hide his confusion. Why in the world would Kamil speak for the Tartar and Turk army? Such a momentous role was usually reserved for an *aga*, a Muslim general.

While both armies held their breaths, Mathis rode out to Kamil. They stood next to one another, their horses facing opposite directions. Mathis gripped his reins tighter. "You certainly go to a lot of trouble to organize a meeting, Kamil."

"What reports have you received on Sarah and Simon Oppenheimer?"

The question was so direct, Mathis blinked. "All I know is that they were abducted, but are being returned. Samuel Oppenheimer is making arrangements to ransom them from a band of Hungarians."

Kamil gave Mathis an odd look, one that appeared tense. "Do you know who captured the Oppenheimers in the first place?"

Mathis shook his head. "I have no idea."

Feeling uneasy for reasons he couldn't explain, Mathis looked over his shoulder, then gazed back toward Kamil. "Do you know who was responsible?"

"I will look into it." Kamil smiled and seemed to relax. "Perhaps we can exchange information."

"I suppose you want to know everything I discover about the treasure."

"Suppose I tell *you* something about the treasure."

Mathis' horse whinnied and pawed at the ground. "I'm listening."

"Rumors are circulating about a small delegation

of calligraphers from the sultan's court that travel to Transylvania every five years. They are sworn to secrecy concerning their duties, and their families are held hostage until they return. If they take too long, their kinfolk are slain."

Mathis patted his horse's neck to calm her. "You seem to be telling me something about the whereabouts of the treasure. The treasure we both know to be a book, and believed to be inside the door panels to the royal palace."

"Don't be dense, infidel. We both know those doors are no longer in Buda. If someone has the treasure in Transylvania, they're making sure the sultan knows about it. I must investigate more about these rumors."

Mathis tried hard not to give an outward show of triumph. It was as he had suspected. The treasure was no longer in Buda. But what did Kamil's message mean? "Are you implying the doors are in Transylvania?"

"I'm saying that someone in Transylvania might know where the treasure is. You and I can work together to find it and mutually profit. When I imprisoned you in Visegrad, you said 'What if your enemies knew a secret that would put the sultan's life in jeopardy? What do you think would happen if you brought this knowledge to the sultan in time to save his life?' This so-called secret is the treasure you speak of, isn't it?"

"*Ja.* Exactly."

"I am your best source of information about this. Maybe now you'll let me resume my coffee operation?"

Mathis pointed toward the long, crescent-shaped formation of horsemen behind Kamil. "That's why you brought your army here, to ask me about your coffee operation?"

"No, they are just a little distraction. While your army takes to the field here and sends some of your musketeers to face our raiders to the west, you have drawn off important men from the defense of Buda. By the time we withdraw, our defenders in the citadel will have retaken most of the city below."

Mathis turned around toward Buda. Already, red Turkish flags unfurled over the lower city. He ground his teeth. "Damn your worthless hide, Kamil. Why would I want to have dealings with a serpent like you?"

Kamil pulled his pony away. "Your armies will never take Buda, infidel. But if you cooperate with me, you might still rescue the slaves."

The Tartar turned his mount toward the Mohammedan lines and called over his shoulder. "Tell your commanders I am ready to send another shipment of coffee through."

"No one trades with the enemy in the midst of a war. We'll talk about it later, Kamil."

"Tell them now, infidel."

Kamil was nearly out of earshot when he turned around and cupped his hands to his mouth. "The next time you see your Jewish woman...the one named Oppenheimer... tell her I discovered her little story about Mount Peca was a folk tale. She's a shrewd vixen, if there ever was one."

As Kamil rode back, the line of Muslim horsemen started to turn and leave.

Mathis rode his mount back to his regiment with mixed emotions. He had no idea what Kamil meant about Sarah Oppenheimer. Could he have been the one who kidnapped her? He had deceived Mathis by leading the Mohammedan cavalry against the Habsburg army with no intention of doing battle, and had created a diversion allowing the

Buda defenders to pounce on Mathis's comrades. Kamil's trickery had undoubtedly cost the Habsburgs many lives this afternoon.

On the other hand, if Kamil told the truth about the treasure, a very big if, perhaps Mathis was closer to finding what he had searched for all these months. That hope provoked suspicion. Was Kamil manipulating him and lying about the treasure to save the man's coffee business?

Savoy dismissed his bodyguards and rode back to camp alongside Mathis, who shared everything Kamil had said, except the information about the treasure. Mathis couldn't risk anyone outside his closest confidantes knowing where the treasure was, or they would surely turn the information over to Brother D'Aviano. The friar wasn't precisely sure what the treasure was, but he knew it contained information powerful enough to make the sultan do whatever the emperor wanted—including giving up territory. Gaining Hungarian land was more important to D'Aviano and the emperor than saving the women and children abducted by the Tartars.

Savoy growled. "Not that damned coffee, again." He reached for a tin of snuff and inhaled. "Your Tartar is probably more concerned about making a profit than saving Buda for the sultan. Do you trust this Mohammedan?"

By now, Mathis gave up on his hopes for using Kamil to find the treasure, and could only think of exacting revenge on him. "Not a whit, beyond his own self interest. The question is, is he telling the truth about wanting to do business with us? Forgive me for speaking bluntly, but I wouldn't be surprised if the emperor wants to do business with him."

Savoy slowed his horse and looked over his shoulder.

"Watch who you say that in front of, or you'll lose more than your command. You're talking about a state secret. Understand?"

"*Ja*. My lips are sealed."

Savoy nodded. "We will seek out Brother D'Aviano, and you can give him the message."

■ ■ ■

Considering how often he fought the Mohammedans, it was a miracle Mathis had stayed alive so long. Despite being undernourished, the beginning of August found him in relatively good health. Rather than reassure him, however, the passage of time made him increasingly anxious when he thought about Endre's absence.

After celebrating Sunday mass, he hopped on his horse and rode to Count Ezterhazy's regiment. He approached the tent he had visited every Sunday for the last month, and saw an officer sitting on a rock, cleaning his saber. "Greetings, *Herr* Major."

"*Wie gehts es ihnen*," the Hungarian replied in flawless German. "There is still no word about Lieutenant Bakos. He left here in June, and has not been heard from since."

Mathis wrinkled his brow. "I hope he is safe. No man ever had a more loyal friend than him."

The officer sheathed his saber. "Pray that he is safe, and has a good explanation for not returning sooner. If not, he will be considered a deserter."

The next day, Mathis and his regiment clashed with the Turks again. Despite achieving victory, Mathis was so drained from the encounter he caught himself nodding off in the saddle on the ride back to camp. His fellow dragoons seemed barely capable of holding on to their reins.

When he retired, the wounded lay on blankets strewn over the ground. Only a few occupied one of the rare cots. The cries of the injured filled the air. The surgeons and officer's wives who tended the casualties seemed lost in the sea of patients. Mathis heart grew heavy with every step, knowing only half would survive the night.

"*Herr* Captain, would you please take a rag from that pile over there and help me dress this man's wounds?"

Mathis looked into the pleading eyes of Private Weber, transformed back into *Frau* Lang, the surgeon's wife. As captain, it wasn't his responsibility to tend the wounded, but her humanity and the suffering around him overcame his physical exhaustion. He went to the pile and brought back an armful. "Let's take care of these men."

They worked together for hours, pausing only at dusk to light lanterns to continue through the night. Mathis cut the rags to size, while *Frau* Lang bandaged the wounded.

"It will be difficult for these men to recover," she said, wiping a man's arm. "They only have biscuits to feed on, and sometimes spoiled fruit. They're weak as kittens."

He nodded ruefully. "Our supply ships have slowed to a trickle ever since Simon Oppenheimer went missing. The men are hungry and exhausted. Our army can barely stand on its feet."

Mathis prayed that night, as he had for weeks, that Simon would soon return.

CHAPTER SIXTEEN

INSIDE THE BARN, ENDRE WATCHED ONE OF Constanta's sons submerge a gourd-shaped retort into a deep pan of water, and poke a long tool inside it, one that appeared a combination of scraper and tweezer. After working the utensil back and forth, the man extracted a brown substance from the container and inserted it into a jar of butter, also underwater.

Constanta stood beside Endre. "That's how we keep the phosphorus from combining with the air."

"And how we keep ourselves safe," her son interjected without looking up. "Despite army invasions over hundreds of years and the Saxons in Brasso, we've always found a way to keep outsiders from molesting this farm."

Endre was in the eye of a storm. The sons and daughters of Orban had concocted a myth of invincibility that created a miraculous safe haven. He had wanted to leave for several weeks, but his curiosity got the better of him whenever Constanta revealed a new secret. Each time, he decided against his better judgment to stay a while longer.

But now he realized he had stayed too long. "I really should leave and return to Count Ezterhazy's regiment," Endre reluctantly announced to Constanta. Though he wasn't sure if his words urged her or himself more. "I've done what I could to rescue Simon Oppenheimer."

A dinner bell sounded not far away.

"Come, dine with our family." Her eyes sparkled. "Decisions like this are best made on a full stomach."

The gnawing in his belly made him readily agree. Leaving on an empty stomach was never a good idea, anyway. He followed her from the barn to the bridge.

As they crossed over the moat, Constanta pointed to the rope he had used to swing onto the bridge weeks ago. "We enjoyed watching you hang from that like an overweight squirrel."

"You watched me go through all that? Why didn't you help me?"

Her lips pressed into a mischievous smile. "And miss your manly display of courage? Not for a sack of florins. Besides, you had to prove yourself worthy, if not intelligent enough, to appreciate our settlement."

They passed through the door at the bridge's entrance and it slammed shut behind them. "Besides," she continued, a hint of merriment in her voice, "we wondered how long it would take you to discover the secret of how to conquer the bridge."

Close to the dovecotes, two young men and three girls giggled.

Endre looked closely at the latch on the door. He didn't know how, but the padlock appeared to have snapped into place as soon as the door shut. "It would have been nice if you had told me how to open that padlock before I risked

145

my life swinging over the ditch," he grumbled, pointing to the door.

Constanta's face grew serious. "Do you want to know the secret of the padlock?"

"Of course," he snapped.

She walked to the door and put her hand on the latch. "Very well, but you must swear to never reveal it to another soul."

"Yes, yes, I swear."

She raised the latch. The padlock lifted with it. She pulled on the handle below and the door opened. "Now you know."

A chorus of laughter erupted from the onlookers. Endre rolled his eyes skyward. "The padlock is a fake."

Constanta waved her hand dramatically. "The mystery...is...solved."

"*Sst.*" Endre clicked his tongue.

Constanta laughed. "Now, now, don't be so hard on yourself, dear boy. The greatest wonders of the world depend on illusion. You're not the first one to be led astray by this padlock."

"Or the Komondor, who blended in with the sheep until it bit you," one of the young men chimed in.

"Nor the benign appearance of pigeon droppings," one of the young girls chirped. The maiden next to her clapped her hands and yelled, "Boom!" causing Endre to give a start and step backwards, touching off another round of laughing.

Constanta laid a gentle hand on his arm. "Don't fret, my young hussar. You're amongst friends here. Just laugh along with them."

Embarrassed, Endre nevertheless bowed his head

politely and smiled. "I didn't realize how entertaining I could be."

Constanta patted his shoulder. "Consider this your initiation, Endre."

Endre's smile widened, and became genuine. He realized, in some inexplicable way, although he had never been to this farm before, he was home.

■ ■ ■

The next day, on a flat plain beyond the range of the Turk's guns, Mathis inspected his men's weapons. After finishing his review, he called out, "Return to your tents, but remain on full alert. When it's decided where we fight today, our company trumpets will sound."

As the men disassembled from the field, a familiar man wearing a long wig and a breastplate limped toward him with a cane. "I sympathize with your men, *Herr* Captain. One day it's on the battlefield facing the Tartars, the next day it's fighting house-to-house with the Mohammedan foot soldiers."

Mathis saluted. "True, Commander Starhemberg. But I sympathize more with your men. Every day, it's battling man-to-man in that cursed city. As soon as you get past one line of defense, the Mohammedans throw up a new one and push you back."

Starhemberg arched his bushy brows. "From what I hear, Captain, you're about to fight on a new battlefield. One where your enemies are in your own army."

"What do you mean, commander?"

■ ■ ■

The barge lurched and fell with the waves of the Danube.

147

Sarah anticipated the rocking, bent her legs and sprang off, landing on a dock. Simon followed a few seconds behind, grabbing the side of an upright timber to steady himself. He let out a long breath. "On land again, blessed be the Lord."

Armed soldiers milled around the pier located just north of Buda. Sarah looked downriver, where the citadel loomed above the Danube. Guns blasted from its ramparts. A cannon ball exploded against its wall, a hit from a Habsburg gun, then another landed on a nearby market. The acrid smoke from the explosions reached her nose even from a distance.

A soldier holding a halberd approached them as a laborer tossed their bags from the ship to another man on the dock. "You are Simon and Sarah Oppenheimer, are you not?"

"Yes, we are, in the emperor's service," Simon boomed.

"Charles of Lorraine sends his warmest welcome. After you have placed your bags in your tent, you are to come with me."

"May we take a brief rest, first?" Sarah wiped her brow. "We were captives of the Hungarians only two days ago, and have traveled continuously since then."

The soldier turned to Simon. "You'll have an opportunity to wash up, but Brother Marco D'Aviano expects you within the hour."

The two laborers carted the bags to the Oppenheimer's tent.

Sarah and Simon stopped at a tent near the edge of the camp. Sarah smiled at the line of armed guards surrounding their quarters. Obviously, Charles of Lorraine did not want them abducted a second time.

The soldier pointed to a bucket of water with a dipping pan in it next to the tent. "Use this for the wash basin inside to refresh yourselves. After you have finished your meeting with Brother D'Aviano, the Duke has arranged a kosher meal for you both."

Sarah and Simon nodded approvingly. Finally a meal prepared according to the law. Neither Kamil nor the Hungarians had provided such services.

Half an hour later, Sarah and Simon were ushered into D'Aviano's tent. The brother rose from a cushioned stool. "Welcome back, Simon and Sarah Oppenheimer. The emperor sends his heart-felt appreciation for your labors in his service." He gestured toward two stools with red cushions. "Please, be seated."

A servant parted the opening flaps to the tent and brought in a platter carrying three cups. D'Aviano smiled. "Please, drink. The wine is kosher."

Sarah gasped. Never in her life had she experienced such a gesture from a member of the clergy. "Thank you, Brother." *Beware of Greeks bearing gifts*, she told herself. *What does D'Aviano want?*

The servant went out and returned moments later with a decanter filled with wine.

At D'Aviano's request, Simon relayed how a Tartar had abducted them, omitting references to the treasure of the Raven King. Both he and Sarah had agreed to keep from mentioning such secrets to others. Simon finished by saying they had been rescued by Hungarian horsemen who demanded ransom from Samuel Oppenheimer, who had had several sacks of silver coins delivered to their hosts.

D'Aviano's face folded into troubled creases. "Why did this Tartar abduct you?"

Simon shrugged, and per his habit answered the question with one of his own. "What could be a Mohammedan's worse enemy than the Habsburg army? Remove me from the scene, and the army starves."

D'Aviano leaned forward, resting his chin between his fingers. "That's exactly what's happened. Still, the Tartar spared your lives. Why?"

Simon frowned and tapped the inside of his little finger. Sarah knew he didn't like D'Aviano's cross-examination, and nerves started to take over. "As you saw with the Hungarians, we're worth more alive than dead. Especially when it earns someone bags of silver."

D'Aviano raised his hands. "I am gratified you are both safe, no matter what the reason behind that Tartar's actions. But tell me…the Hungarians intercepted you not far from Lake Balaton. Why was the Tartar taking you *toward* Austria, when he was safer taking you in the opposite direction nearer his army?"

Mathis had told Sarah that D'Aviano was a relentless inquisitor. She had to keep Simon from revealing too much about the treasure. She put her hand over his wrist to interrupt him and spoke quickly. "We told Kamil there were gems buried inside the caves near Mount Peca. That's what lured him into the arms of the Hungarians." She was amazed at how quickly she could come up with such a lie. "We were on our way there when the Hungarians rescued us."

D'Aviano smiled slyly. "Gems beneath Mount Peca? How clever of you. I am familiar with a local legend in that area about the Hungarian king Matthias Corvinus riding out of that mountain one day to rescue the people from the Turks. Perhaps you have heard of it? Or some such story about him and his lost treasure?"

Sarah involuntarily twitched. D'Aviano grinned. He was probing her for something more than the kidnapping. And he was sly enough to rely on her reactions as much as the words she used. Pausing a moment, she regained her composure. "The story was fabricated, Brother. Nothing more than a ruse to buy my cousin and I some time. Fortunately, it worked."

D'Aviano's smile faded into dead seriousness. "An interesting turn of events. Tell me something, *Fraulein* Oppenheimer. Before the siege of Visegrad, Captain Zieglar was seen in your company, discussing books I lent him about the royal palace in Buda. He, too, was kidnapped by the Tartars and ended up in the Tower of Solomon, where he attempted to unravel a code inscribed on the walls. That code spoke of a certain treasure inside the royal palace in Buda. What do you know of all this?"

Simon waved an angry finger. "She has nothing to do with Captain Zieglar. His name is odious to our family."

D'Aviano's smile returned. "Well, now. What could our Captain have done to anger you so? Did he violate your trust?"

Sarah dug her nails into Simon's arm so hard he snorted, but said nothing. "Please, Brother," she pleaded. "There are things that go on between a man and a woman that only they should know about. We do not have a priest in our tradition to confess to, we have other ways to atone for our misdeeds. What happened between Captain Zieglar and me was corrected. So…please…embarrass us no further on this subject."

D'Aviano's gaze shifted to pointed daggers. "If Zieglar has acted in lust, he must answer for his transgression."

Sarah's throat tightened, her frustration put her on the edge of tears. "No, Brother. No. I have no accusation to bring against Captain Zieglar. Please disregard my remarks."

"Hmm." D'Aviano's scrutiny traveled toward Sarah's fingers clutching Simon's arm. "What about you, *Herr* Oppenheimer? Do you have a charge to lay against Captain Zieglar?"

Sarah released her hand, but she stared hard at Simon. He cleared his throat. "No, I have nothing of which to accuse the Captain. Nothing at all."

D'Aviano licked his lips. He looked like a tiger attempting to corner his prey, but unsure of his next move. Suddenly, he threw back his arms and relaxed in his chair. "Good, then. Our captain presents no difficulties. There is something else I'd like to discuss with you, *Herr* Oppenheimer. Something you may find profitable."

D'Aviano's change of pace seemed to eject Simon out of his chair. "Profitable?"

"*Ja.*" The brother snapped his fingers, and his servant appeared from a corner and poured more wine into their cups.

After the wine was replenished, D'Aviano continued. "What I have to tell you must be kept secret, agreed?"

CHAPTER SEVENTEEN

SARAH DIDN'T TRUST THE WAY D'AVIANO SPOKE TO them like adversaries one minute and confidantes the next, yet she politely agreed to his request for secrecy. Simon nodded as well.

D'Aviano resumed. "You are both familiar with the court martial that took place earlier this year, when one of our officers was exposed for his role in selling women to Mohammedan slavers?"

Simon nodded. "*Ja*, he exchanged women for Turkish coffee. Some of that coffee included unroasted beans, suitable for planting."

"You remember well, *Herr* Oppenheimer." D'Aviano wiped the wine from his mustache with a cloth. "It is my belief God has brought your father to the emperor's attention so His Majesty has the means to deliver food and war material to the army."

"I am sure that arrangement has deteriorated in our absence, but I will revive it."

"*Ja*, and we rejoice over your return. Heaven has

blessed us."

Simon looked dubious. "So, what is the problem?"

"There is no problem, *Mein Herr*. Only an opportunity. An opportunity for you to make additional income carrying something back to Austria on your return trip. Something a disgraced officer failed to deliver."

Sarah saw the light dawn in Simon's eyes. "Coffee? You mean you want to trade coffee with the heathen at the same time we make war on them?"

"Only with some of them. Just a small faction of people within the Ottoman Empire. And your ships will be protected by Habsburg vessels on their return trip. Think of the revenue it will put in your family's pockets."

Simon blinked from the spell he seemed under. "Why is coffee so important to the emperor? How does this aid the cause of the Cross?"

"The emperor's greatest allies are his family, the Habsburgs of Spain. If they gain the ability to cultivate this bean in their American colonies, it could very well revitalize their declining empire. A strong Spain will make a strong Vienna."

"But Vienna's greatest threat comes from the Ottoman Empire. How will the coffee trade affect the struggle against the Mohammedans?"

D'Aviano smiled slyly, his eyes shone. "In exchange for giving you a monopoly over the transportation of coffee, you will help us obtain the intelligence that will weaken the sultan's grip on Hungary. You must help us squeeze every drop of information possible out of Captain Zieglar about the treasure of the Raven King."

Sarah squirmed in her seat. Before arriving in Buda, she and Simon had heard D'Aviano recently put Mathis back on the front lines. That could only mean D'Aviano had given up having him help find the treasure, since it was obvious that Zieglar was suddenly considered expendable. Now it sounded like D'Aviano had rethought matters and wanted Zieglar's cooperation again. What changed?

D'Aviano continued. "We want to know more what this treasure is before our army invades Buda and we go looking for it."

Simon shrugged and appeared to play dumb. "What is the treasure of the Raven King? And what difference does it make to the emperor?"

D'Aviano looked annoyed. "I am sure Captain Zieglar will inform you of that, if he hasn't already. Just know this, when you receive the information from Captain Zieglar and we know exactly what the treasure is, the emperor will be able to dispose of the sultan once and for all." He swept his finger in Simon's direction. "We will see to it that your father, the emperor's *Kreigsfaktor*, will become very, very wealthy."

Sarah didn't like the idea of becoming a funnel for draining information from Mathis—the man she was fond of, despite her ambivalence about his past conduct. She didn't relish betraying Mathis to serve the interests of a cleric who made her skin crawl. "Brother D'Aviano, what makes you certain you can strike a deal with these Mohammedans?"

"They are people who respond to greed."

"I see." Sarah wanted to ask hard questions, but coming across as an aggressive woman would only antagonize D'Aviano. She put her anxiety aside and forced herself to speak in her softest voice. "Have you contacted the Mohammedans who traffic the fertile beans? They risk their lives by smuggling them, and are not likely to take the first step unless it's toward someone they trust."

D'Aviano maintained his relaxed position. "We were hoping Simon might help us do that."

Simon grunted. "What makes you think I know these people?"

Sarah tugged on her vest and cleared her throat. "Do you remember a Tartar by the name of Kamil?"

"Kamil? Kamil?" Something in D'Aviano's display of surprise told Sarah it wasn't genuine, especially the way he continued to express it. "*Ja,* I do. Isn't Kamil the Tartar Captain Zieglar released from prison? The one who exchanged a hundred women and children to us for some document?"

"*Ja.* Kamil returned those hostages in exchange for a tax document, a *ferman.* Captain Zieglar saved many lives because he was able to negotiate with this Tartar."

D'Aviano's small brown eyes glowed with intensity. "How do you know this, *Fraulein*?"

Now it was Sarah who felt Simon's nails digging into her arm, urging her restraint. "The point is, Brother, Captain Zieglar has a working relationship with Kamil. Kamil was one of the principals in the coffee trade before our army shut it down. If you want to revive the coffee shipments, especially the fertilized beans, you need Captain Zieglar."

A deep tone of consternation rumbled in D'Aviano's throat. He looked at the floor. "I suppose you and your cousin are willing to enlist *Herr* Zieglar's cooperation?"

"You are asking a lot from us," Simon protested.

"Of course we would, Brother. Under the proper circumstances." Sarah smiled. "So, if we carry out our end of the bargain, may we assume you will treat us as friends, including Captain Zieglar?"

D'Aviano smiled knowingly. "I think that could be arranged."

Sarah spoke as innocently as she could. "We will be happy to ask Captain Zieglar to help you with this coffee business. And we will also ask him about the treasure. All we want in return is your kindness, and for you to protect Captain Zieglar."

D'Aviano straightened up in his chair. "Anyone can *ask* him questions. What I need are *answers.*"

Sarah grew serious and lowered her voice. "We cannot guarantee results. Only that we will put in a good word for you and encourage Captain Zieglar's cooperation."

"And see to it in the meantime the army gets fed." Simon emphasized his point by hitting his palm with the edge of his hand.

D'Aviano sank back in his chair. "If you help me, I will help you."

Sarah gave her best smile. "May I ask where Captain Zieglar serves now?"

"Where every dragoon is serving." D'Aviano snapped. "On the front lines."

Sarah drew in her breath, her eyes widened. "You mean he's risking his life, fighting the Mohammedans?"

"That's his duty."

"But you said you would help him, Brother."

"What kind of help do you mean?"

"Captain Zieglar won't be able to negotiate the coffee agreement for you if he is fighting on the front lines."

D'Aviano's voice lifted, he spoke casually, too casually. "I will request his removal from combat and give him a chance to strike a deal with this Kamil."

Sarah pretended not to notice Simon's scowl. "Thank you, Brother."

D'Aviano hunched forward, his voice steeled. "Don't forget: Zieglar's privileges depend on him showing results."

"We will do our best, Brother."

Sarah's chest tightened. Even though she had wangled good treatment for Mathis Zieglar from D'Aviano, she was left with the feeling that everything she had said was exactly what D'Aviano had wanted.

■ ■ ■

"More wine?" Constanta pushed a pitcher closer to Endre.

He wanted to refuse, but it lay so sweet on his tongue he couldn't. He poured himself another cup and grew much warmer and more relaxed.

As the young men and women who'd run the farm sat around the table with Endre, all eyes riveted on him, only Constanta spoke.

"What did your mother tell you about our farm, Endre?"

"She said if I ever needed help in times of trouble, I should come here. But I must ask for help in the right way."

Constanta beamed a radiant smile. "And so you have, Endre. You are your mother's son and you have done well to come to us. Tell us about your family."

"Well…" he cleared his throat. Talking about himself made him uncomfortable. "My father joined Count Ezterhazy's regiment in order to provide for my mother and I. As a boy, I hardly saw him." Endre lifted his eyes up, and then lowered them again. "But when I was about fifteen, he was wounded in a border clash with the Turks.

158

From that time on, he could no longer serve."

Constanta's smile dimmed. "You felt responsible for your parents."

Endre's mind wandered to the times he helped his father out of bed and onto his cane, just so the man he had looked up to all his life could walk. He tensed his jaw. A soldier never showed tears or sentiment. "It was my duty."

"What did you do to take care of them?"

"I joined the count's regiment and took my father's place."

"Surely not when you were fifteen."

Endre's gaze traveled to the tablecloth. "A year after. I was large for my age. My father had taught me horsemanship and how to use a sword. Out of compassion for our family, the count allowed me to join as a private, but I learned fast. It was my duty."

"That's how you took care of your father and mother."

"Yes, until my father died shortly after I joined the regiment. Now, there is only my mother and I."

Constanta motioned to one of the girls, who disappeared into the kitchen and soon returned with a fragrant cup of herbal tea. She laid it gently in front of Endre, but he didn't feel like drinking.

"Only your mother survives." Constanta smoothed her hair. "Did you ever wonder where your aunts, uncles and cousins were?"

Prickly heat crawled up Endre's neck, accentuated by too much wine. "All my life, I've wanted to know what people I belonged to. My father was the only one in his family who escaped the plague…and my mother…my mother told me her family lived in a land far away. And that some day, I would meet them."

"Your regiment gave you something to belong to." Constanta spoke softly, in a near whisper. "Did it make you happy to be with them?"

"It used to." The steam rising from the cup before him dissolved from focus. "Until our unit was ordered to move against our own people. Then I was expected to follow orders, bad orders."

"You mean you had to persecute Protestants?"

Endre's lips cinched together like the drawstrings of a sack. He could only nod.

Constanta rose and pulled her chair beside Endre. She sat and laid her hand on his arm. A few silent minutes transpired before she spoke. "Endre, did your mother ever tell you why she left her people?"

He shook his head.

"She went on a trading expedition with her father to the Habsburg-controlled Hungary. There, she met a young man and fell in love. When it became obvious she was with child, her father—my father—disowned her."

Endre snapped upright as if struck by lightning. "You mean...you mean...?"

"Yes, my boy." Constanta gestured at the men and women seated at the table. "These are your cousins, Endre. And I am your aunt. Welcome home."

It was as if someone had peered inside his head and read the longings he had hidden from all his life. He *was* home. These were his people.

Constanta bent her neck and met his eyes. "I know this is quite a shock, Endre. Your mother has written me many times and described you as a man devoted to his friends, and faithful to his regiment. It's as if you've been loyal to them in hopes they wouldn't leave you...isn't that true?"

Endre stiffened. "I must do my duty. I should leave and return to my regiment."

Constanta slid her hand gently down Endre's arm and let it stop on his wrist. "I am sorry if I've made you uncomfortable."

He gave his head a short, angry shake.

"Did someone else besides your mother have something to do with why you came here?"

He balled his hands into fists. Dare he reveal too much about his friend, Mathis Zieglar? "A friend of mine had an interest in rescuing Sarah and Simon Oppenheimer. I came here as a favor to him."

"Yes, out of loyalty to your friend. Who is he?"

Endre cleared his throat. "A captain of the dragoons in the Habsburg army. Not anyone you would know."

Constanta smiled. "You would be amazed at how much we know about the Habsburg army. We may appear to live in an isolated spot, but many friends pass through here and keep us current with the events around Buda. What is your friend's name?"

Endre lifted his head and looked into Constanta's eyes. "Captain Mathis Zieglar of the Savoy Dragoons."

Constanta gave a warm, satisfied smile. "I see. Captain Zieglar is fortunate to have a loyal friend like you willing to make the journey here, fortunate indeed. Allow me to ask you to indulge me with one kindness."

"What would that be?"

"Our pigeons brought us a message this morning from a man who will arrive here in a few days. Please wait for him before you depart. What he says will help you and your friend."

Endre winced. "I appreciate the warmth of your

hospitality, but my comrades face death every day in Buda. I should be with them."

"What if I told you this man could tell you about a secret treasure. A treasure that could change the fate of Europe?"

Constanta was full of shocking revelations. Was she talking about the same treasure Mathis Zieglar had confided in him about the day the two of them were in the Tower of Solomon? Perhaps he should wait and find out.

CHAPTER EIGHTEEN

AFTER A ROUGH AND TUMBLE DAY DEFENDING THE Habsburg trenches against the Mohammedans, Mathis shuffled wearily back to his tent. His left shoulder ached from a Mohammedan slamming his musket butt into it during one vicious encounter. His ears still rang from cannon balls exploding over his head. He needed rest and decent food to regain his strength, but based on past history, he had little hope of either.

As he neared his tent, he stopped his nose to avoid the stench of two horse carcasses that needed to be dragged away. He didn't notice a private standing next to a rounded sack until the man greeted him. "Good evening, Captain."

"Good evening, Private. What brings you here?"

The soldier handed Mathis a rolled up paper fastened with a colored string. "*Fraulein* Oppenheimer sends you her best wishes."

Mathis' heart skipped a beat. He untied the paper and eagerly scanned the script inside. Her elegant handwriting instantly warmed him.

"Dearest Captain Zieglar. Thank the God of Israel you have endured the Mohammedan arrows, and are still alive. Simon and I are also safe and would like to see you. After you have taken your meal, we would be pleased if you would allow this gentleman to escort you to our quarters."

Your obedient servant,

Sarah Oppenheimer

Frowning, Mathis folded the letter and put it inside his coat pocket. "You're going to wait until I go to the mess and eat?"

"No sir." The man grinned and lifted up the sack. "As soon as you can find us a table, I'm going to join you. *Fraulein* Oppenheimer cooked us dinner."

They soon found a table made of two rough hewn planks lying on top of saw horses set aside for the soldiers in Mathis's section of the camp. Mathis dove into the sack, his mouth salivating from the fragrance of freshly baked bread. He and the private stuffed themselves with cheese, mutton, and guzzled sweet Jewish wine. They emptied the sack in minutes.

The private wiped his mouth and chortled. 'You can send me to run a message to the Oppenheimers anytime, Captain."

His hunger satiated, Mathis allowed himself a moment to think. "Private, you and I have probably eaten better than Charles of Lorraine this evening." He stroked his chin. "Where did the Oppenheimers get these victuals?"

The private rose and raised his palms. "Why not ask them yourself?"

"Lead the way, man."

■ ■ ■

When he first saw them standing outside their tent, Mathis fought hard to keep his jaw from dropping. Sarah and Simon were so thin and gaunt. Sarah's laced vest hung over her like a wet bag, and Simon moved inside his robe as if it were a canopy. "Sarah, are you well?"

"Never better." A warmth in her eyes glowed like a stove heating buttered rum on a winter's evening. Her voice was musical, and genuinely pleased. "It's wonderful to see you, Captain."

He wanted to sweep her into his arms and cover her face with kisses, but Simon's terse greeting restrained him. "Captain Zieglar."

Mathis bowed low. "The Lord in his mercy has brought you both back from the dead. This is one of the happiest days of my life."

"*Ja*, well, so it is." Simon coughed into his fist as if it were difficult to get the words out. "We'll see how happy you remain after we discuss business."

Sarah winced. "What my cousin is trying to say is we heard you and Lieutenant Bakos were responsible for our rescue. There were times when we wondered whether or not Kamil would kill us, but he didn't, thanks to your quick-thinking. Please give the lieutenant our thanks."

"Mathis smarted. *Kamil*? *Kamil* abducted you?"

"*Ja*. The same man you met months ago in that deep ravine when I watched you from behind the bush. Remember? You told him if he didn't help you get into Visegrad, you'd inform the sultan's men he was smuggling coffee and get him into trouble. We have much to tell you about him."

Simon glanced nervously over his shoulder. "*Ja*, but not here. Let's take a walk by the river."

Together, the three found a path that edged the Danube. There were enough soldiers standing on nearby docks and at various buildings that it was safe from the Mohammedans.

Sarah recounted her and Simon's kidnapping by Kamil, and all they had learned. But Simon kept to himself. Mathis assumed he still festered over Mathis's decision to seek the *Mishneh Torah* for his own ends, rather than to share it with the Oppenheimer family.

But when the conversation turned to D'Aviano's proposal for Mathis to help restore Kamil's coffee smuggling, Simon's demeanor warmed. "It's an opportunity you shouldn't pass up, Captain. You need to get back in the emperor's good graces if you want to be moved from the front lines and survive this war."

Mathis's face hardened. His gaze landed on the hill where on the other side the cannonades continued to thunder in Buda. "I have friends in the regiment that don't have the luxury of avoiding combat. Men who are starving from want of food and ammunition."

He turned to face Simon. "Where did you get the food the private brought me?"

Simon's face reddened, he twitched ever so slightly. "We obtained it honorably, I assure you. Just before we were kidnapped, I ordered supply ships to bring us food and assemble a few miles downstream. We had to do it that way because General Halliweil ordered us to cut back on requesting supplies. After Sarah and I returned, I ordered the ships to deliver their cargo."

"Such a stroke of luck. Your timing was excellent."

"Hmpf." Sarah rolled her eyes skyward. "Someone's timing *was*."

Simon's face fell. "My decision…was…the result of someone's suggestion."

"Thank you for acknowledging my assistance," Sarah said with an impish lilt.

Mathis's lips curled into a smile. "So, our men will soon enjoy this shipment of food?"

Simon nodded; a twitch betrayed his apprehension. "Some of them will. But it's only a drop in the bucket. We need to order a great deal more—if we can--before things get worse."

"Does Lorraine know to act?"

"Ahh." Simon lifted his hand to his forehead. "We…we have been running like mad men since we arrived in Buda and forgot to cover it with him. Perhaps you can discuss it when you speak to Brother D'Aviano?"

"Very well." Mathis almost preferred returning to the front lines and battling Mohammedans than the prospect of sparring with D'Aviano over another subject, but it had to be done. However, since D'Aviano needed him to revive the coffee trade, Mathis would at least hold some of the cards this time.

Still, Mathis couldn't resist needling Simon. He openly winked at Sarah. "I feel better knowing Sarah will be close by when I negotiate with the good brother."

She flashed him a smile that illuminated the river beside them. "Dearest Captain, you flatter me."

Mathis never heard a man grind his teeth as loudly as Simon. But it only served to heighten Mathis's awareness that, even though she was Jewish, he never desired a woman more than he did Sarah Oppenheimer.

■ ■ ■

"You and I have had our differences in the past. Severe differences, Captain," D'Aviano said, welcoming Mathis into his tent that evening. "But, if you assist the emperor in renewing the coffee exchange, he will extend his gratitude to you."

Mathis savored this rare moment of D'Aviano needing his help, the man who had threatened him with torture only weeks ago. Perhaps Mathis could exploit the occasion to soothe Simon Oppenheimer's hurt over his separate pursuit of the *Mishneh Torah*. "I am always happy to be of service to His Majesty. Would his gratitude include allowing me to be among the first to enter Buda's citadel after our troops storm it?"

D'Aviano stared hard. "Why is that important?"

"I expect there will be a treasure trove of sacred texts and literature there. If some of it is Jewish, turning it over to the Oppenheimers would reward them for their loyalty to His Majesty."

"That would depend on two things." D'Aviano held a finger erect. "First, since you no longer serve on the front lines, you must be willing to command the supply ships that sail to Vienna and back."

Mathis couldn't resist a snort. "You want me—the man who uncovered the coffee smuggling—to transport those beans to Vienna?"

D'Aviano raised another finger. "Second, your access to the citadel depends on your subordination to Count Marsigli. Not only will you help him find the treasure of the Raven King, you will support his personal mission to salvage King Matthias's library for the emperor."

"What?" Mathis sputtered. "No. You cannot assign me to that arrogant—"

"Calm down." D'Aviano snapped. "Marsigli's quest is more important than the taking of Buda itself. His task is close to the emperor's heart."

"I see." Mathis gained his composure remembering the treasure was no longer in Buda. "Whatever you decide, good brother. I shall convey your agreement about recovering Jewish literature to the Oppenheimers."

There was no mistaking the flash of anger in D'Aviano's eyes. He went silent a few minutes before responding in a cold, deliberate voice. "Then we shall negotiate the matter. The count will be in charge of finding the treasure, but you will have the freedom to accompany him into any synagogue you wish, as long as you give what you find to the Oppenheimers. But you must first agree to assist the count in searching the palace for the treasure of the Raven King."

"Agreed." Mathis laughed inside. In the palace. Small chance of that amounting to anything.

"Splendid. Your first responsibility will be to contact Kamil and make preparations to obtain the coffee. After that, make the ships ready for the voyage to Vienna. They must be able to withstand enemy attack. We've already lost some to combat."

Alarm bells rang inside Mathis's mind. "Wait, that's not the first time I've heard it's dangerous for our ships on the Danube. Are you going to give me sufficient protection for our trip to Vienna?"

A coy smile formed on D'Aviano's lips. "Trust me, Captain. You will have all the protection you need. Which reminds me, make sure you deliver the coffee to Johannes Diodato's warehouse. It is across the river from Vienna in Leopoldstadt."

Mathis held his breath. "Johannes Diodato? The

man who originally gave me the books about Matthias Corvinus's palace?"

"*Ja*, the very same."

Diodato was a man whom Mathis held mixed feelings. Diodato was an Armenian, born in Greece, and used his warehouse to store the smuggled coffee beans Mathis had tracked during an investigation into corruption. Though some of Diodato's associates were responsible for murdering Mathis's wife, Diodato was innocent of the crime. The merchant was a close confidante of D'Aviano and strongly loyal to the emperor.

Mathis thought it strange the way D'Aviano had brought up Diodato's name. "Excuse me, Brother. Why should discussing protection of our ships remind you of *Herr* Diodato?"

D'Aviano hesitated, then spoke haltingly. "What? Oh, nothing. I forgot to mention your destination is *Herr* Diodato's warehouse."

"Are you implying that *Herr* Diodato will participate in escorting our ships?"

D'Aviano's face turned to granite. "The only thing you need to know is five galleys and five barges depart tomorrow with you aboard. Neither *Herr* Diodato nor his ship will be in that number. The peace of Christ be with you. Now, be gone."

"The peace of Christ be with you." Mathis bowed, turned on his heel and left. He was baffled. D'Aviano's less than forthright answers revealed he was hiding something. But Mathis was sure of one thing. As long as the war against the Turks raged, whether in Buda or on the supply ships, D'Aviano would see to it Mathis never left the front lines.

CHAPTER NINETEEN

ATHIS HAD JUST TAKEN OFF HIS WAISTCOAT TO prepare for the evening's rest when he heard a hushed call outside his tent. "Captain Zieglar? May I speak to you?"

That voice belonged to only one woman. His heart raced. "Let me put something on."

There was a giggle. "That would be advisable."

He pulled the tent flaps apart. A slight figure stood before him, a tell-tale locket of honey-brown hair fell out from under the hood. "Sarah, what are you doing here without an escort? Simon will send you back to Heidelberg if he sees you."

"Right now, I'm afraid he's had so much wine he can't see the door to his tent."

She looked around. "Is there a place we can talk?"

Mathis motioned to a collection of bushes a short distance from the table he had eaten supper. "There."

Fortunately, the wind had picked up and promised to muffle their conversation from anyone's potential hearing.

171

Clouds gathered above; an occasional crack of thunder in the distance conspired to assist their secrecy.

Once they found a clearing sheltered by the bushes, Sarah let loose a torrent of words as if a dam had broken inside. "Oh, Captain Zieglar, if you only knew how close Simon and I came to death. There is so much I want to tell you about the treasure. And the danger Kamil put us…."

Mathis steadied her with a hand on her upper arm. "Take your time, Sarah. You're safe now."

A sinister laugh rumbled in the foliage behind them. "Senseless girl, how can you speak that way about a man who kept you alive under such danger?"

Mathis pulled his sword and moved in front of Sarah. "Show yourself, Kamil, or I'll come and get you."

The bushes parted and Kamil stepped into the clearing. "Surely you can find a better way to greet your future business partner, Captain. I have risked my head to get here."

Mathis sheathed his sword. "Did someone jingle silver coins in a sack? That seems to be your cue, doesn't it?"

Kamil ignored the comment, choosing instead to raise his hand toward Sarah. "Continue your thought about the treasure, Sarah. Will you repeat the lie you told me about its whereabouts?" He snorted. "Mount Peca, indeed."

"Well…." Sarah blushed. "It wasn't easy to be straightforward at the time."

Mathis chortled. "Who could blame a woman for saying anything to escape the embrace of a Tartar?" He rubbed his chin. "Of course, there was no worry of that with someone like you." He laughed again.

Kamil sneered. "We can trade insults all day, or we can trade coffee." He impatiently rubbed his mouth. "Are you ready to receive my ships?"

"Tell me your plan."

"Tomorrow, an hour before dawn, I will send two swift-running galleys past your cannons on the Pest side of the river. Make sure your gunners open up against the Mohammedan artillery in Buda and give my boats cover."

Kamil stopped and looked around before he continued. "The vessels will put in to shore north of Pest, and my crew will turn the craft over to your people. My price is eight thousand florins, including the cost of the galleys—obviously, we cannot bring them back to the sultan's territory after violating his law."

Sarah pulled her hood back. "How much coffee will that include?"

Kamil shook his head irritably. "Never mind. I'm not negotiating with you."

"Very well." Mathis snickered. "How much coffee will that include?"

Kamil bared his teeth. "Don't be thick-headed, that's not the important part. Each vessel will carry a small chest of fertilized beans. They alone are worth the price."

"It *is* important," Sarah said in her sweetest voice, "because Simon's profits will come from the regular coffee, not the chests. And without Simon there will be no transaction."

"Uff." Kamil rubbed his hands impatiently. "I don't have time for this. Tell Simon there will be thirty sacks of regular coffee beans onboard each ship. That should compensate him for his trouble. I must leave."

With that, Kamil noiselessly melted into the darkness.

Sarah smiled contentedly. "That's welcome news. Simon will be happy."

He gazed into her eyes, until she looked away with pink on her cheeks. So sweet, yet so strong. Mathis had never known a woman like her. Then he remembered something she had said. "You had something to tell me about the treasure?"

She recounted everything that happened with Nathan Mendel, the man who had held a *chalaf* to her throat and demanded she turn over the document written in invisible ink.

"Ah, so there was another side to that document." Mathis took a long breath, and let it out slowly. "I remember the poem we had discovered on the visible side that led me to the Tower of Solomon. That's where I found the clue indicating the location of the treasure of the Raven King." He wanted to say more, but wasn't sure if he should tell Sarah the treasure was located in the palace doors, since he doubted they were still in Buda. It might only dishearten her.

"*Ja*, another side." She looked up and met his gaze once more. "It said '"Seek ye the labors of the god? Find the nest where the Raven King's egg hatched. Then descend into the salt.'"

On impulse, he grabbed both her shoulders. "Good Lord in heaven, that's the clue I need. Whatever it means, it holds the key to the treasure."

Her eyes widened, and her face flushed again. Her arms in his hands were warm and soft. Suddenly, he could barely breathe. He'd stepped over a boundary. Sliding his hands gently down her arms, he stepped back.

Sarah didn't say anything. Her gaze was direct and piercing, holding him in place. She moved forward into his arms.

His heart nearly stopped. She fingered the ends of his neck scarf, as he searched for the right words. "You've trusted me with valuable information, Sarah. Why would you do that after I betrayed you about the treasure?"

Sarah returned his gaze without flinching. "I can't give you a reason," She looked away and her voice turned into a ragged whisper. "Maybe I'm a fool, because it goes against everything I was taught. But I can't help it. I trust you."

Her vulnerability caught him completely off-balance. His temple throbbed and his hands turned clammy.

She shrugged again and a few tears escaped from her eyes. Mathis extracted a handkerchief from his pocket and dabbed them away. All other thoughts vanished staring into her glistening gaze. With a gentle lift of her chin, he pressed his lips against hers. She ran her hands along the side of his head and returned his kiss.

After a few minutes, she rested her head on his shoulder. "Mathis, what are we doing?"

Mathis stroked her hair. "I don't know. In all this insanity, you're the only thing that makes sense."

He suddenly straightened and held her at arm's length. "Oh *ja*, I almost forgot to tell you. I talked to Brother D'Aviano this afternoon—we agreed once I get inside the citadel—any older Jewish texts I find will go to your family."

Sarah's eyes widened and her entire face brightened. "Oh Mathis, that's *wonderful* news. Simon and my family will be so pleased." She returned to his embrace. "I knew there was a decency about you."

The promise of bringing the Oppenheimers ancient texts made it easier for him to tell her why the treasure was probably no longer in Buda. Fortunately, it didn't seem to steal her joy. Enduring warmth glowed inside Mathis, yet tempered by the realization he had bitten the forbidden fruit. Both Christian and Jewish laws condemned the affection he and Sarah shared. But he couldn't renounce his feelings for Sarah, no matter the danger.

■ ■ ■

Inside her cottage, Constanta swept her hand toward a wiry man with a black beard and a dusty coat. "Endre, please welcome Nathan Mendel. He's come a long way and will be staying overnight."

The two men bowed their heads politely. Mendel seemed to jump at the chance to talk. "You are an associate of Captain Mathis Zieglar, the adversary of the Tartar named Kamil."

The man spoke perfect Hungarian, Endre replied to him in kind. "Captain Zieglar and I serve together in the Habsburg—"

"Zieglar wants the *Mishneh Torah* so he can intimidate the sultan," Mendel snapped back with a harsh scowl.

Endre frowned. "Who has told you this?"

"I have my sources," Mendel barked.

Endre's face reddened. "And did your sources tell you Kamil is close friends with a slaver named Davudoff?"

"I am aware of that. What of it?"

Endre set his jaw. "Captain Zieglar's only interest in the *Mishneh Torah* is to exchange it for the hundreds of slaves Kamil and his friends took from Christian lands."

Mendel glanced at Constanta. "This is why you thought I should talk to him?"

"You are not each other's enemies." Constanta straightened her back and squared her shoulders. "Tell him about the treasure's resting place."

Mendel's eyebrows furrowed. "Why should I trust him?"

"Because you want to rid your family of slavery. And because he belongs to my family."

Mendel let out a long breath. He pointed toward an open door. "If you'll have someone unpack my mule, I'd enjoy a flask of wine."

Constanta motioned to two upholstered benches facing one another. "Both of you make yourselves comfortable while my sons take Mr. Mendel's luggage to his room."

As they complied, Constanta sat in a nearby chair and spoke in an encouraging voice. "Endre, Mr. Mendel is descended from Jakob Mendel, a man who lived over two hundred years ago and was a friend of King Matthias Corvinus. Since that time, a chosen member of the Mendel family has always inherited a sacred role: keeper of the most important secret regarding the *Mishneh Torah*. Today, Mr. Mendel is that person."

One of Constanta's daughters brought Mendel a small stand with a washbasin, and set it down. Another poured water into the bowl from a pitcher. When she had finished, she handed him a washcloth and a towel. "Please, refresh yourself."

"Thank you."As Nathan dabbed his face, he studied Endre. "What do you know about the *Mishneh Torah?*"

Endre sat back on the bench. "Only that it contains a secret so dark it will compel the sultan to give the person holding it whatever he desires."

CHAPTER TWENTY

NATHAN MENDEL SIPPED HIS WINE. "WHERE DOES Captain Zieglar think this treasure lies?"

"The last I saw of him, he was in the Tower of Solomon in Visegrad, looking for clues."

Mendel shook his head ruefully. "Has he talked to Sarah Oppenheimer yet?"

"It's possible. She must have been freed from Kamil's custody by now."

"Then he may have figured out the treasure is no longer in Buda." Mendel rubbed his chin. "But he still doesn't know where it is. All he knows is the *Mishneh Torah* was packed inside the panels of the palace doors."

Endre leaned forward. "The doors are no longer in Buda?"

"Not any longer."

Constanta leaned forward in her chair. "Nathan, perhaps you can tell Endre about your ancestor, Ezra Mendel."

"Yes, Ezra Mendel." Nathan looked up became very still. "He witnessed the days when Sultan Suleiman removed doors from the palace in Buda, and tried to ship them to Constantinople."

Nathan informed Endre how Ezra Mendel and the *hajdus* had overtaken the barge containing the palace doors as it sailed down the Danube near the village of Paks. "You remember how I told you the galleys escorting them left them the day before the barge was overtaken, right?"

"Yes." Endre nodded. "You said men on smaller boats approached the military ships, and told the Mohammedans there was a nearby town containing dozens of women. Then the military ships left the barge. Am I correct?"

"You listened well." Nathan rubbed his hands together. "But there were no women in that village. Only bands of *hajdus* who rushed onto their decks as soon as the ships put ashore. The *hajdus* took one of those galleys and ripped the back cabin off its deck to make more room for new cargo..." He smiled.

"So, they must have loaded the doors onto the back of the galley where the cabin formerly stood." Endre looked down, absorbed in thought. "But why did they want to use the Mohammedans's galley? Because it was faster than the barge? So they could outrun pursuing Turkish ships?"

Nathan's smile widened. "Each of those makes sense. But there is an even better reason. Are you familiar with the rivers flowing from Transylvania through Hungary?"

"Yes, I am."

"Then you know the Danube connects to another great river flowing from north to south?"

Endre cocked his head. "The Tisza."

"The Tisza," Nathan confirmed, his eyes alight.

Endre leaned forward, the vein in his temple pulsing with excitement. Was he about to find out what happened to the treasure of the Raven King? He knew how much his friend Mathis Zieglar had suffered searching for it. Perhaps now he could solve the mystery of its location. "Are you telling me they needed a galley because a barge would find it difficult to sail north, against the Tisza's current?"

"Yes, that would be a problem for a barge. But a galley could row up the river, against the current. Eventually, the Tisza turned into another river, the Szamos, which in turn flowed into the Someşul Mic."

Endre laid his hand over his forehead. "Following this is giving me a headache. They went to great trouble to transport the doors into Transylvania, but where did they end up?"

"Stay with me. The doors were unloaded in the city of Kolozsvar. Does that name ring a bell?"

It didn't. Endre knew Kolozsvar was one of the principal cities of Transylvania, but nothing else came to him. "I have no idea, sir."

"Pfft." Nathan blew air impatiently. "Who had those doors made in the first place? Whose treasure did they contain?"

"Oh, yes. In both cases that would be Matthias Corvinus, the Raven King" Endre rested his chin on his fist. "Wasn't Kolozsvar his birthplace?"

"Exactly right. Remember that when you talk to your friend, Captain Zieglar. Remember to tell him the doors were unloaded in Kolozsvar—which is the raven's nest. Hopefully, he'll recognize the meaning of that phrase."

"The raven's nest. The doors were unloaded in Kolozsvar, the raven's nest. Is that where they are today?"

Nathan shook his head. "No. After moving between various locations, they were put in one of the many caves that honeycomb Transylvania.

Endre sighed, the convoluted web of this treasure's movement taking its toll on his mind.

"But, there's one in particular your captain should know about. Tell him he should look for the Torda salt mine. Then he will know the meaning of the phrase "descend into the salt.""

"Descend into the salt." Endre repeated the phrase. He had heard the area south of the city of Kolozsvar was rife with caves. "Have you seen these doors, sir?"

Constanta rose from her chair, walked over to Endre's and laid her hand on his arm. "Remember how I told you earlier a member of the Mendel family has always kept the secret of the *Mishneh Torah*? At various times in history, someone from the Mendel family, like Nathan, has been responsible for leading the sultan's representatives once every five years to the *Mishneh Torah* to confirm it is still intact."

Mendel motioned for another cup of wine. "Speaking from a military standpoint, the sultan could have annexed Transylvania years ago when he conquered Hungary. But he didn't, because he feared the Transylvanians would have broadcast the secret inside the *Mishneh Torah* to the world."

"The secret?" Endre blurted out. "What secret?"

"Hmm," Constanta intoned. "It is very complicated. Let's just say the evidence inside shows the sultan has descended from a line of imposters. He is not an Ottoman. If the proof were ever revealed, it would spell disaster for him."

"As long as the Transylvanians in charge of the mines seal their lips, the sultan grants them autonomy." Nathan held his cup as one of Constanta's daughters poured wine. "As long as the sultan gives them their independence, the Transylvanians keep quiet."

Endre squirmed in his chair. "What happens if the Habsburg emperor conquers Buda and sweeps into Transylvania? His rigid Catholicism will make it hard on the Protestant faith."

Constanta returned to her seat, looking grave. "He might very well try. Transylvania is like a sheep living between two wolves—one Catholic and the other Mohammedan. That is why we say we are 'caught between two pagans.'"

"His invasion would not be a happy day for the Mendel family." Nathan sighed. "The Jews do not trust Leopold ever since he expelled us from Vienna in 1670."

Endre turned to Nathan. "Why don't the Turks just torture you and force you to tell them where the treasure is?"

"They had plans to try that once, with one of my ancestors." Nathan gave a grim smile. "My family's friends at the sultan's court heard about it right away because no one keeps a secret there very long. Our Transylvanian friends acted on the information, and transferred the *Mishneh Torah* to a secret location before the Turks could send a military expedition to retrieve it. They let it be known if the attempt ever happened again, the secret would be made public."

Constanta smiled. "Our contacts keep us one step ahead of the sultan. None of his men can outrun our messenger pigeons."

Endre stirred in his chair. "You're not afraid the Turks will use their spies to find the *Mishneh Torah*?"

"No, I am not." Nathan wiped his lips. "The *Mishneh Torah* is hidden inside a series of caves through which few people know how to navigate."

Endre realized if all this were true, Nathan and Constanta had given him a gift beyond description. One Mathis Zieglar would die to obtain. But was it too good to be true? Could he really trust what he had heard, or was it a way to ensnare his friend Captain Zieglar? "*Herr* Mendel, you've said you are doing this because you want to rid your family of slavery. What does that mean?"

Nathan grimaced and went still in his chair. The room silenced, until Constanta smiled at him. "It's all right, Nathan. Tell him."

Nathan covered his heart with his hand, as if it pained him, and sighed. "I live with my family in a small town in eastern Transylvania called Bozodujfala. Earth has seen few places like it. Jews, Catholics, Unitarians, even members of the Reformed Church live in peace with one another."

Endre stirred. "I have never heard of such a thing. How does the town prevent war and riots from breaking out?"

Nathan's lips formed a sad smile. "As I said, Earth has seen few places like it. People of each faith join in and celebrate one another's holidays. We respect and defend one another's freedom."

Endre couldn't believe his ears. "If the Imperial army comes to Transylvania, they won't like that."

"Perhaps, but we have a more immediate problem." Nathan played with his cup's handle. "Even though the sultan protects us against the Habsburgs, he has a harder time controlling his Tartar allies."

Endre gave a sour look. "The Tartars are the Devil's

spawn. Wherever they go, they pollute the land with their slaving."

"Exactly right," Nathan responded. "In Transylvania, it is not unusual for a Jewish man to marry a Unitarian woman, or a Reformed woman to marry a Lutheran. It is common for the son to follow the faith of his father and the daughter to do the same with her mother."

Constanta nodded to one of her daughters who brought over a tray of fresh bread and butter. "So it should not surprise you Nathan's nephew, a Christian, was kidnapped a few weeks ago when the Tartars swept through his town."

Nathan's face darkened. "That little boy came to our house every day and sat on my lap while I would tell him stories from the good book." A lump threatened to crawl up his throat. "I loved him."

"I am sorry." Endre's voice was somber. "The Tartar's curse has touched the people of western Hungary, too."

"Anyway." Nathan sniffed. "I know Kamil is friends with a member of my family, a man involved in the slave trade. Davudoff. I met with both of them not long ago, and asked for their help in recovering my grandson. Kamil told me that months before, he had traded a hundred slaves to Mathis Zieglar for a *ferman*—a document that gave our family a tax exemption."

"Mr. Mendel, what does that have to do with your grandson?"

"Bear with me, sir. As the person in charge of the secret of the *Mishneh Torah*, I knew one of my ancestors had inscribed a hidden message on the back of another document sewn inside the binding of the *ferman*. This message was a code that directs the possessor of the secret to the hiding place of the *Mishneh Torah*, the treasure of

184

the Raven King."

"I see." Endre thought he saw where this was heading. "When Captain Zieglar gave Kamil the *ferman*, was this secret document still inside the binding?"

"No, it was gone. Kamil knew from his spies that Sarah Oppenheimer originally gave the *ferman* to Mathis Zieglar, before Zieglar exchanged it with Kamil."

Nathan fingered his bread. "So Sarah Oppenheimer must have had access to the document before him. She must have taken it."

"Forgive me, sir. But how do you know Captain Zieglar didn't take it?"

"Because Kamil told me he talked to Captain Zieglar during the siege of Visegrad. It was clear from their conversation Captain Zieglar thought the *Mishneh Torah* was still in Buda. He didn't know about the secret code." Nathan looked down at his bread, and licked his lips. "Once Kamil and I figured things out, I paid a nasty visit to Sarah Oppenheimer and warned her she had better hand the document over. I thought she might still be unaware of the secret because it was written on the back of a paper in invisible ink."

Constanta took a piece of bread for herself. "But you still haven't told Mr. Bakos why you are now willing to share the secret with him."

Nathan held up his hand. "Very well. In my conversations with Kamil, and Constanta, I've finally come to the conclusion Mathis Zieglar is not trying to find the treasure of the Raven King to help the Habsburgs. He intends to use it to free innocent people, like my grandson, from slavery. I will do anything I can to help him spare as many people as possible from this curse."

185

CHAPTER TWENTY-ONE

North of Buda
Early August

AT MORNING'S FIRST LIGHT, MATHIS WAS ON BOARD the first of five galleys—two supplied by Kamil—to set sail for Vienna. As men loaded supplies on the ship, Sarah ran alongside the banks toward the docks, well ahead of Simon.

"Mathis," she called out, waving both hands. "Mathis, come here. I've got something to show you."

Knowing Sarah was not someone to get excited over something trivial, Mathis excused himself from his conversation with a quartermaster and hoisted himself over the side of the ship. "What has you so worked up, Sarah?"

She grabbed his hand and pulled him away from people milling around, although Simon stood in the distance. Her fingers slipped inside the laces of her vest and extracted a paper. She held it in her hand like a gemstone. Sarah kept her voice low in between pants. "Do...do you...remember the verse...about the raven's nest ...and the salt?"

186

Mathis looked over his shoulder and assumed no one was close enough to eavesdrop. "*Ja*, I remember. What is going on?"

Sarah's eyes widened. "Well…I just remembered when I was rescued from Kamil. You know…the Hungarians who chased him away…they…they told me they heard about me by getting a message from a carrier pigeon."

"*Ja*, you told me that. So what did you do?"

Sarah put both hands on Mathis's shoulders, bowed her head and took a deep breath. "So… when you told me your friend Endre was in trouble for desertion. I…I went to a man who sends messages to different areas by carrier pigeons."

"Good idea."

Sarah took in another breath, less deep this time. "I sent out a request for Endre to contact us and tell us if he's well."

She pressed the paper into Mathis's palm. "This is what arrived today."

He unfolded the sheet and read it in a muffled voice. "Have Vadasz lead you to the raven's nest in Kolozsvar. Then I will show you the labors of the god in the salt."

The world turned fuzzy, everything save the words on the paper. Mathis nearly lost his balance, and had to steady himself. He swept Sarah into his arms and kissed her firmly on the lips. "The treasure, dear woman, the treasure. You've found the treasure!"

Sarah wept and hugged him.

"Stop," Simon shrilled from a distance. "Take your hands off her, *now*."

Mathis cleared his throat and reveled in Sarah's ecstatic gaze. The hope in her eyes reflected his own. Finally, the treasure was within their grasp and even Simon's indignation couldn't dampen the exhilaration of the moment.

Later, as Mathis stood on the fore deck, Simon and Sarah took their seats in the aft cabin. Simon's scowls and aloofness made it clear he did not approve of Mathis's relationship with Sarah. He continued to express his resentment over Mathis not agreeing to turn the *Mishneh Torah* over to the Oppenheimer family.

Somehow, she escaped Simon's watchful eye a few precious moments, and approached Mathis. Stopping by one of the railings, she sniffed and wrinkled her nose. "Hmm. Wherever I go, I smell this peculiar odor. Pleasant, but peculiar."

The ship's pilot stopped in making his rounds and nodded toward her. "That's the smell of oakum, *Fraulein*. We just had the ship caulked a few days ago to make her waterproof."

"Oakum?" She squinted. What's that?"

"Petroleum and pine resin mixed with fibers from old ropes."

Simon came forward and stepped between Mathis and Sarah. "Sarah-h-h. You need to sit in the back of the ship."

Sarah laid a hand on her cousin's arm. "Just in time, Simon. I've found the perfect freshener for you in between ablutions."

She explained the pleasant odor rising from the hull until he threw his hands up and sulked away. "Your saucy tongue is too much for me, woman. Too much."

As the galley pulled away from the dock, a sailor tossed a tow line to a waiting barge. Sarah held on to the rail next to Mathis. "Won't pulling another vessel slow down our speed?"

Mathis winced. "*Ja*. But it's the best way to fight the current. Unfortunately, our army needs every supply ship we can get our hands on brought back to Vienna. The barges must stay close to the galleys because they need guns for protection."

Together, they watched a second galley depart and link up to another barge. Sarah repositioned her grip on the rail and faced Mathis. "What if our army storms Buda while we're making this voyage? Won't that prevent you from searching for the manuscripts?"

The rowers' rhythmic chanting filled the air, and they pulled the oars in unison. The ship gained speed, and soon the ride was smooth enough for Mathis to release the rail. "Missing out on taking the citadel *is* a possibility, but not one I'm worried about. Considering the shape our army is in, I don't think it's ready to storm anything until they're better fed."

"I've seen the number of tents reserved for the sick multiply each day. What's going on?"

Mathis waved his hand toward the banks along the Danube. "This terrain is hard on our men. Lack of food leaves them vulnerable to diseases that drift in from the marshes. We're starting to see our men come down with sweats, fever, and black tongues."

"Oh, no." Sarah's face creased in concern. "That sounds like *morbus hungaricus.*"

"*Ja*, the Hungarian disease. That's why we're towing ships to Vienna, to bring back more food. Our success depends on more than just carting sacks of coffee for the emperor. These starving men depend on us returning with something to eat."

Mathis's gaze traveled down the narrow deck,

inspecting the vessel. Ten rows of men, three to a bench, sat on either side and put their hands on the oars. Many of them had tucked swords beneath their seats.

He lifted his eyes to the mast in the middle of the ship. A crossbeam hung at a forty-five-degree angle holding a folded sail. It wouldn't unfurl until the wind blew behind them. He breathed in deeply, and prayed God would give them safe passage to Vienna.

A convoy of five galleys soon towed five barges, straining against the current. The creaks of wooden beams and oars stretching in the rushing water filled the air, and the breeze washed away the heavy stench of tar and sweat. They headed north up the Danube. Mathis took out his telescope and scanned the west bank.

Sarah raised her voice. "What are you looking for?"

"Mohammedans. They roam freely here."

"Seen any?"

"An odd scouting party here and there."

An hour later, Mathis spotted a dozen ships coming toward them from the north, sails full and oars dipping rapidly. He scanned their decks. His blood ran cold. Enemy galleys, well-armed. Their decks were crammed with troops.

Mathis cupped his hands and shouted. "Enemy ships approaching! Enemy ships approaching!"

Two men from the aft cabin handed muskets and powder to the oarsmen. Mathis took two wheel-lock pistols out of the backs of his boots. Even with a cannon on the fore of each Habsburg ship, they were hopelessly outgunned.

The captain came up to him. "We have to cut our tow lines to the barges, and scatter as best we can."

Mathis shook his head. "We will not abandon our

men." He handed his wheel-locks barrel-first to Sarah. "Hold these a moment."

Mathis made his way past the oarsmen, through the aft cabin, and climbed up a raised platform on the ship's stern. The pilot used his knife to saw the knot that fastened the tow-rope to the galley.

"Leave it." He put his hand on the handle of his sword to show he meant business.

"But they're slowing us down," the pilot protested.

"Your job is to steer the ship and obey orders."

The man shook his head at Mathis, but complied. "*Ja*, sir."

Mathis turned around and departed to the fore cabin housing a one-pound cannon. A private and a sergeant stood at attention, and saluted Mathis.

He returned their salute "Prepare your *falconet*."

The galley's pilot did his best to avoid the Mohammedan vessels speeding their way. But the ship was soon hemmed in by two enemy craft before the Habsburg gunners had a chance to fire off a shot.

A voice boomed from the starboard side. "*Shalom*, Captain Zieglar. Your situation is beyond hope. Surrender, and you will live."

Mathis knew that voice. It belonged to the adversary he had interrogated on several occasions. Kamil's partner, the slaver, Davudoff.

As Davudoff's ship pulled alongside Mathis's galley, Mohammedans with scimitars and bows prepared to jump on board. Mathis gnashed his teeth. Davudoff would throw him and Sarah in chains. He would spend the rest of his short life rowing a galley. Sarah's fate would be worse. Like all captured women, she would be raped and sold.

191

Mathis held out his palms to Sarah. She laid his wheel-locks in them. Sick to his stomach, he realized they were overwhelmingly outnumbered. How could God do this to him? Just when he was on the verge of finding the treasure of the Raven King. Now, everything would be lost. He tried to keep the panic from his voice, but his short breaths betrayed him. "I'm sorry this has happened to us. Sarah. Know you mean everything to me...."

Sarah's eyes stretched wide, gazing at something over his shoulder. She gasped. "No, Mathis, look."

An ominous lone ship pulled around the bend upriver, and knifed through the water toward them. Mathis caught his breath. He hadn't seen anything like it. Three decks of oarsmen plunged their paddles into the water and powered it forward. The vessel was nearly twice as long as his galley.

Mathis's heart pounded. The intruder's huge, triangular sails stretched as they caught the wind, one of them displayed the double eagle Habsburg emblem.

"Captain Zieglar," Davudoff's insistent voice rang out. "Surrender your ship before we seize you by force."

Mathis ignored Davudoff and scanned the newcomer's deck. A metal dragon head on the end of an upturned neck stood erect on the prow. Two more heads posed threateningly—one stationed on the middle of each side. Fumes rose from each dragon's mouth as the vessel slid next to an enemy craft.

By now, the two Mohammedan ships had lashed themselves to either side of Mathis's galley. Mathis turned toward Sarah and barked. "As long as I live, stay in back of me."

"I will," she choked on her reply.

Soldiers poured on board and charged toward the

rowers. The Habsburg crew leveled their guns and fired. The boom echoed across the deck and deafened the screams. When the smoke cleared, seven attackers lay twisted and bleeding. Scimitars flashed in the sunlight, and Habsburg musketeers began to fall. The Mohammedans were on the verge of swarming the crew. A short, muscular man led the enemy on the starboard side toward Mathis. It was Davudoff. "Last chance, Zieglar."

Mathis leveled his wheel-locks. "Have you lost your mind, Davudoff? You could make a fortune off of this coffee trade."

Davudoff shook his head. "Kamil has betrayed our partnership. He wants to forsake slavery and turn to trade. I can't let him destroy my family's business."

A vicious roar interrupted the conversation. All on board held their breath as rivers of flame shot out from the newcomer's dragons and bathed the deck of a nearby Mohammedan galley. Men screamed and ran across their decks, their clothes on fire and burning their skin. The stench curdled in his stomach, until they plunged over the side and into the water.

A second galley appeared, identical to the first. It, too, sidled up next to another Mohammedan galley. Flame billowed out of the dragon's nostrils and lit the craft into a torch. Davudoff turned, disbelief shadowing his eyes

Meanwhile, the pilot of Mathis's galley appeared, brandishing a long dagger.

Visibly shaken, Davudoff turned his attention to his men. "Work quickly. Spare the captain and the girl. I'll deal with them personally."

Mathis aimed his wheel-locks carefully. He winged Davudoff's thigh and cut down a man beside him. They both dropped to the deck, clutching their wounds.

Five more pressed forward.

Mathis screamed and jumped into the air, turning completely around. As he landed, his blade sliced into an assailant's shoulder. Cold steel bit into Mathis's cheek. He sunk his saber into the attacker's neck.

Meanwhile, three Mohammedans surrounded the pilot and cut him down. Mathis ran to the nearest one and ducked his swinging scimitar. He buried the point of his saber into the man's torso. Then he kicked the legs out from another assailant. Before the man could rise, Mathis ran him through. The surviving intruder took one look at Mathis, turned, and climbed back over the side.

As the rescuing Habsburg galleys closed in, the Mohammedan vessels blocking Mathis's ship withdrew.

Davudoff leaned against the rail, panting. He tried to lift his leg up repeatedly but stopped each time with a grunt. Mathis waved off two Imperial soldiers who closed in on him, ready to finish him off. "Put him in chains and tend to his wound. He's worth more to us alive."

Davudoff's face twisted in anger. "What do you think you'll get from me, *goyim*?"

Mathis threw a linen cloth at Davudoff. "More than you're worth, dung heap. Keeping an eye on you will ensure the hostages taken from my people will stay put until I can free them."

Davudoff was too busy staunching his bleeding to reply. Two soldiers bound his hands and feet and carried him off.

Mathis sheathed his saber and climbed halfway up the sail's rigging. He called out in Turkish to the retreating vessels. "Gentlemen, surrender before your vessels become kindling. I guarantee you the same terms your friends offered us."

Men scurried frantically on the decks of the Mohammedan ships as they ignored the warning and ran for it.

Mathis ordered the rowers back to their stations, and the captain to fill in for the dead pilot.

"Gunners." Mathis commanded. "Make your cannon ready."

"*Ja*, sir."

"After the ship comes about, aim it at the rudder of the retreating ship. Then fire."

Their shot missed and punctured a hole in the sail. Another blast from the cannon ripped timbers from the helm cabin. By the time the gunners reloaded for a third try, the target slipped out of range.

Just as well. The report they would take back to their friends would keep the Danube free from enemy attack for a while. Their casualties would reinforce the message.

Sarah returned to Mathis's side and gently touched the side of his head. She winced for him, and drew back her hand, dripping in blood. "Mathis, you're hurt."

"*I* will dress the captain's wounds." Simon appeared, a doleful expression on his face. "As soon as I can get my hands on linen and water."

As Simon wiped and bandaged Mathis's wound, the first rescuing ship pulled alongside them. It was a behemoth that dwarfed Mathis's vessel. Unlike the smaller ship, the rescue craft sat twelve feet higher in the water, and stretched nearly twice the seventy-foot length of the galley.

"Captain Zieglar?" a familiar voice rang out. "This is Johannes Diodato. Can you hear me?"

Mathis cupped his hands to his mouth. "Greetings Johannes Diodato. May I come aboard?"

Diodato's rotund, bearded face peered down at Mathis. "Unfortunately, my friend, that is not possible. We cannot allow anyone to rediscover the secrets of producing Greek fire. I went to great pains and expense to find out how the Byzantine Empire created it."

"Greek fire?" Mathis's pulse raced. "That secret has been lost for centuries." He whistled low as he passed his eyes along the length of the ship. "Good heavens, Diodato. You've recreated the ancient Byzantine navy."

"Just two ships. But we can't use Greek fire too many times on the Danube."

Mathis put his arms on his hips and walked back a few steps. "Why not, now that you've built these monsters?"

Diodato smiled ruefully. "Because, many years ago, the Mohammedans learned how to suppress the fire. After the word gets out about us bringing the weapon back, they'll remember how they did it. But it was fun taking the weapon out for a surprise. We'll use it again when the Mohammedans least expect it."

As the larger ship inched away, Mathis grimaced across the deck at the casualties. Eight oarsmen and the pilot would have to be buried. Thank God, Mathis, Simon and Sarah had escaped the slaughter. The ships would make it safely to Vienna, and Davudoff's captivity would ensure the twenty-seven hundred hostages his family imprisoned were kept together.

CHAPTER TWENTY-TWO

The Habsburg Camp outside Buda
Early November, 1684

NEARBY CANNONS OCCASIONALLY SHATTERED the autumn air around them where Mathis sat in the officer's mess, sharing a beer with his friend, Frederick Tannenberg. Despite the continuous shaking and battering of walls, they remained tranquil. Their new normal.

Tannenberg seemed to have trouble keeping his eyelids open, and his usually buoyant tone was gone. "Good to see you back with us, Mathis, even though it's not under the best of circumstances."

"Good to see you, too, old friend." He read the latest results of the siege on Tannenberg's face. "I've run so many convoys from here to Vienna in the last several weeks, I've almost forgotten what it's like to stand on firm ground."

Tannenberg gave a weary guffaw. "You've led ships back and forth non-stop for over a month. But we're still short of food. How can that be?"

Mathis's stare drifted down. "The War Council seems more concerned with sending shot and powder. Food and medical supplies are less important. It's killing us."

"*Ja*, it is." An undertone of anger crept into Tannenberg's voice. "We've lost half our army since June. We can't keep this up."

"What about the reinforcements we received in September? The Bavarians were supposed to beef up our forces."

Tannenberg stretched back in his chair. "Ahhh, that. Well, it seems they have done very little against the Mohammedans. As soon as we batter down one wall, the enemy throws up a new line of earthworks. They're better protected today than when the siege began."

Mathis breathed a sigh of resignation. "Undersupplied and undermanned. This is turning into a disaster."

"It will be if we don't withdraw. The Mohammedan field army is getting stronger every day, and will soon overwhelm us."

Tannenberg rested his chin on his jaw. "Whatever happened to Davudoff? Are you letting him rot in prison?"

"For now. We don't want him interfering with Kamil. Davudoff is an expert at making a mess of things."

A corporal walked up to them. "Captain Zieglar? His Excellency, Duke Charles of Lorraine wishes to see you in his tent. Follow me, please."

Mathis excused himself and trailed the soldier to the Duke's tent. As he neared the sentries standing guard, he heard Lorraine's exasperated voice through the flaps. "Can't you see, we've come too far to break things off now?"

"If you were going to take Buda, Field Marshal, it should have happened back in September when the

Bavarians reinforced you," a deep, gruff voice replied.

"The reinforcement we need most is an adequate food supply."

Mathis was about to request permission to enter, when one of the sentries pressed a finger to his lips. "Wait until the chief of staff leaves," he whispered.

The gruff voice sounded close to the tent's exit. "I've had enough of this bickering. It's time to let the emperor decide. We wouldn't have ended up this way had Leopold appointed me to this command in the first place."

With that, the tent flaps were thrown open and a tall, older man wearing a *cuirassier* stalked out of the tent. Two bodyguards followed. "My Lord," each of the sentries uttered as the man walked past.

Mathis recognized the older man, Hermann of Baden, head of the War Council. By the conversation he had just overheard, Lorraine was on Baden's blacklist. That agreed with reports that Baden was disappointed he had not received Lorraine's appointment for commanding the siege.

"Captain Mathis Zieglar wishes entry," a sentry announced as he nodded to Mathis.

"Allow him in," came the weary response.

Mathis entered the tent and bowed. "Your Excellency." He and Lorraine were alone in the small quarters.

Lorraine walked out from behind a table and grasped Mathis affectionately by his forearms. "Captain."

"How may I be of service to Your Excellency?"

Lorraine pointed to a chair. "Be seated, and keep your voice low."

The two men sat opposite one another. Two lamps lit the table, their candles short with weak lighting.

In the flickering light, worry lines etched Lorraine's

face. Pock-marks dimpled his forehead, a tell tale sign of a previous bout with smallpox. He leaned forward in his chair and whispered, "I remember the service you rendered back in Visegrad when you negotiated peace with the *aga*. I need your skills again, Captain Zieglar."

Lorraine's commendation was dubious, at best. Mathis feared he knew what Lorraine had in mind. The prospect of carrying a white flag into the face of the Mohammedans defending Buda made his stomach weak.

Lorraine wiped the sweat off his brow with a cloth. Mathis strained to hear his voice. "There are forces at work who would like nothing better than to call off this siege and blame me for the failure. I need you to go the *pasha* of Buda and persuade him to agree to something that will leave my command a shred of dignity. I need you to carry out a mission inside the Buda citadel."

Mathis let out a slow breath, a heavy dread filling his stomach. Perhaps Lorraine had contracted the Hungarian disease and become delirious. "May I speak freely, Excellency?"

Lorraine's lower lip curled above his upper one. "Granted." He sighed.

"I will gladly lay down my life in exchange for all you have done for me, and more if need be. But, considering the run-down state of our army and the strength of our enemy, how will this mission accomplish anything?"

Lorraine straightened, his eyes sparkled. "Listen to me, Captain. You will ask the *pasha* of Buda if you can take a look at 'the hard substance that adorns the arch in the library.' That is an order."

Mathis stared in disbelief. Lorraine quoted from the etchings Tannenberg had counterfeited from Dracula's cell.

200

D'Aviano must have put Lorraine up to this. Realizing it was going to be longer than he had originally thought to take Buda, D'Aviano was trying to locate the treasure before the siege collapsed.

"What if I find the information we are looking for? Surely the *pasha* won't let me walk out of the citadel holding it in my hands."

Lorraine's eyes became blackened sockets as he leaned back into the shadows. "He may be receptive to the idea if we promise to call off the siege."

Mathis's throat tightened, his heart sank. He never thought anyone could use Lorraine, his family's benefactor, against him. Maybe the prospect of losing the siege had put him under immense pressure.

A light seemed to go on inside Mathis's brain. "Wait… what if I don't find the treasure inside the palace? Will you question me or my honor if I tell you I haven't found it?"

Lorraine pressed his palms on the table's edge. "That would be hard to believe, considering the clues you've provided us."

Mathis's face flushed. The treasure wasn't in the palace, and he didn't want to look for it there. He didn't like being backed into a corner like this. "Then may I propose you send masons with me to inspect the palace's arch, men whose word you trust? If we find it there, you'll have the report of multiple witnesses. If not…."

"You can't be accused of making it up."

"Exactly." Mathis nodded. "But if I'm going to stick my neck out, I want something in return."

"What is that?"

"I want to be released from duty for six months. Also, I ask you request a man's services for me from Count

Ezterhazy's regiment. His name is Vadasz Bakos."

"You are a captain in the emperor's army and your duty is to serve with your regiment."

"Indeed. And after this, I will have earned six month's furlough."

"What do you intend to do for six months?"

There was no getting around it. He had to reveal his plans. "Travel to Transylvania and negotiate for the freedom of our people. Innocent people taken hostage by the Tartars."

Lorraine's jaw hardened. "You cannot possibly succeed in such a foolhardy mission. Your journey will take you through territory in rebellion against the emperor. Six week's leave for yourself and no one else."

Mathis kept his expression even, and refused to blink. "If it pleases Your Excellency, six months and Vadasz's companionship."

Lorraine hit the table with his fist. "Six weeks for you and no escort. I will not let you endanger another man's life. That is my final offer."

Mathis rose. "Then six weeks it is. Will Your Excellency give me a few days before I take a white flag to the citadel? If I work through an intermediary, our chances of getting an agreement with the *pasha* will stand a greater chance of success."

Lorraine's sigh came from deep in his throat. "Make it as quick as you can. I will find masons to accompany you."

Mathis saluted and left. Six weeks without a guide wouldn't work. He had to find a way to get around Lorraine, and go to the city of Kolozsvar on his own terms.

■ ■ ■

Kamil usually showed up in camp within a day after Mathis returned from transporting coffee to Vienna. That evening was no exception. Lorraine had instructed the sentries stationed on a small peninsula jutting into the Danube to admit Kamil, no questions asked.

Mathis waited for the Tartar at the table outside Mathis's tent and next to a stand of poplars. As the afternoon turned to dusk, the trees rustled and a voice calmly queried, "Was *Herr* Diodato pleased with the last shipment?"

Mathis turned to make sure no one was close, then got up and walked into the trees. Kamil stood in a clearing, dressed in a wooly vest and a leather cap covering both ears.

"*Herr* Diodato was happy we encountered no attacks from Turkish ships this time," Mathis half-whispered. "You will soon be rich, considering you no longer have to split the profits with Davudoff."

Kamil shook his head. "On the contrary, I still have to do business with his family. Though I am withholding some of the proceeds to convince them not to betray me."

Mathis pursed his lips. "Indeed."

Kamil gave a wry smile. "I have to remain involved with them if they are going to refrain from selling off the twenty-seven hundred Christian slaves they own. It has been all I can do to restrain them. You need to give them a reason not to lose patience."

"*Ja*, well, I may soon have good news about that. But don't forget the money all of you are making through the coffee trade in the meantime." Mathis ran his fingers through his hair. "I need a favor from you."

Mathis explained what he needed from the *pasha*.

Kamil couldn't suppress a snicker. "You want me to convince him to prove to Lorraine there's no treasure hidden in the palace library? What a stupid waste of effort."

"I know, I know." Mathis waved his hands. "But at least it will bring an end to the siege."

"For how long, infidel? Until they return next year?"

"I am no prophet, Kamil. The *pasha* should be happy his city will have relief for the foreseeable future."

"You are asking much and giving little, infidel. I still have only a vague idea of what this treasure is you seek. It makes me wonder what I stand to gain from this arrangement."

"Patience. You will receive your reward within six or seven months. I will let you know more after the siege ends."

Kamil's eyes narrowed. "You had better do that. In the meantime, tell your commanders the next shipment of coffee will arrive in a week. It will be regular beans this time."

"Regular coffee? No more sprouted beans?"

"You have enough to supply a hundred farms, already." Kamil turned and left.

■ ■ ■

Two mornings later, Mathis awoke to a note written in German lying on the ground inside his tent. It read "the *pasha* of Buda invites you to the citadel tomorrow at dawn. Prepare to deposit Sarah Oppenheimer as his hostage."

Mathis crumpled the paper in his fist. "Never," he seethed. "That will never happen."

Later that morning, Lorraine summoned him to his tent. When admitted, he found himself standing in front of Lorraine and D'Aviano. Lorraine greeted him. "We received a note from a courier this morning that said the *pasha* agreed to our terms."

It was all Mathis could do to tamp down his rage. "Only if we leave Sarah Oppenheimer as their hostage. That's unacceptable. She's an innocent and has nothing to do with this."

"You have no say in this, Captain," D'Aviano growled. "The Oppenheimer girl has already been notified."

Lorraine's tone was more conciliatory. "Don't worry yourself. Leaving a hostage is just a routine matter, a negotiating tactic. Nothing out of the ordinary."

Mathis's hands knotted into fists. He looked D'Aviano in the eye. "Does His Eminence think so little of the niece of Samuel Oppenheimer, the man who has single-handedly financed this siege? Would he be so quick to sacrifice one of his own nieces?"

"Watch your tongue, or I'll have your commander run you through the gauntlet," D'Aviano warned.

Mathis waved his finger. "Have you considered the etchings that led us to the palace were probably made a hundred and fifty years ago? Isn't it possible the treasure's location might have changed since then?"

D'Aviano folded his hands over his waist. "We will leave no stone unturned finding out. That is the emperor's wish. Now go. Sarah and the masons will wait for you tomorrow on the path leading to the citadel."

Mathis growled, and stomped out of the tent, not caring what the consequences would be for his display of disrespect. The fools were happy to gamble with Sarah's life for a treasure that wasn't in the palace. He realized he was partly to blame, and that made it worse. Tannenberg had doctored the etchings on the stone to save Mathis from the Inquisition and it had put Sarah at risk.

CHAPTER TWENTY-THREE

SARAH'S EYES ANXIOUSLY SCANNED THE CITADEL IN the early morning light as she, Mathis, and seven masons led donkeys laden with lumber up the slope. Every step echoed in Mathis's mind, his insides on fire ever since D'Aviano ordered him to escort her into the hands of the enemy. The walls above them were ringed with archers, all of whom seemed to aim their arrows at him.

One of the donkeys lost its footing and collapsed, sending timbers rolling down the hill. The party halted until the masons retrieved the spilled lumber and reloaded some of it on the animal, and the rest of it on their own shoulders. It seemed like a bad omen to Mathis.

When they reached the city gates at the top of the hill, soldiers surrounded them, led by an officer. "What's the meaning of this?" Mathis translated his words for the benefit of those who spoke German. "Why are you bringing wood here?"

Mathis bowed. "If it pleases you, sir, the *pasha* has given us permission to work on the entryway to the library in the royal palace. This lumber is for us to construct scaffolding."

The officer scowled beneath a dark turban. "I expected you, but know nothing about these beams. Let me consult with the *pasha*."

A messenger was sent running to the fortress's commander. The servant returned in minutes, panting. "The *pasha* will permit it. However, he demands you tell him what kind of literature you expect to find inside the arch."

Mathis was stunned. Why had this become an issue at this late juncture? He couldn't deceive his way out of the situation this time. "We are looking for Maimonides's *Mishneh Torah*."

The messenger ran away, and returned again. Mathis's answer didn't seem to make any difference to the *pasha* as they were escorted by soldiers to the steps of the royal palace, where another officer waited. "Sarah Oppenheimer?"

She nodded hesitantly.

He pointed to five soldiers. "You will go with these men to the *pasha*'s quarters."

"Sarah," Mathis cried. They locked hands a moment before their escorts pulled them apart.

Her hands still extended, she called out. "Don't worry Mathis. The God of Abraham, Isaac and Jacob is with us."

He felt a lump in his throat as the men led her away.

The officer turned to Mathis. "You are not permitted to take anything out of the library. Bedding and meals will be provided for you, as you are not allowed to leave the building under any circumstances. If you do, you will put the hostage's life in peril."

Mathis nodded. "I understand."

"Good, then unload your beasts and take your wood

to the place I will show you."

Mathis and the masons loaded beams on their shoulders and followed the officer up the steps to the entrance of the palace. It was stripped of the beautiful statuary and artwork Mathis had read about that existed in the days of Matthias Corvinus. He noted plain wooden doors opened into the palace instead of paneled bronze gates. They followed their guide through a series of rooms with faded paint, until they came to an early Renaissance-style arch supported by two pillars. "Build your scaffold here."

Mathis slowly appraised the structure. His gaze traveled up the narrow, fluted pillars that rose beneath an arch made up of marble sections of tile. The keystone at the top of the arch had a bas-relief image of a raven carved on it. "The emblem of the Raven King," Mathis whispered reverently.

As the masons walked back and forth to the donkeys unloading the lumber, Mathis wandered beyond the library entrance into a huge hall with a ribbed vault ceiling. Stacks of chests lay on top of one another, turned so the ancient books contained within were visible to the outside. Two vertical windows with broken glass bathed the area with sunlight.

Mathis dusted off several dozen titles and suddenly caught his breath. There, in front of him was a copy of the *Mishneh Torah*. He eagerly started to pull it out of the chest when something powerful gripped his arm.

He turned to face a stern, bearded guard holding a long dagger. The man motioned his weapon in warning. "You cannot touch anything here, or harm will come to the hostage."

Mathis shoved the leather-bound volume back. "I will

leave, then."

He departed from the library with the guard following him. Despite the man's admonition and the potential danger to Sarah, Mathis was elated over his discovery. If he could find a way to obtain this version of the *Mishneh Torah*, it would go a long way toward repairing the rift between he and the Oppenheimer family. It might also make break down Simon's resistance for Mathis to spend more time with Sarah.

Within hours, the masons built a scaffold that rose toward the crown of the arch. Mathis fought against the urge to leave and request an audience with the *pasha* so he could negotiate acquiring the famous document. But he knew his departure would look like he was apathetic about finding the treasure inside the arch, and he had to look interested. Otherwise, D'Aviano would hear about it and think his actions suspicious.

After bracing the area on either side of the keystone with lumber, the masons carefully chipped beneath until they could remove it. The trapezoid-shaped stone dropped into the arms of a worker, revealing nothing underneath but bare wall.

The foreman—a man with a black beard and curly hair—turned to Mathis and shrugged. Mathis pursed his lips and lifted his hands. "What can one do?"

The masons plastered the keystone back in place, buttressed it with lumber, then took a rest.

The foreman approached Mathis. "We'll let the keystone set for a few hours while we start on the other sections.

Mathis nodded. "Carry on."

By sundown, they had removed two sections in

addition to the keystone. Mathis estimated they had a day and a half to go. He found himself looking longingly into the library. What other treasures lurked inside those chests?

■ ■ ■

Two days later, the masons removed the last section of the arch and fit it back into place. No hidden manuscript was found. The *pasha* walked in with a retinue of soldiers and Sarah as the final repair took place. "Well, Mathis Zieglar," he scoffed, "so much for your quest for the treasured document."

Mathis looked at the hefty figure before him and his white shock of beard. Mathis bowed. "Yes, Excellency, it is a disappointment." His mind returned to the *Mishneh Torah*. "But perhaps something good has come out of it."

The *pasha* raised a brow. "Please elaborate."

"On the first day of our visit, I wandered into the library and spotted a copy of the *Mishneh Torah*. Perhaps Your Excellency would like to conclude the siege on a happy note by generously gifting it to the Oppenheimer family? It would heal the disappointment in not finding the treasure we sought."

The *pasha* studied Mathis carefully. "I thought you were looking for *The Mishneh Torah* within the sections of the arch. And now you have discovered something by the same name in the library? Why didn't you tell us three days ago and spare yourselves the effort?"

Mathis was caught off guard. He couldn't reveal the text he originally sought would prove the *pasha's* master, the sultan, was a fraud. He struggled for words.

"May I explain?"

All eyes turned toward Sarah, who smiled, despite being flanked by two armed guards.

The *pasha* nodded. "You may."

"In the beginning, we hoped to find a specific edition of the *Mishneh Torah* inside the arch. Doubtless, there are several copies of the book, but the one we hoped to find was once owned by Hekim Yakub, physician to His Majesty, Bayezid II."

"Why would this edition mean more to you than the one in the library?"

"A good question, Excellency, one that requires a careful explanation. She smiled. "We sought Hekim Yakup's document because it is unique—signed by Maimonides himself. It has been reported there are notes attached to it revealing many of Maimonides's thoughts that did not appear in later editions. Which makes that *Mishneh Torah* invaluable."

The *pasha* looked skeptical. "All well and good, young lady, but why would Charles of Lorraine care about a piece of Jewish literature? Why would he call off a siege to acquire it?"

Putting aside his admiration for Sarah's skillful manipulations, Mathis interjected. "As a military officer, I can speak to that, Excellency."

The *pasha* sighed. "Make it short. This is more complicated than sitting in on a conversation conducted by the *ulema*."

"Thank you, Excellency, we will do our best to avoid sounding like Islamic jurists. The emperor owes Samuel Oppenheimer, Sarah's uncle, a great deal for his financial support. Releasing the *Mishneh Torah* into his hands will go towards repaying him for his investment."

"Financial support, eh?" The *pasha* frowned and looked at Sarah. "Perhaps I should hold Samuel Oppenheimer's niece for ransom. The money would compensate many widows in Buda whose husbands have fallen, thanks to the weapons Samuel Oppenheimer provided."

"Excellency," Sarah's voice pleaded. "We mourn the loss of life in every home. Many Jews live here in Buda and have also suffered. Please know we only want you to extend the same generosity you offered when you allowed these masons to search the arch. Put an end to this siege, and heal the wounds with your liberality."

"Hmpf." The *pasha* looked at Sarah and then at Mathis. "You two should be professional diplomats." He waved his hand. "Let it be so. You may take the copy of the *Mishneh Torah* with you today."

Mathis could scarcely contain his jubilation. Sarah gave him a look he would never forget. They had performed a miracle.

The *pasha* allowed Sarah to leave her guards and accompany Mathis into the palace library. Sarah spent an hour studying the book and confirmed it was an ancient copy, though it contained no code like the edition that was the treasure of the Raven King. After they wrapped the document in a linen blanket, Mathis whispered, "Sarah, I want you to do me a great favor."

"*Ja*, Mathis?"

He looked around to make sure they had privacy. "Let's see how things play out with D'Aviano before we announce our acquisition."

Sarah's forehead wrinkled. "What about Simon? Surely we can trust him."

"Let's not for now. If he were to let his enthusiasm get

212

the better of him and mention our find to others, it might put a weapon in D'Aviano's hands."

Sarah's eyes widened. "I'm scared, Mathis. Does this mean we are in danger?"

Mathis stroked her hair. "No, that's not what I'm saying. D'Aviano has a way of using things I value against me, and the less he knows the better. Can you keep it secret for awhile?"

She nodded, her lip trembled. "This will return an ancient artifact to our community. If you only knew how much I want to tell the whole world about it. But for you... I'll remain silent."

■ ■ ■

The setting sun cast long shadows by the time Mathis and his party reached the Habsburg camp. Mathis and Sarah were invited into Lorraine's tent where the Duke and D'Aviano greeted them. Another friar stood close to D'Aviano, his face obscured by a cowl.

After hearing about the fruitless search inside the library's arch, the friar made no effort to conceal his disappointment. "You have nothing to show for all the trouble our men went to in dismantling the arch. I wonder if you knew this would be the result before it happened."

Fear prickled the back of Mathis's neck. "I have been faithful in discharging my duties to the State and the Church. I have done nothing for myself."

But D'Aviano was not satisfied. "This outcome makes no sense. The engravings from Dracula's cell specified 'the hard substance that adorns the arch in the library.'"

Mathis mustered all the sincerity he could inject into his voice. "Brother D'Aviano, we don't know how many

213

years those inscriptions were in Dracula's cell. Many things could have changed since they were written...perhaps someone else discovered where the treasure was."

D'Aviano's eyes traveled up and down as he studied Mathis in silence. Finally, he spoke. "What was the name of the private who assisted Captain Tannenberg on the day those inscriptions were handed to us?"

"Private Weber," whispered the friar inside the cowl.

"Bring him and Captain Tannenberg to my tent."

The hooded friar bowed and left.

Out of the corner of his eye, Mathis stole a glance at Sarah. Her calm demeanor betrayed no hint of the apprehension setting his teeth on edge. But, then, she had no way of knowing Private Weber's true gender.

CHAPTER TWENTY-FOUR

"CAPTAIN TANNENBERG IS AT HIS POST, AND will not be available until this evening." Lorraine informed D'Aviano. "As for Private Weber, he was reported missing several weeks ago. He is suspected of desertion."

D'Aviano's jaw dropped. "When did this happen?"

"Captain Tannenberg informed me of this shortly after he produced the inscriptions from the Tower of Solomon for you."

D'Aviano's eyes flashed. "I was wondering why I never heard anything from the army when I asked how long it had been since the private's last confession."

"That request never reached me." Lorraine sighed. "My apologies for the misunderstanding. May I ask why you wish to question Captain Tannenberg?"

"I want to know why he supplied us with faulty information about the treasure's location."

Lorraine frowned. "Captain Tannenberg is an officer with a spotless record. I request you question him respectfully."

"Hmm." The corner of D'Aviano's mouth quirked up. "Very well, commander. But, question him I shall."

D'Aviano and his assistant turned toward the tent entrance. "The peace of Christ be with you."

After they left, Lorraine turned to Mathis. "Although your search was unproductive, I will keep my end of the bargain with the *pasha*. I will command the army to begin withdrawing in three days."

Mathis saluted and followed D'Aviano out the door.

When Mathis retired to his tent, he was surprised to find Sarah and Simon sitting at the table where he often waited for Kamil. Sarah laughed. "We've brought you a flask of sweet wine."

Mathis couldn't help fidgeting. "I don't want to seem ungrateful, but I have to leave as soon as possible. There's something important I must do."

Seeing disappointment in their faces, he briefly told them of the danger Tannenberg faced from D'Aviano. "That friar almost sent me to the Inquisition not long ago. I need to give Tannenberg a chance to think of something to say."

"Why should we keep you and make things more difficult?" Simon urged. "Don't worry about us. Go to him."

Mathis jumped on his horse and sped to the country west of the citadel where Tannenberg's battery was. As the afternoon light thinned, fewer cannon sounded as their crews prepared to retire for the day. He hoped he could make it to Tannenberg before D'Aviano summoned him.

He ignored the whistling of a cannonball until it struck the ground yards from his horse. The explosion tossed him like a rag out of his saddle. Everything went black.

Eventually, a searing pain across his chest forced him

to open his eyes. A huddle of men peered over him. "Are you well, *Herr* Captain?"

Someone sat him up while another offered him water. He drank it until a lump in his stomach made him choke, then vomit. His ribs hurt. "Get...get Captain Tannenberg, commander of a *saker* on the western heights. Tell him it is urgent he comes immediately." With every breath, the pain ricocheted down his spine.

Mathis tried to stand up but fell back down. "Get Captain Tannenberg, *now*."

Someone left. The sound of hooves riding away followed. Mathis tried to get up again, but strong hands restrained him. "Rest, *Herr* Captain. Someone has gone to fetch Captain Tannenberg."

Mathis's vision swam, and the world tilted around him. "Where's my horse?"

One of the faces in front of him grew long. "A piece of shrapnel injured your horse. He will have to be destroyed."

"No...this can't be. I've ridden that mount into battle too many times. He's saved my life...You can't destroy...." The ache magnified a thousand fold, and his vision blurred. Mathis blacked out again.

When he came to, someone mopped his face with a wet cloth. "Where is Tannenberg?" he mumbled. "You have to get Tannenberg."

The beating of hooves came near. The man that had left rejoined the huddle. "Captain Tannenberg cannot come. He has a meeting with Brother Marco D'Aviano."

■ ■ ■

Mathis was carried to his tent in the back of a mule-drawn wagon. All the while, self-loathing tormented him.

He should never have allowed Tannenberg to lie for him in the first place. If Mathis had only ended the conversation with Sarah and Simon earlier, he could have reached Tannenberg and warned him to prepare for D'Aviano. Now his friend faced the horror of the Inquisition.

The wagon knocked and bumped all the way back to Mathis's tent. Two soldiers carried him inside and laid him on a cot. One bent over him. "I will ask a camp surgeon to look you over. Take courage, *Herr* Captain. He will be here before long."

After a while, Mathis managed to painfully sit up on the side of his bed. When he tried to focus on the wall of the tent, it remained a blur. He hung his head and surrendered to the daze. Just as the remaining light turned into night, a voice sounded outside his tent. "This is Simon Oppenheimer. Are you well, *Herr* Captain?"

"Uh, oh. I ammm…I ammm here…I am…." Mathis couldn't overcome the slur in his voice.

The tent flaps parted and Simon entered, holding a lantern. "We heard of your little accident, *Herr* Captain. And we thought, who else is there to nurse you back to health?"

Mathis laughed weakly.

Sarah followed him, holding a black pot with a lid. "Wait 'til you try these lintels. They're goodness for the soul."

Simon placed the lantern on a stand next to the cot. Sarah pulled up a stool and dipped a ladle into the pot. "Take and eat, *Herr* Captain."

Mathis guzzled a few mouthfuls. Little by little, he felt his strength return. The details of his visitor's faces sharpened and the blurriness receded. "I…I have to help Tannenberg. D'Aviano…will destroy him."

"Now, now." Sarah patted his wrist. "First you heal, then you worry about others."

His speech returning to normal, Mathis told Sarah and Simon of the peril Tannenberg faced. "He...he saved me from the Inquisition...and now he faces it himself."

Simon sat on the ground and pulled his hands over his legs. "But doesn't Captain Tannenberg have proof the emperor's friends trafficked women to the Mohammedans? Not to mention he could expose their secret trade in fertile coffee beans."

Mathis buried his head in his hands and waited for his thoughts to clear. "I doubt that will stop D'Aviano. That just gives him another reason to get rid of Tannenberg."

Sarah's voice quavered. "Then you're not safe either."

"That depends on...on whether D'Aviano thinks I can help him....find the treasure of the Raven King. He must be thinking that over...right now." Mathis sighed. "And if he gets Tannenberg to confess...he made up those inscriptions, then D'Aviano...he may come after me. He's convinced I'm withholding information...and he's right."

"Then we must think of something to save the captain," Sarah said firmly. "Something quick."

■ ■ ■

The next morning, Mathis regained the use of his legs and walked haltingly over to the outdoor table near his tent. He was in no mood to give a friendly greeting when a surgeon finally arrived. The man explained Mathis had probably suffered a concussion, which he'd already surmised. "Perhaps you can make yourself useful and arrange for a cane," Mathis snapped.

"I can do that," the man said with a good natured

smile. "But it will cost you a couple of *kreutzers*".

"Which I will pay when you provide the cane."

The surgeon walked over to his horse-drawn wagon, and reached inside the box behind the bench. He returned with three walking sticks of varying lengths.

Mathis grasped each one, testing his weight.

He felt guilty he had spoken arrogantly to the surgeon. Pulling a few coins out of his pocket, including an extra one, he pressed them into the man's hand. "This one will be suitable, *Herr Feldscher*. Thank you."

The man nodded amiably and mounted his wagon. "Make sure you do not ride a horse in the meantime."

"I will try my best."

Shortly after the surgeon left, Simon and Sarah met Mathis by the table.

After looking around, Mathis turned to Simon with a low voice. "What news do you have?"

Simon's face was grave. "Nothing hopeful, *Herr* Captain. According to what I can gather, Captain Tannenberg denied he forged the inscriptions on the stone that saved you from the Inquisition."

"How did D'Aviano respond?"

"He insisted the Captain was lying. He informed the Captain his spies had located *Frau* Lang, er, Private Weber this morning. D'Aviano taunted Tannenberg with the news she would suffer dire punishment for impersonating a man, unless, of course…."

"Umm." Mathis grimaced. "Unless she admitted that Tannenberg coerced her into creating false evidence. Did either of them confess?"

Simon looked down and folded his hands over his chest. "*Ja. Frau* Lang has implicated Captain Tannenberg in the fraud."

After a moment of silence, Simon looked up. "*Herr* Captain, knowing what you did yesterday, why did you ride toward Captain Tannenberg on the front lines? What were you trying to accomplish?"

"I was hoping to get him to tell me where *Frau* Lang was, so that we could put her out of D'Aviano's reach. Maybe hide her on a boat traveling to Vienna."

"Ah, I see. That might have succeeded at the time." Simon looked flustered. "But now she's in the stockade."

Mathis concentrated and spoke slowly. "They will probably show Tannenberg the instruments of torture today to make him talk. If he doesn't comply, they'll start breaking his toes and fingers tomorrow. Then he'll tell the truth and I'll be next."

The bushes next to them rustled and Kamil's voice chided. "Well, Captain. Did you really expect D'Aviano to take your deceptions at face value? My spies have told me much about this churchman."

Mathis started to walk inside the foliage, but Sarah and Simon stood deathly still.

Simon glared at Mathis. "You think I don't have enough troubles, you would wish that Tartar on me, again?"

Sarah shook her finger. "That man brings us evil, Mathis."

Sniggering came from the bushes. "'That man' has given your family so much in trade, you can't count the money you've made. Now, you need me more than ever."

Using his cane, Mathis parted the branches and found Kamil by himself inside a clearing. "It's all right," Mathis called out softly to his friends. "You can come in."

"Do you think I am a glutton for pain?" Simon

protested. "Not on your life."

Hesitantly, Sarah pushed back the bushes and stood beside Mathis. He was in no mood for the usual verbal sparring with the Tartar. "We need a solution to our problems, not your taunts. So, if you have something to contribute, make it quick."

Kamil grinned. "That's better, now that most of us are here. It seems we have a mutual interest in releasing our friends from the stockade. Perhaps we should pool our resources."

Mathis narrowed his eyes. "What're you saying? You're willing to help me spring Tannenberg if I help your friend Davudoff?"

Kamil nodded. "I and one of my men will assist you."

"Wait a minute...." Mathis lifted his head at Kamil as if the Tartar cheated him at cards. "Why do you want to free Davudoff? So that you can have the pleasure of killing him?"

Kamil's expression saddened. "No, nothing like that."

Mathis wasn't sure if he should accept what Kamil claimed. "Davudoff is the man who tried to destroy the coffee shipment you sent to Vienna. Why *don't* you want to kill him?"

Kamil heaved a deep sigh. "Because you keep caring for the one you love, even when they act badly. I want to free Davudoff."

Looking as if he had forgotten himself a moment, Kamil reverted to his characteristic smirk. "Anyway, it's in your interest to help me."

"You must be jesting, Tartar. I'm the one that stopped you and Davudoff when you impersonated an Imperial soldier back in Vienna. And now you want me to help you pose as a soldier all over again? So I can betray the army?"

Kamil cocked his head to one side. "I'd say your army has betrayed you, Captain. After all the battles you have fought for them and all the Mohammedans you have killed...how do they reward you? By locking up your friend, Tannenberg, and torturing him until he points the finger at you? Is that the army you want to serve?"

Pale as a bed sheet, Sarah laid her hand on Mathis's wrist. "That's horrible. Tell me you won't let that happen, Mathis."

Mathis scowled. "I'll do my utmost. But we haven't much time."

Sarah removed her hands. "For what?"

Mathis steadied himself against his cane, and looked her in the eye. "You know the spot where the soldiers bathe on the banks of the river?"

Sarah averted her eyes and looked down. "This is, so... embarrassing."

"We can't worry about propriety under these circumstances. Sarah, I need you to steal two uniforms and bring them back to me."

"But before you go," Mathis pointed in the direction of where they had left Simon, "have your cousin bring me Private Vadasz Bakos."

"Where are you going?" Kamil demanded.

"To visit some of Tannenberg's friends. He needs them, now."

CHAPTER TWENTY-FIVE

ATHIS'S SIDES STILL ACHED WHEN HE WALKED, and he had to stop on occasion to regain his strength. But he resumed and pushed into a swift gait, hoping a Tartar raider wouldn't spot him. "I've got to make it to Tannenberg's men," he repeated over and over through clenched teeth.

"Mathis, please stop."

He turned around to find Sarah a few paces back, her face troubled. "Mathis, are you going to take the uniforms I gather and give them to Kamil and his friend?"

He turned back and resumed his walk. "It's better you don't know. Go back to camp."

She caught up to him and laid her hand on his arm. "Mathis, if you're going to ask me to break the law, shouldn't you be honest with me?"

Mathis snorted his frustration. "If you must know, I've got to break Tannenberg and Davudoff out of prison. The uniforms are for the two who will help me. There. Are you any better off knowing?"

"Mathis, Mathis," she intoned softly. "I know you're hurting, and that's why you speak so sharply. Let me help you."

Fury reddened his face. "Why must you do that? Every time you talk to me that way I forget I'm a soldier. If I don't act quickly, Tannenberg will die…and maybe I will, too."

Sarah looked at him, her voice tender. "Don't you realize, Mathis, I can't help speaking that way to you because…."

Mathis stopped. The anger melted from his body. "Sarah, don't you see? As much as I care for you, I'll never be right for your family and your religion. I'm about to defy my country and emperor. I can't ask you to follow me into something so completely unknown."

Sarah stroked the hair away from his temple, her face creased in tension. "You're right for me, Mathis Zieglar, and that's all that matters."

Mathis clasped her other hand and stared deeply into her soft, brown eyes. "Are you willing to leave your family behind and follow me to another land?"

"Anywhere, Mathis Zieglar. Anywhere."

■ ■ ■

That afternoon, Mathis led four uniformed men toward the stockade. He raised his hand and they halted. He whispered to Sarah beside him, "Remember, let me do the talking."

Would the makeshift document he had cobbled together work? He had stamped a glob of wax at its bottom with Lorraine's medallion, hoping it would pass the scrutiny of the prison officer.

Two soldiers stood guard on each side of the structure,

eight total. A lieutenant sat at a desk near the entrance. He looked up from his paperwork, rose and saluted as Mathis approached. "Welcome, *Herr* Captain. What business have you here?"

Mathis returned his salute. He unfurled the document. "As you know, the army is preparing to lift the siege. I have an order from Charles, Duke of Lorraine, directing you to release the prisoners named here to us. We will take them to ships and transport them back to Vienna."

The lieutenant took the paper and read it. "*Frau* Lang, the Jew named Davudoff...." he dropped the page to his side. "And Captain Tannenberg? What is going on, here? I thought the Captain was going to be tortured tomorrow."

Mathis gave him an icy look. "That is for the Duke to decide. Will you comply, or will you tell him you know a wiser course of action?"

Fear fleeted over the lieutenant's face. He glanced over his shoulder, and lowered his voice. "How do you want the prisoners prepared?"

"Just chain their hands. We'll take care of the rest."

Within minutes, the prisoners were escorted down to Mathis, their chains clanking together with every pace. Just as the inmates were turned over to Mathis's men, the lieutenant cocked his head. "Say, aren't one of those soldiers *Herr* Lang, *Frau* Lang's husband?"

Mathis reached inside his greatcoat and pulled a wheel-lock from his belt. He discretely poked the barrel's mouth through his coat's buttonhole. "Careful, Lieutenant," he said softly. "Now, calmly explain to your men you are going to accompany us to the docks. Make sure it's convincing, or my little friend here will send a round through your heart."

The lieutenant's face quickly drained of all color. He did as instructed.

The party departed the stockade in the direction of the river. On the way, Mathis led everyone into a clump of birches where Sarah waited. He nodded to the lieutenant. "Release the prisoner's padlocks, with the exception of Davudoff."

Soon, Tannenberg and *Frau* Lang were free of their shackles. Tannenberg lifted Mathis up in a bear hug. As he sat Mathis down, Tannenberg shook his head in wonder. "You risked your life for me, *Hauptfeder*."

"As you did for me, brother. Now, I need your help."

Mathis snapped his fingers and three stable boys brought them nine horses, the number needed for Mathis, Sarah, the uniformed men, and the three sprung from prison. Sarah reached into a sack, pulled out coins, and paid them.

After the boys departed, Mathis took a length of rope and looked at the lieutenant. "Stand against that tree while I tie you up. Tannenberg, gag him."

Soon, the party proceeded at a canter so as not arouse suspicions over their departure, heading northwest. Sarah rode on one side of Mathis, Tannenberg flanked on the other.

Sarah sighed. "This is the hardest thing I've ever done, Mathis. All I did was leave Simon a note explaining as best I could."

"You did well, my love. Simon would not have wanted to accompany us." The words *my love* from his lips in open air felt better than he dared hope.

"I know, but Heidelberg is the only life I've known. I'll never see it or my family again."

227

Mathis grinned. "I wouldn't wager my life on that. If you want to hear Heaven laugh, just swear something will never happen again."

"But it goes deeper than that, Mathis. My faith is my life, as well."

Mathis reached over the reins and put his hand over Sarah's wrist. He sensed it wasn't the time to be dismissive. "You've sacrificed everything, Sarah. I vow I'll do everything in my power to make you happy. Including creating a life where you can observe your faith."

Tannenberg called out. "You recruited four men to join this prison break…including *Herr* Lang. Who is that man in a Hungarian uniform?"

"Vadasz Bakos."

Tannenberg's eyebrows rose. "A relative of Endre?"

"*Ja.* His cousin."

Tannenberg frowned. "And the other two?"

Mathis chuckled. "Think of them as mercenaries. They'll ride with us to a place we'll be safe from the Turks and the Habsburgs."

"Where? Paris?"

Mathis laughed at the improbability of crossing Europe to find refuge. "No, jester. Transylvania. They accept people of all backgrounds."

Tannenberg nodded toward Sarah. "Even a Jewish and a Christian couple?"

Mathis smiled. "Yes, even that unlikely pair." He winked at Sarah.

Tannenberg turned back again and looked quizzically at Mathis. "Say, is one of those 'mercenaries' your friend, Kamil?"

Mathis laughed. "How did you know?"

"He looks as if he's never sat in this kind of saddle. He rides like a Tartar."

"That's right, Tannenberg. Two of our band are Tartars."

The tightness in Mathis's body slowly dissipated. He had succeeded in rescuing Tannenberg, but at the expense of his career. What more sacrifices lay before him?

■ ■ ■

"You Germans ride like old women," Davudoff exclaimed. "It will take us days to reach Eger."

Mathis and his companions had rode two hours as hard as they could away from the Habsburg camp, and the party halted next to a cool, babbling stream, to water their horses.

"Eger?" Tannenberg wiped the sweat off his horse. "I've heard that's an Ottoman fortress. Why are we going there?"

Mathis leaned back and stretched. He spoke in a voice low enough so only Sarah and Tannenberg could hear. "Kamil and I made a deal if I helped him release Davudoff from jail, Kamil would get us through Mohammedan territory. We have to do that to reach the treasure of the Raven King. He guaranteed our safety if we stayed overnight at Eger. Better for us to make our presence known to the Turks, than to cut through their territory and have them surprise us."

Frau Lang and her husband, Dietrich, led their horses toward Mathis. "We're lucky to have escaped without running into an Imperial patrol," Dietrich said. "What are our plans? Head north?"

"*Ja*, north." Mathis replied. "Ultimately, we aim to reach Transylvania, out of the clutches of the Habsburg army."

Dietrich shook his head as if he'd contracted a chill.

"Transylvania? We don't speak Magyar, and don't know anyone there. How will my wife and I make a living?

Vadasz waved his hand at Dietrich. "The same way you earn a living now, as a surgeon. There are many cities in that country populated by German-speaking Saxons. You'll do fine."

Mathis lifted his eyes toward his friend, and laughed. "Don't worry, Tannenberg. There are plenty of vineyards and breweries there for you, too."

Tannenberg took a draught from his water skin and wiped his mouth. "There'd better be, I'm running out."

■ ■ ■

The party continued traveling through forested land. Dietrich Lang began to whine. "If I had known participating in this escape would take us to Transylvania, I would have thought twice about this."

As he repeated the complaint the third time, Mathis brought his own horse to a stop. He stared at the surgeon with a cold eye. "Would you prefer taking your wife back to the Inquisition and explain to them why she wore men's clothes and served as a cannoneer? It could be arranged."

Dietrich was unimpressed. "I would rather be in the hands of our own people than take our chances with the Mohammedans."

Disgusted, Mathis threw his arm westward. "Then go home, you miserable dog, and rot. Leave any time you wish."

Frau Lang rode up to them, wearing a horrified look. "Are you mad, Dietrich? We have no future back in Vienna. Transylvania is our only hope."

Dietrich called out as he steered his horse westward.

"Ever since you became Private Weber, my life has been cursed. I want it normal again. If that means answering to the Church for what I've done, so be it. *Auf Wiedersehen*, wife, or whatever you are today."

"No, Dietrich. Come back, please," *Frau* Lang sobbed. "We can't go back. Think of our families, our home."

But he rode off, deaf to his wife's pleas.

No sooner had Dietrich left their company than Davudoff's chiding at their slow progress resumed. "Pick up the pace, or I'll be a year older when we get to Eger. Take these chains off my hands and I'll show you how to ride."

"I should have never let you out of prison, when I traded you for the *ferman*," Mathis responded. "You're damned lucky we didn't leave you in the stockade back there, where you would have contracted a disease."

Davudoff sneered. "You help me only because you need me."

Sarah patiently explained that Mathis's injuries kept him from riding any faster, but Davudoff was unforgiving. "Excuses, excuses. What kind of soldier is he?"

Mathis couldn't tell the protestor to go his own way the same as Dietrich because Mathis needed Kamil and Davudoff to guide them through Turkish territory to Christian Upper Hungary. On the other hand, he wanted to shut the man up permanently. He fumed and seethed until the third day of travel.

In the morning, after the party broke camp, Mathis walked up to Davudoff. "I want to make you and your loud mouth a bet."

"If it would make you ride faster it would be worth it, *goy*. What kind of wager?"

No matter how much pain it produced, Mathis would silence Davudoff once and for all. He pointed to Davudoff's crown. "Fluff your hair up and place your *yarmulke* forward on your head. I'll bet all the food I have with me that I can knock your cap off your head without using my hands. If I win, there'll be no more complaints from you about our pace, and you'll cooperate for the rest of the journey."

Davudoff repositioned his cap and snickered. "I would love to make you go hungry. Then you will know what it's like to be in a Habsburg cell. You're on, *goy.*"

As the party formed a circle around Davudoff, Mathis removed his greatcoat and took his walking stick from where it was lashed to his saddle. Kamil looked at Davudoff and clicked his tongue. "You shouldn't bet against that infidel, my friend."

"We'll see," Davudoff cackled.

Mathis tossed his stick up in the air and somersaulted, completing the motion by laying on the ground and holding his legs erect. The stick landed on his soles, and he kicked it on top of Davudoff's head. Plunk. The stick and the *yarmulke* rolled to the ground.

Davudoff's jaw dropped and his hands flailed. "*Oy. Oy gevault,*" he stammered.

Frau Lang and Sarah stood still, their expressions incredulous. "Didn't I tell you?" Kamil chortled.

Tannenberg roared from his belly. "He moves like a watches' mainspring. That's why he's called *Hauptfeder.*"

CHAPTER TWENTY-SIX

Traveling toward Eger, Northwestern Hungary
December, 1684

AFTER THEIR JOURNEY HAD COMPLETED FOUR DAYS, Mathis's companions approached the towering walls of Eger, looming on a hill. The calls of a *muezzin* rang out from a minaret, signaling they were close to the Ottoman Empire's northernmost border.

They were within five-hundred feet of the city gates when Davudoff rattled his chains. "Turn me loose. Set me free now, or I'll tell the authorities you have no right to hold a Jew against his will."

Mathis's heart raced. On one hand, if he released Davudoff, freeing the hostages would be more difficult after he located the treasure. On the other hand, if Mathis kept Davudoff bound and he attracted too much attention, they could all end up in a Turkish jail and their mission would fail.

Kamil turned to Mathis. "If he makes a fuss, there's little we can do. Holding a Jew without a hearing before a

233

judge is unlawful."

"The man is a hemorrhoid," Tannenberg groused. "Knock him unconscious and tell the authorities he's sick."

Without a word, Mathis fished inside his coat pocket for the key and rode over to Davudoff. Seconds later, the man was free.

As Davudoff threw off his bonds, Mathis raised his finger. "Before you ride off, use your brain a moment."

"There's nothing you can say to make me stay."

Mathis stuck out his lower lip. "Maybe yes, maybe no. But ask yourself, why do you think I didn't cooperate with the Church and tell them what they wanted to know?"

Davudoff cast an angry glance at Kamil and back toward Mathis. "Is this concerning your delusion about finding Matthias Corvinus's lost treasure? Kamil has told me of your insane notion."

Mathis spread his hands. "*Ja*, it is *all* about the treasure. Do you honestly think we would be here if I wasn't sure about its location in Transylvania?" He gestured toward Tannenberg. "Do you think I would risk my best friend's life for a delusion?"

Mathis grabbed the inside of his greatcoat above the buttons and lifted it up. "Do you think I would turn my back on my career and risk the Inquisition if I didn't think I was on the trail of the treasure?"

Davudoff wetted a cloth with his water skin and rubbed the chain rust off his arms. "Why should I care about this treasure, even if you lay your hands on it? How does it benefit me?"

"It affects you, *mein Herr*, because you hold the slaves Captain Zieglar wants." Sarah's voice rose with each word. "The sultan will fill your pockets with gold when you turn the hostages over to Captain Zieglar. You and your family will be rich."

Davudoff sniffed. "That sounds very far-fetched. Why would the sultan pay me anything more than market value for my slaves?"

"Because, if you help me, I will demand he pay you extra for your efforts." Mathis knew he had to make his argument strong. He pointed to Kamil. "This man knows I do as I say. If you trust him, trust me."

Davudoff and Kamil stared at one another silently. Kamil nodded.

Davudoff softened the edge in his voice. "What do you want from me, then?"

"I want you to accompany me until I find the treasure. Then, I want you and Kamil to take the news back to Constantinople."

■ ■ ■

The second they approached the city gates sentries surrounded Mathis's party, pointing spears at them. The commander of the guards shouted in Turk, "Look at those uniforms. They are infidel soldiers. Seize them."

Kamil held up his hands in surrender. "*Salaam alaikum*, brothers. I am a Tartar leading these deserters to the true God. Please make them welcome."

Within minutes, the weapons were withdrawn and the party was allowed to seek lodging. Davudoff winked at Mathis. "Lucky for you, Kamil is with us."

Kamil turned to Davudoff. "Lucky for us a dozen Imperials have already come here, seeking sanctuary. They're used to taking in deserters."

Then it hit Mathis as if a mountain fell on him. He

actually felt safer surrounded by Mohammedans than if he was with his own army. The realization he had left his regiment, his country and the hope of ever seeing his mother alive again kicked the breath out of him. He was a man without a home.

■ ■ ■

Mathis's party left Eger the next day and rode through rolling valleys between low-lying mountains. The agreeable terrain had less jolts and bumps, giving Mathis's aches a chance to heal. But three days later, when they reached Upper Hungary, with its higher mountains and changing elevations, it was a different story.

As they climbed through a pass between two mountains, with the ruins of a stronghold on one side, Mathis turned to Vadasz. "This land has more fortresses than my greatcoat has buttons."

Vadasz laughed. "Only thing this country can count on is war and invasion."

Mathis looked at Vadasz's colorful laced shirt beneath the man's jacket and hat sporting a high, erect feather on the front. "Wouldn't we fit in better if we all dressed like *hajdus*?"

"Maybe. Or maybe local people speak in Hungarian and some of us answer German while we dress Magyar. Then people really suspect us." His broken accent was thick, but Mathis easily understood him.

"So, you think it better if we keep wearing our Habsburg uniforms and tell them we're deserters?"

"Hope so, Captain. People here led by Hungarian nobleman, Imre Thokoly. He rebels against Habsburgs, and is supported by Turks."

Mathis scratched his chin. "Thokoly, I've heard of him. He hates the emperor persecuting Protestants and forcing Catholicism on Hungary. He wants to make Hungary—at least Upper Hungary—independent."

"*Ja.* Turks help him against Habsburgs. But Turks suspect Thokoly for negotiating with Habsburgs for peace. Alliances in Upper Hungary very slippery."

Tannenberg rode on the other side of Mathis and leaned in on the conversation. "This doesn't sound like much of a safe haven you're leading us into."

Mathis gave a pained smile. "Better than taking your chances with the Inquisition."

■ ■ ■

The group was a day's journey out of Eger, headed east toward the Transylvanian border, when a motley collection of people, some walking and others in wagons, approached them.

Mathis took out his telescope. "They're people of all ages, including infants. Families like this generally don't travel much in the winter. What has befallen them?"

"Might be refugees." Vadasz squirmed in his saddle. "Will ask what happened."

He rode ahead to the approaching group. By the time Mathis neared the oncoming people, Vadasz finished a conversation with one of the elders. He returned to Mathis. "They're fleeing the Tartars just east of here. We should take a more northerly route to Transylvania, and avoid the trouble."

Kamil walked his pony to the two of them. "I'm familiar with this country."

Mathis flashed him a look that said "of course you are."

"It might be safer to go northeast through Kassa," Kamil advised. Mathis and Vadasz agreed, even though such a journey would prolong their travel several days.

The weather turned colder as Mathis and his companions tracked northwest. Five days past Eger, approaching the medieval city of Kassa, he looked up, stuck out his tongue and tasted snowflakes.

When they came to a bridge spanning the Hernád River, six *hajdus* surrounded them. "What is your business in Kassa?" their commanding officer demanded.

Since he spoke Hungarian the best, Vadasz answered. "Do not fear us, brothers. We are merely deserters fleeing the Habsburg army. My name is Vadasz Bakos, and we are friends of your cause."

The officer smiled broadly and puffed out his chest. "And what is the cause of our army?"

Vadasz spoke deliberately. "To drive the pagan Habsburgs from the land, and provide freedom for every Hungarian."

The officer, clothed in a wooly sheepskin coat, looked at one of his subordinates. "What do you think, Sandor?"

"They look like who they say they are," Sandor replied.

The officer looked Mathis's party over carefully. "There's a place to lodge at the end of the first street in town. Do you read German?"

"Yes," Vadasz answered. "We all do."

"The inn has a sign above the entrance of an ale cup with the word 'Essenhaus.' Stay there until we give you permission to leave."

Vadasz thanked the sentries and doffed his cap. Mathis, held his breath throughout the conversation, and didn't exhale until the party rode slowly away. He turned to Sarah. "That's Eger and Kassa down, only a few more Transylvanian villages to go before we're in Koloszvar."

Sarah nodded and cast a nervous glance over her shoulder. Mathis took her cue and noticed two of the sentries following them at a distance. "Don't worry," he muttered. "We'll be fine as long as we don't cause trouble."

Kamil pulled his horse alongside Mathis. "This inn is owned by German-descent people, Saxons. Their allegiance may be dubious. I would advise everyone to keep their mouths closed about anything political, especially how they feel about the emperor."

"Agreed," said Tannenberg, riding behind Mathis.

"A wise policy," Mathis agreed. "Considering many in the Holy Roman Empire consider Leopold their enemy."

The innkeeper turned out to be a large proportioned man. He greeted Mathis as he entered the door of the inn. "Welcome to the *Essenhaus*," he said in German with a hearty chuckle. "I am the proprietor, Roland Dengler."

"Good afternoon," Mathis bowed, slightly. "I am Mathis Zieglar. I have two women and four men in my party. Can you put us up for the night?"

"Indeed, I can."

He turned to a young boy who was serving a guest a drink. "Hans, after you finish, get your brother and help our lodgers stable their horses."

Soon, the party sat at a long table and sipped cups of warm ale.

A young girl, wearing a vest laced in the front and a long apron over her dress, waited on them. "I am Hilda," she said. "You are in for a special treat tonight. Because my mother is Magyar and my father is Saxon, we prepare cuisine from both areas. For those of you who prefer German food, we have bratwurst and sauerkraut. My advice, how-ever, is that you indulge yourself with our Hungarian of-fering: *Hortobagyi* pancakes. They are savory crepes filled with tender veal, with garlic and onions on the side. Or, you may choose *slambuc*, potatoes and noodles boiled over an open fire, and flavored with bacon."

"I'll have the pancakes," Kamil and Davudoff said simultaneously.

"Me, too," Sarah chimed in.

Mathis smiled. No need to explain to Hilda that Muslim and Jewish dietary laws forbade the pork in bratwurst and *slambuc*. He noticed with a touch of irony, though the Qur'an forbade alcohol, Kamil didn't seem to have a problem consuming ale.

It seemed as if the preparation of the food took forever for Mathis, ravished after being on the trail for four days. He drank one draught after another and soon felt woozy. Tannenberg laid a soft hand on him. "Easy, brother. You're not built like me, remember?"

Yet Hilda insisted he imbibe more. She brought him two mugs at a time and plopped them down in front of him. "Drink your fill, *mein Herr.* You need something to keep you warm this evening."

The room reeled around Mathis. He felt dizzy, and had to hold onto his chair.

He heard Sarah's concerned voice. "No more drinks, please." She whispered in his ear, "Are you well, Mathis?"

"I, uh…don't feel very good."

As he faded, Mathis felt Vadasz and Tannenberg hoist him up and put their shoulders beneath his arms. They half-walked, half-carried him into a room. Then he drifted off.

When he awoke, it was early the next morning. He lay in the back of a wagon, next to Tannenberg and Vadasz, bound with ropes. Mathis vainly struggled against a cord wrapped around his wrists.

CHAPTER TWENTY-SEVEN

A BURLY MAN WITH A LONG MUSTACHE TWISTED around in the passenger seat. "Don't worry, you'll be warm tomorrow in Regec Castle. Count Thokoly would like to have a little chat with you."

Mathis managed to sit up despite the bone-rattling ride. His horse and those of his wagon-mates were tethered to one another and the wagon. Kamil and Davudoff were in the back of a second wagon, their horses also trailing behind. Oddly enough, their hosts appeared less worried about Sarah and *Frau* Lang, permitting them to follow the wagons on separate horses.

The ride jarred Mathis's teeth. Riding over frozen ground was never pleasant.

By the following evening, the travelers were at the base of a road that spiraled up the side of a mountain and led to an imposing white, limestone castle. A series of towers with pyramid-shaped roofs peered over curved, crenellated walls.

Tannenberg sat up. "Medieval looking, isn't it?"

242

Mathis grunted assent.

After the party ascended the mountain and entered the castle gates, birds cooed in the distance. As the prisoners were ordered out of the wagons and walked between a series of multi-storied buildings, Mathis spotted the source of the sound. There in a courtyard, three dovecotes stood atop long poles. Pigeons fluttered their wings and preened themselves, hopping in and out of their shelters.

The captives climbed wooden stairs and were led onto a long porch with ornately carved pillars. Soon, they stood in a great hall with fireplaces on three walls radiating heat. The burly man went up to each and sliced their bonds with a dagger. "You are free to roam the castle grounds, as long as you do not attempt to escape. For your own safety, obey any directions the soldiers give you."

"How long will we be obliged to stay here?" Mathis asked.

"Count Thokoly will discuss that with you in the morning."

As their captors left, eight armed *hajdus* entered, carrying the prisoners' bags. One of them, obviously the leader, lifted up his voice. "Welcome to Regec Castle, visitors. Identify which bags are yours and we will show you to your rooms. Dinner will be served after you settle in."

Still curious, Mathis spoke out. "Why are we being detained? How have we offended the ruler of this place?"

The *hajdu* in charge smiled grimly. "You are recipients of Count Thokoly's hospitality for reasons he will explain."

That evening, the party dined on beef and fruit preserves. Sarah sat next to Mathis and spoke in a near whisper so as to avoid nearby guards from overhearing. "Why do you think they're detaining us?"

Mathis finished his wine. "I'm not sure. I noticed the dovecotes, so maybe they received some message about us. But aside from their enemies, the Habsburgs, who wants to stop us?"

Sarah shook her head. "I don't trust Davudoff. Maybe our host's allies, the Turks, have discovered our search for the treasure. The Mohammedans would like nothing better than to destroy it before it could be made public."

Mathis gave a sardonic smile. "Destroy it...and us. By the way, has anyone rummaged through your valuables?"

"No, Mathis. Everything is safe."

■ ■ ■

The next morning, the party was seated at a table in the middle of the hall, warmed by the glow of three fireplaces. Without warning, four *hajdus* threw open the entryway door. One announced "His Excellency, Count Imre Thokoly, King of Upper Hungary."

A striking man with a cleft chin and a pointed nose strode into their midst, removing his gray fur gloves. After scanning the faces of all seated, his eyes traveled to a vacant place set at the end of the table. "Ah, good, you have saved a place for me," he said in German.

One of his retainers pulled the chair back, and Thokoly sat. "Well, well," he said to Mathis and his companions. "I trust your accommodations last night were comfortable?"

They all nodded.

"Good." Thokoly rubbed his hands together. "Then please, eat your breakfast. No doubt you are wondering why I have invited you to Regec Castle."

Again, the table voiced their assent. Mathis found Thokoly remarkably accommodating, considering the man's rank.

As everyone ate breakfast, Thokoly spoke. "As you know, the people of Upper Hungary have chafed under the Habsburg yoke for many years. They have chosen me to lead them in their struggle to worship as they please."

The table's response was again positive, but more subdued this time.

Mathis put his food down. "How may we be of service to your Excellency?"

Thokoly smiled. "You must be Captain Zieglar, am I correct? Until late, of the Savoy Dragoons?"

Mathis hid his surprise, and concern at how this man already knew who he was. "*Ja,* at your service, Excellency."

Thokoly continued. "Well, a good friend of our cause recently contacted me and asked that he speak to you before you leave our country."

The hackles went up on Mathis's neck. How could Thokoly know they were headed out of Hungary?

"So, when you ask 'how can we be of service,'" Thokoly's eyes twinkled, "you can promise you will wait patiently for this gentlemen and answer his questions truthfully."

Mathis did his best to remain calm. "Of course. Might your Excellency share with us the man's name, and how long until his arrival?"

Thokoly gave a slight shake of his head. "Ah, well, my good sir, this man you have never met, so I will leave introductions until his arrival. In about two weeks or so."

Mathis's hands tensed into claws. The travel time Thokoly cited would coincide with a journey from Vienna.

■ ■ ■

Keeping themselves amused while they waited for the

mysterious visitor to arrive proved quite challenging. Mathis and Sarah spent hours poring over the *Mishneh Torah* together; Sarah taught him some finer points of Hebrew grammar and interpretations of the many idioms in the text.

Davudoff, however, wanted nothing of it. Once, when he walked into their study session, he snorted. "Listen to yourselves, like a couple of nattering rabbis. Whatever you're reading, unless it's the books of Moses, it is a waste of time."

Mathis looked up from the document. "We're in Hungary now, *Herr* Davudoff, where people are free to believe as they like. Our deliberations are our business."

Davudoff snorted and walked off.

At other times, Mathis would practice mock saber fights with Kamil and Vadasz. On one occasion, Vadasz swept his foot in back of Mathis's ankles. He started to fall backward and threw his saber behind him, but instead of landing, did a backward handspring. After he finished, he picked up his weapon just in time to parry Vadasz's thrust.

"Where did you learn that?" the Magyar wondered, awe-struck.

Kamil laughed. "He spent time practicing with Polish Tartars. Now, he fights like one."

After two weeks and three days, a man arrived at Regec, dressed in German-style leather pants and a dark grey greatcoat. Thokoly was away at the time, so one of his officers introduced the stranger to Mathis. "*Herr* Captain, this is Franz Steiner, the man Count Thokoly spoke of."

Steiner, was of medium height, dark hair, with eyes that frequently darted in different directions. He removed a leathered glove and offered Mathis his hand, which when pressed, felt clammy. "Good to meet you, *mein Herr.* We have much to discuss."

The officer showed them to a private room, and underscored the seriousness of the occasion by posting a guard outside. "See they are not disturbed," the officer told the sentry.

Steiner motioned to two chairs behind a table. "Let us sit here and keep our voices low."

He kept his eyes glued on the entryway. "Now, as to the purpose of our meeting, for which I have traveled many miles...."

Mathis decided to get straight to the point. "You mean straight from Vienna, don't you?"

Steiner's mustache twitched. "Among other places, *ja.* I represent *Herr* Ezekiel Ludwig Vogel and Bishop Kollonitsch."

Mathis froze. He knew nothing about Vogel, but Bishop Kollonitsch had promised to excommunicate Mathis when he had intervened to save Samuel Oppenheimer's life. The bishop had only been thwarted when Brother Marco D'Aviano delayed the excommunication to induce Mathis to deliver the treasure of the Raven King. If Steiner was an associate of Kollonitsch, he must bode evil. "What do you want from me, Steiner?"

Steiner's eyes stopped moving for once, and fixed on Mathis. "Calm down, Captain. You might enjoy hearing what I have to say."

CHAPTER TWENTY-EIGHT

Regec Castle
Late December, 1684

"You're so far away from home, Captain Zieglar," Steiner mocked his predicament with fake pity. "Don't you miss your mother and home in Grinzing?"

Mathis blocked the images Steiner attempted to conjure from thin air, like a dark necromancer. "I accepted that price when I became a soldier."

"And what a soldier you were…until you deserted your regiment. How badly you must feel…estranged from the army, cut off from your people."

"I'm getting older, waiting for you to get the point, Steiner."

Steiner sat back, a slight smile peaking through his affected sympathy. "What if I could make things better for you and the *jungfrau,* Sarah Oppenheimer? Think of her sadness, leaving her family and religion behind. Shouldn't you want to help her?"

"Still getting older, Steiner."

Steiner's smile turned malicious. "Your deception is over. Simon Oppenheimer and Charles of Lorraine have told us everything. You're going to Transylvania to recover the *Mishneh Torah*. There's a code inside it pinpointing the treasure of the Raven King."

Mathis buried his face inside his hands. After a moment, he spoke between his fingers. "How did they get Simon to confess? Did they torture him?"

"No need for that. He was so filled with anger when you took his cousin away, we couldn't stop him from talking. He despises you."

Mathis let his hands slip to the table, and he hung his head. "Why have you come here, Steiner? To rub my nose in my misfortune?"

Steiner's laugh exuded menace as he reached inside a pocket and pulled out an envelope with D'Aviano's wax seal on it. He extended it to Mathis. "Here, open it."

Mathis's spine tingled with dread as he broke the seal and pulled out a sheet of paper. His forehead wrinkled in surprise. He read it silently to himself.

"Let all know that Mathis Zieglar has the emperor's pardon for all crimes related to his role in his performance at the Buda siege and finding the Mishneh Torah. He is also excused for his conduct in Vienna in 1684. He and Sarah Oppenheimer, Vadasz Bakos, Endre Bakos, Frederick Tannenberg, and Frau Lang will also have the emperor's protection if they choose to return to their former stations. This forgiveness is conditional upon Mathis Zieglar turning over the Mishneh Torah to Brother

Marco D'Aviano upon Herr Zieglar's return to Austria by the year 1685. Signed, Brother Marco D'Aviano."

Mathis gasped. "I cannot believe it."

"Hmpf." Steiner's waved his fingers nonchalantly. "Just remember, you must return the *Mishneh Torah* by next year, or the agreement is off."

"Wait a minute," Mathis growled. "Why would Count Thokoly allow you into this castle? Bishop Kollonitsch is a staunch defender of the House of Habsburg. And you are his representative."

"And *Herr* Vogel's as well."

"So how are Kollonitsch and Vogel able to work together with Thokoly?"

Steiner snorted. "Never mind. This is more complicated than you could understand."

Mathis made no effort to disguise his anger. "If you want me to cooperate, you had better make me understand."

"Some things are better left alone."

Mathis stood and tossed the letter at Steiner. "Drop dead."

Mathis started to walk away when Steiner called out, "All right, Zieglar. Come back. I'll explain."

Mathis returned, but remained standing.

"Sit down," Steiner demanded.

"I'll stand, you talk."

"All right, all right." Steiner's amiable tone sounded forced. "Just listen."

"Again. Why are Kollonitsch and Vogel in bed with Thokoly?"

"Good God, man. At least move close enough you can hear my whisper. Good, that's close enough. There are two things at work. First of all, the Count's loyalty is…shall we say…fluid at this point? He doesn't care for the Ottomans, or the Habsburgs, only what either one can do for his independence. He and the rest of Hungary say they are caught between two pagans."

Despite himself, Mathis couldn't suppress a snicker. "An apt turn of a phrase, if I ever heard one. Between the Church's worship of saints and the Turk's denial of Christ, I'd say the Hungarians describe their situation perfectly. They're caught between two pagans."

"Now, before you go Calvinist on me," Steiner waved his hand, "listen to the other factor at play here. Vogel and Kollonitsch would give their left arm to sever the emperor's dependence on Samuel Oppenheimer's financial backing. Kollonitsch hates that a Christian emperor depends on a Jew for funding his war effort, and Vogel is his best hope for replacing Oppenheimer."

Mathis paced. "You're asking me to turn the treasure of the Raven King over to D'Aviano, to save my own skin."

Steiner's eyes flitted rapidly again. "I'm saying you should surrender to the inevitable. In a few months, Generals Caprara and Schultz will invade Upper Hungary and Transylvania. You can either extract the treasure peacefully, or you can let the Imperial army rip the Torda salt mines apart."

The Torda salt mines. Yes, of course. That must be what Endre alluded to when he said "Have Vadasz lead you to the raven's nest in Kolozsvar. Then I will show you the labors of the god in the salt."

That, in turn, recapitulated the information in the note

Sarah had found in the *ferman*, "Seek ye the labors of the god? Find the nest where the Raven King's egg hatched. Then descend into the salt."

'The labors of the god' referred to panels on the palace doors depicting the twelve labors of Hercules. D'Aviano and Marsigli could have looked that part up in the book D'Aviano lent Mathis illustrating the doors. 'The salt' must mean the Torda mines. By now, D'Aviano and Marsigli had added things up, too. D'Aviano just needed Mathis to get to Transylvania, something a Habsburg soldier couldn't do—yet.

Mathis moved to the room's shutters, opened them slightly, and spied a *hajdu* removing a canvas sack off the back of a packhorse. As he shouldered his load, Mathis heard the sound of clinking coins. "Those bundles are filled with silver."

He wheeled around at Steiner. "So, now I know why Thokoly's willing to arrange this meeting. Money. What did Kollonitsch have to do to get D'Aviano to write that letter?"

Steiner shrugged. "Nothing. Their interests coincide, and they were willing to work together." He stood up. "Watch your tongue or I'll rip up D'Aviano's paper."

Mathis grabbed Steiner by the throat and pinned him against the wall. "Watch *your* tongue or I'll let the world know Vogel and Kollonitsch are sending silver to Thokoly—the man who paved the way for the Turks to lay siege to Vienna."

At that point, the sentry walked in, his saber drawn. "Let him go, now."

Mathis released Steiner and patted him on the cheek. Chuckling darkly, Mathis scooped up the letter and walked past the guard. "I'll have the *Mishneh Torah* to the emperor by year's end," he called out.

■ ■ ■

A blinding snowstorm pelted Mathis's group as they lashed their bags to their mounts outside Castle Regec. Thokoly stood on the parapet above them, and called out, "The roads hold many perils between here and Transylvania, not the least of which are Tartar raiding parties. There are also many unemployed *hajdus* along your path who have turned to banditry. I will insure the safety of your journey by having ten armed men accompany you until you reach the city of Zilah, deep in Transylvania."

"You are most kind," Mathis tipped his hat.

Thokoly's expression stiffened into granite. "Make sure you succeed in your mission, *Herr* Captain. Your lives depend on it."

Mathis realized that Thokoly must also have a stake in him finding the treasure of the Raven King, an odd proposition considering Thokoly and D'Aviano respectively represented the opposing interests of Protestants and Catholics. Once the party was out of Thokoly's earshot, Mathis took Sarah aside and shared his thoughts. "Thokoly must be trying to strike a deal with the Habsburgs by helping us find the treasure."

Sarah nodded. "*Ja*. One thing I picked up from my conversations with people in Regec Castle is that Thokoly knows the Habsburgs are on their way here, shortly. He has to try everything he can to avoid their wrath."

"Hmpf." Mathis snorted. "Even if it means double-crossing his Turkish allies."

The little band set their faces to the southeast and

253

Kolozsvar. As they progressed toward Transylvania, the snowfall stopped and the ride became easier. The mountain passes of Upper Hungary gradually surrendered to small hills and plains dotted with neat rows containing the twisted limbs of vineyards. The wind stopped howling and they took their heavier wraps off.

Near the Transylvanian border, columns of smoke spewed from a small village. Flames stretched heavenward from the homes' rooftops, and many structures had collapsed to the ground. The party rode through the destruction and came across bodies scattered on the ground, festooned with arrows. The surviving men appeared in a daze—some wandered aimlessly, others wailed uncontrollably.

Sarah turned to Mathis. "What…what happened here? Was it war?"

"In a sense, *ja.*" Mathis moaned inwardly. "Look around, Sarah. Who do you not see?"

Sarah lifted trembling fingers to her cheeks. "In the name of the Lord, Mathis. There are no women, or children."

"It's war, all right. The kind of war the Tartars wage every time they raid for slaves. They take the women and children, and leave the men."

Tears rolled down Sarah's cheeks. "My family's seen too much war in Heidelberg. But, this is even worse. It's just…*horrible.*"

The ground shook beneath their feet, and a building crumbled to the ground. A spray of sparks rose into the air in its wake. Mathis breathed heavily. "Maybe now you can understand why I've fought so hard, against my army and my emperor. So I can pull the hostages out of the hands of these Tartar monsters. Can you see why I was willing to trade something valuable for their freedom, something like the *Mishneh Torah*?"

"*Ja.*" Sarah sobbed, choking on tears.

Kamil turned in his saddle. "You Christians are no different. Your army crosses the Turkish border all the time and enslaves Mohammedans."

"That happens on occasion, *ja.*" Mathis raised an accusing finger at Kamil. "But there's a world of difference between that, and emptying entire regions like the Tartars do."

"Stop your preaching, infidel. Have you never heard of Portugal's African slave trade?"

Mathis smirked. "Oh *ja,* I know of it all too well. Do you remember why the pope allowed Christians to take slaves? To counteract the Turkish slave army that invaded Europe. He did it to protect Christendom."

Frau Lang, who had been silent since she lost her husband, now grew agitated and waved her hands. "For the love of heaven, still your tongues, the two of you. My family has lost women to slavery, also. It is wickedness, no matter who practices it." She, too, dissolved into weeping.

Sarah wiped away her own tears and rode over to *Frau* Lang and consoled her.

Several more miles down the road, Kamil nudged his pony next to Mathis's. "Perhaps the time has come to curtail this curse as much as possible. Slavery rots the guts out of my people."

Mathis studied at him. "Sarah told me about your conversations with her and Simon when you abducted them. Are you sincere about wanting to turn your people away from slavery? Toward trade?"

255

"It may cost me a great deal to oppose the way my people make their livelihood, but in the end, life will be better for everyone. What do you want me to do?"

The winter cold nipped at Mathis's fingers. He struck the palm of his hand to stimulate circulation. "Just make sure the message that we've found the treasure of the Raven King reaches the sultan's calligraphers. I'll let you know when that is."

■ ■ ■

Mathis's group rode sixteen days to reach Koloszvar, stopping only a few hours each night for rest and to replenish their supplies. Sarah never complained once about their arduous journey, and her resolve to help Mathis rescue the hostages was as strong as his.

They found the city nestled in a valley, at the base of several rolling hills of farmer's fields and vineyards. Rows of homes lay outside the older, medieval city contained within its gates, threatening to intrude on the nearby farmland.

Soldiers barred their way at the city gates. A sergeant demanded, "Who are you, and what is your business in Koloszvar?"

After giving him their names, Mathis leaned forward in his saddle. "We're here to meet a man called Endre Bakos. Do you know where we might find him?"

The sergeant gave a shrill whistle through his teeth, echoing through the arch leading to the city. A lanky figure appeared behind the soldiers. "Let them in, brothers. They've come for me."

"Endre Bakos." Mathis swung out of his saddle, made his way past the soldiers, and embraced his friend.

Endre's smile stretched across his face and he opened his arms wide. "Good to see you alive, brother."

The two patted each other on the back.

Mathis held him at arms-length. "How did you know when to greet us?"

Endre gestured to the road they had traveled. "Army tell us who comes before they arrive. Knew you would be here, soon."

The others dismounted and the soldiers let them pass. Mathis introduced each one, except for Endre's brother, Vadasz, who also embraced Endre. The man led them to a nearby inn where they stabled their horses.

Endre took Mathis aside and grinned. "Sarah look too good for wreck like you. How you convince such beautiful woman come with you?"

Mathis mock-punched him in the ribs.

"Now, the moment you wait for." Endre grandly unfurled one arm. "I take you to Nathan Mendel. He will guide to treasure of Raven King."

CHAPTER TWENTY-NINE

Inside the Torda Salt Mines
Early October, 1685

LIEUTENANT MARTIN EBNER DUSTED THE SALT DUST off his coat threatening to envelope him and turn him into a ghost. He and his group of twenty men covered their mouths and noses with damp kerchiefs, yet his nostrils dried out after only half an hour beneath the Earth's surface.

After plodding through an endless maze of winding passageways, the miner leading them stopped. He pointed at a stout door, secured by a bronze padlock. "This is the forbidden area." The Hungarian's words were translated into German by one of Ebner's assistants.

"Ask him who has the key," Ebner demanded.

"He has heard the door is opened once every five years by a Jew, who leads a group of blindfolded visitors here."

"Every five years? I doubt that anyone has survived this place long enough to know that. Tell him to give us the truth, or I'll slit his throat."

The translator scowled but conveyed the message. "He says you can ask other miners about this. It is well known among them."

"Bah." The lieutenant waved his hand toward the door. "Sapper, come forward. Blast the lock off the door."

Using linen cloths and rope, the sapper hung an explosive charge from the padlock. As he attached a long wick, Ebner led his men away.

A minute later, the charge exploded. Chunks of salt fell from the overhead dome; a saline cloud choked the air. Ebner and his men waited for the dust to settle, and then made their way back to the door. The padlock was a shard of metal, the portal sagged on weakened hinges.

Ebner pried the door open with an iron bar, taking care not to touch the smoldering ledges seared by the explosion. As the portal swung open, the lieutenant's men gasped. Before them stood two halves of a magnificent bronze door, suspended from jambs cemented into the mine walls.

Ebner walked closer, inspecting the panels. The engravings portrayed the twelve labors of Hercules. He grabbed the end of one door and cautiously swung it open. As the edge became visible, he stood paralyzed.

"*Herr* Lieutenant, are you well?" the translator asked.

Ebner turned with a harsh scowl, and screamed, "Bring me that cursed miner. Bring him now."

The translator inched backward. "What is wrong *Herr* Lieutenant?"

Ebner laid a finger on the side of a panel. "Come here. What do you see, man?"

"I…I see a compartment with an opened seam…and nothing inside."

Two soldiers jostled the miner and shoved him before Ebner. The lieutenant stabbed the hapless man in the chest with his finger. "There were documents inside this chamber. Ask him where they have gone."

The translator asked the miner the question. The man responded in desperate tones. "He says the Jew who comes here every five years changed his routine ten months ago, when he arrived with a Habsburg captain and a woman. He says he has never been in this room before and knows nothing about the documents."

"What?" The lieutenant seized the miner by the shoulders and shook him. "He's lying, again. Damned criminal."

The miner sputtered and tried to push away, but it only made Ebner shake him more violently.

"Sir, sir," the translator pleaded, raising his voice. "He says he has no reason to lie to you. He begs for his life, for your mercy."

"Bah." Ebner threw the man against a nearby salt pillar. "Let's get out of here and report to General Caprara. The emperor will want to know about this immediately."

■ ■ ■

Constanta's Farm
Early October, 1685

As Mathis and Endre walked their horses over the bridge toward the barn, Sarah and Constanta's family rushed to greet them. Mathis and Sarah embraced one another. "How were the negotiations, Mathis? Are we safe?"

"We'll know shortly. Kamil lived up to his promise and

brought the sultan's delegation here. They're a few hundred feet up the road. We should keep our eyes open at all times."

Mathis's eyes traveled up the bluff topped by the pole and the crow's nest. A few feet from the pole, ledges were recently carved on four sides of the mound. A brass cannon on each shelf gleamed in the sunlight. "Our men look ready, Constanta."

A confident smile crept across her lips. "Our men *and* women are prepared."

Mathis laughed to himself. Somehow, Constanta had convinced Michael Apafi, the Prince of Transylvania, to sell her three guns. Who would have ever thought that Tannenberg and *Frau* Lang could have given Constanta's daughters advanced lessons in the cannoneer's trade? They must be the only female battery in all of Europe. *Ja*, they were ready.

Sarah and Mathis approached, and stood in front of the cottage before the bridge

Four men walked briskly to the bridge. The leader dismounted: Kamil. One of the others wore a silk turban with an opal pinned above his forehead. With a thick Turk accent, he asked, "I have been told you speak Turk, is this true?"

Mathis nodded and gestured to the cottage. "It will be my pleasure to take you to the *Mishneh Torah*."

The man in the silk turban looked at Sarah, and back at Mathis. "It is not fitting a woman be part of this conversation."

Mathis stared at him with cold eyes. "Sarah represents the Oppenheimer family. She stays."

The door to the cottage swung open, and Nathan

261

Mendel joined them. "Hussein, the woman will do you no harm. Come inside."

The man looked flustered, his chin jutted out in determination. "No women."

Mathis whispered to Mendel. "How are we going to get around this? Besides, if he speaks Turkish, how can he decipher the code inside the *Mishneh Torah*?"

"Don't worry about that," Nathan reassured him. "He is fluent in Turkish and Hebrew, and the two men beside him are Talmudic scholars. My guess is they don't appreciate Sarah's presence, either."

Sarah touched Mathis's arm. "Let's compromise. Perhaps I can stand outside the open window and listen in."

The visitors accepted Sarah's compromise. As they filed inside the door, the man in the turban held up his hand. "I was the one who verified it last, so it shouldn't take long."

Everyone sat at Constanta's table and put on kid gloves. Nathan brought out the *Mishneh Torah* for each one to take turns inspecting it.

"Yes, yes," the turbaned man said matter-of-factly after a few minutes. "Everything's here, this is the document. We can authenticate it."

"Fine." Mathis breathed in as if a weight fell from his shoulders. "I have been to your ships and seen the twenty-seven hundred hostages. Now we can discuss exchanging the document for our people."

"Come quickly, Mathis," Sarah called through the window. "There's treachery out here."

Nathan and Mathis both stood, the latter scooping up the *Mishneh Torah*. They ran out the door. Kamil greeted them, holding up his hands. "I had nothing to do with this, nothing."

Spahis thundered through the forest on their horses, headed straight for the bridge.

"Come quickly." Constanta waved Sarah, Mathis, and Nathan over to the span. As soon as they made it across, Constanta lit two wicks that protruded out of the supporting beams on the far side.

Two *spahis* cantered onto the bridge as the beams exploded. The bridge tumbled down in a vicious roar. Screams rose from the moat as one of the riders impaled upon the spikes.

The other made it over the span, and headed toward Constanta. She reached for a flask hanging from her apron's sash, and tossed it in front of the rider. A burst of flame erupted, and threw him off his horse. He didn't get up again.

"Quickly, to the hill," Constanta urged. Arrows whooshed past them as Mathis and his friends ran to the mound where the cannons sat.

"Mother," a man in the crow's nest called out. "The Mohammedans are surrounding us."

Mathis' heart dropped. Over a hundred men from all directions neared the edge of the moat. Instinctively, he pulled his wheel-locks out of his boots.

"Save those for another time." Constanta called. "You won't need them, today."

She covered her ears and yelled out, "Cover your ears, everyone." Then she turned to the ones manning the cannons. "Prepare to fire."

"Guns are ready."

"Fire the wick."

"Cannon is lit."

The guns belched flame and acrid smoke. The balls

exploded on four sides of the moat. Black billows blotted out the sun, and shrieks of agony wailed from all directions.

"Take this." Constanta handed cloths to Mathis and Sarah. They put the linen over their noses.

Long minutes passed before the haze receded enough for Mathis to see the results. Thirty feet back from the moat was on fire and the grass singed up to the trench. Piles of smoking bodies littered the ground, the ugly stench of burning flesh infiltrating the air.

■ ■ ■

Two days later, the man in the silk turban returned and called across the moat. "We are here to discuss arrangements to transport the hostages to Vienna."

"No doubt you are," Mathis snapped. "And I am prepared to prevent a repeat of your deceit."

The man bowed his head. "How can we assure you of our good intentions?"

"You will ship the hostages to Habsburg territory, and allow our people on board to send messages back to us as soon as they have arrived safely. Only then will you be given the *Mishneh Torah,* at this location."

"That will be arranged." The Mohammedan appeared chastened. "Anything else?"

"Your expedition is headed by an *aga*, is it not?"

"Indeed. *Aga* Ali Arslan is our commander."

Mathis smirked. "Then he will be my honored guest aboard the lead ship. I will insure his safety as long as you comply with my terms."

"All this shall be done."

Mathis scowled. "One thing more."

"Yes?"

"You will deliver two hundred pieces of silver to the woman named Constanta, for all the damages your people have done to her farm."

The man looked as though he sucked on a bitter pepper. "Agreed."

EPILOGUE

Mathis's ancestral home of Grinzing, Austria
Early November, 1685

MATHIS AND SARAH LED THE HUGE CROWD OF women and children from the banks of the Danube, where the ships unloaded, all the way to the Vienna woods, the Wienerwald. As the sea of humanity plodded up the mountainside, men poured out of the villages to reunite with their loved ones. They embraced the women and children midst a roiling cacophony of tears and joy.

Mathis's mother and his Uncle Christoph ran down the mountainside as fast as their aged legs could carry them. She reached Mathis first and kissed him repeatedly on the cheek, while Christoph wrapped his arms around them both.

Finally, the column stopped at the outskirts of Grinzing, where Father Lebsafft, the commander of the nearby fortress of Klosterneuberg greeted Mathis. The priest climbed a boulder and lifted his voice for the masses to hear.

"Welcome home, Mathis Zieglar. I knew God would watch over you, no matter how impossible the task. But, with God, all things are possible."

The crowd roared its approval. "Mathis. Mathis. Mathis Zieglar!"

The chanting and celebration continued until Sarah desperately tugged on his sleeve. She pointed to a section of the crowd, parting for a hooded man on a black stallion and a dozen *cuirassiers*. When the man spoke, Mathis's blood ran cold. The voice belonged to Marco D'Aviano. "Mathis Zieglar, unless you can produce the *Mishneh Torah*, you will come with us."

This was the moment of truth. He had found the treasure and returned the hostages, but would he survive the Church's wrath?

He recovered his composure and turned to Sarah. "Let's give the brother what he wants, shall we?"

Sarah smiled nervously, reached inside her satchel, and pulled out the book Mathis had retrieved from the Buda palace. "Here you are, Brother."

D'Aviano raised his hand. "You must come with us. I am unable to validate its origin without my reading glasses."

The crowd grew restive with the discussion. A few jeered the friar.

Lebsafft extended his hand. "Here. I have spectacles, and can read Hebrew."

The priest put on his reading glasses, and read the beginning pages to himself. "Hmmm, *ja*, this is a very old copy of the *Mishneh Torah*."

D'Aviano's agitation boiled over. "Is it signed by Maimonides? Are there lines of new text over the original inscriptions?"

"Come on." The crowd surged forward, ready to storm the *cuirassiers*. "Let Zieglar go."

"Hmm," Lebsafft mused. "No, not in this edition."

D'Aviano raised an authoritative finger. "Then in the name of the Holy Church and the Inquisition, I demand that Mathis Zieglar submit to the men that accompany me."

"No! No!" The crowd chanted. "Let him go! Let him go!"

Mathis climbed up on the rock beside Lebsafft, and raised his hand for silence. The chanting slowly ceased. Mathis reached inside his pocket and handed a paper to Lebsafft. "Father, will you read this document, please?"

In a clear and commanding voice, the priest thundered out the words.

"Let all know that Mathis Zieglar has the emperor's pardon for all crimes related to his role in his performance at the Buda siege and finding the Mishneh Torah. He is also excused for his conduct in Vienna in 1684. He and Sarah Oppenheimer, Vadasz Bakos, Endre Bakos, Frederick Tannenberg, and Frau Lang will also have the emperor's protection if they choose to return to their former stations. This forgiveness is conditional upon Mathis Zieglar turning over the Mishneh Torah to Brother Marco D'Aviano upon Herr Zieglar's return to Austria in 1685. Signed, Brother Marco D'Aviano."

Mathis lifted his head. "Now, Father, as you understand this contract, have I fulfilled my end of the bargain?"

The priest looked down and mumbled. "There's nothing there about a *Mishneh Torah* signed by Maimonides. Nothing about newer text over old."

He straightened his back and raised his voice. "*Ja*, Mathis Zieglar, you have carried out your end of the contract. You have legally secured the emperor's pardon."

The crowd cheered and shouted in unison. "Mathis. Mathis. Mathis Zieglar!"

D'Aviano spat and turned his horse around. He and the *cuirassiers* disappeared down the mountainside.

■ ■ ■

That night, the crowds celebrated in the streets, dancing and eating. Between all the festivities, Sarah and Mathis stole back to the ship that had carried them to the base of Wienerwald. Mathis took turns hugging Tannenberg and Vadasz goodbye. "Now, you two can return to your regiments with the emperor's blessing."

"You will always be my brother," Tannenberg half-wept as he lifted Mathis up in a bear hug one last time. "Always."

"Please give my love to Endre when you return to Transylvania," Vadasz said softly.

The two soldiers disembarked from the ship as Sarah embraced *Frau* Lang. "Now you can return to your family."

"But you...." *Frau* Lang sniffed. "How can you leave your people behind?"

Sarah embraced her ever more tightly. "I will be fine. I'm going to be with Mathis Zieglar. That is all I need."

After everyone left the ship, Mathis took Sarah into his arms and kissed her. "You don't know how much I love you for giving up the *Mishneh Torah*. You made an incredible sacrifice."

Sarah frowned. He caressed her cheek, consoling her.

Until she smiled. "Mathis, did you ever see D'Aviano take the *Mishneh Torah*?"

269

"Well…" He stopped and tried to remember. "No…."

"Do you think Father Lebsafft had a reason to keep it?"

Mathis lifted a curious brow. "I can't say he would."

Sarah opened her satchel. "Look inside, my love."

"Oww." He groaned. "You have it after all."

"I don't let go of things I love. That's why I agreed to go back to Transylvania with you. So no one could forbid me to have you as my husband."

Mathis caressed the back of Sarah's hand, holding it like a precious jewel, and kissed it. "Here's to keeping the people we love close to us."

VIENNA'S LAST JIHAD

CHAPTER ONE

June 20, 1683

MATHIS ZIEGLAR PACED BETWEEN THE LIMESTONE pillar and the shaded side of the lecture hall, clasping and releasing his hands as he strode back and forth. A summons from the Jesuits meant they were going to either honor or threaten him.

He paused a moment to gaze over the vibrant orange tiles of Vienna's rooftops. Beneath them, laughter floated upward from young men leaving class. Despite the peacefulness of the scene, his stomach knotted. Instead of holding this senseless meeting, the priests should busy themselves by pulling the students aside and warning them that the largest Muslim army in eighty-seven years was marching toward the Holy Roman Empire.

A latch at the far end of the colonnade clicked and a door opened to reveal a black robed Jesuit. The hem of his garment hung so close to the floor that Mathis couldn't see the man's feet. The figure seemed to float toward him like a flashing ghost, appearing dark and bright as it passed through shade and sunlight.

Does he bring me ill or welcome news? Mathis asked

himself, squinting to make sure he had the right man. "*Grüss Gott*, Reverend Father Schneidermann."

"And to you," the priest replied, licking his lips nervously. "The council is ready, Doctor Zieglar."

Mathis followed his escort into a room filled by four men sitting on each side of a cherry table. The rector of the College of the Jesuits, Father Sistini, rose to his feet at the far end, followed by the others. His eyes glowed like a blacksmith's forge above expressionless, sphinx-like lips.

"The peace of Christ be upon you," Sistini said, his greeting echoed by the others.

Mathis nodded. "The peace of Christ be upon you."

They all sat. Mathis took the chair at the end facing the rector. The men on Mathis' left were dressed in dark secular academic gowns. Those on his right wore narrow white cloths draped over black cassocks; the stoles were emblazoned at the bottom with a solar disk containing IHS—the Jesuit emblem. He pressed his fingernails into his palms. Some he knew were friends, others were strangers.

Sistini cleared his throat. "The purpose of this meeting is to review your progress toward tenure, Doctor Zieglar, and to see if you should continue another year. There is no denying your accomplishments. At age nineteen, you mastered the requirements for a professorship. These are things rarely achieved by one so young."

Once again, Mathis nodded. "Thank you."

A faint smile crept over the rector's lips. "We are pleased to tentatively endorse your appointment to the School of Oriental Languages and Koranic Law. All that remains is for us to determine the correctness of your spiritual beliefs. After all, if the ability to teach Turkish were the only qualification, we would hire a Mohammedan."

A ripple of menacing laughter on the clerical side of the table tightened Mathis' chest. What kind of meeting was this?

The rector continued. "We must be sure you are a son of the church. Do you consider yourself a son of the church, Mathis Zieglar?"

"I do. I do indeed."

"Good. Not all of our professors here are priests, but we look with favor upon those who have taken the vows. Are you called to this vocation?"

Mathis thought of Magda, the sable haired beauty who waited for him outside, anxious to know the outcome of the meeting. He could never deny himself the soft contours of her hips and breasts, the sweetness of her mouth. He would sooner fall on his dagger than sever the psychic bond between them. "When there's a snow storm in hell," he muttered beneath his breath.

"What was that, Doctor Zieglar?"

Mathis cleared his throat. "I am flattered the Society of Jesus would consider me a candidate for their order. But I will best serve the Lord as a married man."

A priest with bushy eyebrows and a sallow complexion crouched forward and shot him a sour look. "Doctor Zieglar imagines himself a son of the church, yet he ignores the examples of our Lord and St. Paul."

"By no means," Mathis said with a pained smile. "I simply prefer to follow St. Joseph and St. Stephen, both of them married men. And I am inspired by your example, Father Bauer. *You* have never let your vows of chastity prevent *you* from ministering to the women of the church."

The secular professors winked and snickered at one another.

Bauer smacked the table with both palms and rose, "How dare you imply I . . ."

Sistini cleared his throat loudly again. "That's enough. Doctor Zieglar. We all know your talent for debate. Do not make another comment like that.

"Let us return to our original question. You say you are a son of the church. A son of the church reveres the Holy Father in Rome and repudiates heresy. Will you therefore renounce Copernicus' teachings about the earth revolving around the sun?"

Warning bells clanged in Mathis' head. He didn't expect this challenge. "I agree with Giovanni Cassini and the Jesuits who assist him at San Petronio. They've studied the planets long enough to know the truth about Copernicus."

Sistini's face flushed. "That's an evasion. Give us your reaction to the book of Joshua, young doctor." He picked up a Bible and read, "'And the sun stood still, and the moon stayed until the nation took vengeance on their enemies . . . Joshua 10:13.' The Word of God says it was the *sun* that stood still, not the earth. Dare you contradict the Pope and teach heresy?"

Mathis' pulse raced. He had debated the subject in a university exercise and saw no reason to repudiate the stand he had taken and been judged the champion. "If the esteemed rector wishes to take this scripture literally, perhaps he understands Jesus the same way. He said 'I am the vine, you are the branches.' I doubt, however, that Christians have become actual twigs *or* that the sun moves around the earth."

Sistini squirmed in his chair and Mathis continued. "If the Jesuits in San Petronio are busy proving Copernicus' ideas, how can you condemn me for refusing to denounce him?" *Let the Reverend Father get himself off the hook on that one.*

"Condemn heresy or be party to it," Sistini bellowed.

One of the secular professors to his left, a giant of a man named Tannenberg who wore a bristling beard, lifted his eyebrows. "No matter what his private beliefs are, Doctor Zieglar has avoided criticizing the church. We shouldn't censure him for that."

"The Pope speaks for God and says that the sun revolves around the earth!" Sistini said. "Doctor Zieglar's implications are blasphemy. Before I conclude this hearing, does he wish to change any of his statements?"

Mathis shot to his feet, shaking with rage. "When I was hired at this university, Reverend Father, you told me to expose my students to the world of ideas. Jesus and Socrates used ideas to spread their message, not the mailed fist of an Inquisition. You should follow their example and open your mind so that God can fill it. The Scriptures say 'Come, let us reason together.' Think about that before you repeat the Jesuit motto *Ad maiorem Dei gloriam.* Only then will you act for the greater glory of God."

Cries of "Aye! Aye!" rose from the left side of the table; angry murmurs rippled along the right.

Sistini tensed. "Listen to me, young doctor. Listen to me well. We will meet here next week and decide your fate. Recant your ideas and embrace the church. Otherwise, we will try you for heresy."

With that, Sistini and all of the men in the hall rose. Schneidemann walked to the door in front of Mathis and opened it.

"The peace of Christ be with you," Sistini murmured half- heartedly, looking down as he departed.

Mathis trudged down the walkway, heaving angry breaths. He found his way out into the street where Magda stood, her shining black tresses flowing in the wind that wrapped her slate blue skirt around sculpted hips. Her almond-shaped eyes lit with anticipation. His cousin, Alfred Zieglar stood beside her, dressed in the pearl gray overcoat becoming popular with the Habsburg army. Their gaze intensified as he drew close.

"Mathis, is everything all right?" Magda asked.

She would insist on the truth. Magda understood him like no one else. Her face sagged in sorrow as he discussed Sistini's impossible demands. "I had no idea the Jesuits were so intent on forcing the secular professors out of the university. Why didn't they make that clear before I slaved like an ox to win that chair? God only knows the sacrifices I made."

"Because they thought they could turn you into one of them!" a voice thundered behind him. It was Tannenberg, the professor who had spoken in his defense. He laid an arm across Mathis' back and squeezed. "But you decided to be a man, instead. And you tied that pretentious rector in knots."

"What will we do now?" Magda sniffed as tears trickled down flush cheeks. "Papa will never consent to our wedding unless you're employed. Why can't you bite your tongue for once instead of proving yourself right? You always have to win."

His heart sank. He had never imagined he could be at fault. Mathis expected Magda to support him against the hypocrites. But now, she wept in disappointment.

"This isn't so bad," Alfred sang out with an optimistic lilt. "The army can use a man of your talents. As a matter of fact, I talked to a *feldwebel* just this afternoon. The Duke of Lorraine put out a call for anyone who knows how to speak Turk or Tartar, offering them a position. You know those languages, don't you?"

Mathis would have to look up the sergeant Alfred referred to.

"No one at the university speaks Turk better," Tannenberg boomed.

"No, Mathis!" Magda said, her eyes growing wide. "I don't want you to run off fighting the Turks. I need you here."

"Darling," he took her hands in his. "We don't have a choice. It's that or the Inquisition."

Magda shook loose from his grasp. "What kind of future will I have with a husband who risks his life for a living? You can't join the army and have a family. Don't do this, Mathis."

Mathis looked her in the eye and set his jaw. "No, Magda.

A man can do both."

■ ■ ■

Two days later, Mathis found himself inside a tent pulling off his overcoat and rolling back his sleeves. It was one of many temporary shelters pitched in the border area of Deutsch- Jahrndorf. A strong gust swept under the walls and stretched them as far as they could expand, scattering papers off a table. As the wind intensified, the ropes securing the canvas groaned. Mathis gripped the back of the chair in front of him. This was his arena, where he would face his opponent. Would he prove his worth, or fail and be sent home?

A soldier pulled back the door flaps. A gaunt, mustached captain dressed in a red great coat with black cuffs stepped inside.

Mathis saluted and clicked his heels. "*Hauptmann* Hauser." Hauser nodded. "This is the last step, Zieglar. I don't know why the duke gave someone so inexperienced a chance at this. Remember, you're under contract and not a soldier. If you fail, we can dismiss you at any time. Yank the information out of the prisoner, or we'll torture him. The Turks are breathing down our necks and we have to know their intentions. Let's see how good you are."

Two soldiers wrestled a threatening, cursing Tartar through the entrance and attempted to tie him to a chair. "Stay put and shut up!" said one, smacking him across the mouth. But the prisoner continued to grab at the ropes until they hit him enough times that he slumped in his seat. Sunlight penetrated the dim space and revealed his solid, muscular features. A reverse U-shaped mustache framed his clean cut chin. Mathis sat down and faced him.

Another Tartar, he thought as an instinctive fury welled up. *A monster who lines his pocket by dragging women and children off in chains. Most of whom die before they reach the slave market. We'll see how powerful his tongue is.*

The Tartar revived and rocked his chair. The longer he struggled, the hotter Mathis' face glowed. He fought against the urge to take one of the ropes and wrap it around the warrior's neck. "*Ghazi*! You say you'll kill these men when your friends attack. When do you plan on doing this?"

The prisoner stilled, apparently stunned. Then his face twisted in contempt. "Christians use boys to question captives? How do you know Tartar?"

Mathis was not surprised at the comment; his boyish

face and lithe frame belied the steeled biceps beneath his tunic, the results of being raised on a farm. He turned to the captain beside him and translated the prisoner's words. After he finished, the officer nodded to one of the soldiers who wrapped a small chain around the Tartar's mouth, drawing it tight across his teeth and squeezing his neck. The captive grunted in agony. It brought Mathis out of his anger and back to himself. *I need to get him on my side.*

"I don't like this type of questioning," Mathis said slowly and deliberately, "because I want to speak to you, man to man. Talk to me so I don't have to turn you over to these men. Once again, when will your friends attack us?"

Mathis motioned and the soldier relaxed the chain. The Tartar growled, "Answer my question, first. Tell me how you learned my language."

After the translation, the captain nodded to the soldiers to resume applying pressure, but Mathis stopped them with a raised hand. "It's all right, *Hauptmann*, this'll help the interrogation."

Mathis turned to the prisoner. "My father served in the army several years ago and brought a Tartar girl home as a slave. Her name was Aglinur, the daughter of Ali, but we call her Mary. She taught me the language."

"Then you were taught by a traitor and a whore."

"On the contrary, she's a member of our household and treated with great kindness. It can go the same way for you. Start by telling me your name."

The captive eyed Mathis suspiciously for a long moment. His eyes darted to the men surrounding him. Finally, he huffed out a breath. "Feth. My name is Feth. I am the son of Galim."

Mathis smiled. "Galim? Your father was considered

wise by his tribe?"

"Yes. He was a village elder."

"Feth, what would your father tell you if he were here? What would he say about your friends, the Turks? They send you into enemy territory in front of their army and expect you to risk your neck, just so they can move in and pocket the loot. Then they show their gratitude by calling you a savage."

The Tartar twitched angrily at mention of 'savage.'

"Feth, we know your army is close to Györ, where we captured you. How many horsemen do the Tartars have?"

Feth's lips pouted in scorn. "Christians are as ignorant as pigs. You only know where we've been after we set your villages on fire. We'll turn you into a land of slaves. Whatever's left we'll toss to the Hungarians."

"How many Tartar horsemen will ride against the imperial army, Feth?" Mathis pressed. But the Tartar clamped his jaws shut.

"Feth, you don't owe the Turks anything. What do the Tartars get for the blood they shed? Half your people go into debt to afford a horse or sword. The Turks overthrow your khan whenever they please. Answer me and you'll get food and water."

Feth's jaw relaxed. "We have enough men to annihilate you."

"Do you Feth? Then your people will have to stop hiding behind the Ottomans and stand up to us on your own. You don't have enough men to do that."

"Stand on our own? We outnumber you by ourselves, infidel."

"With what?" Mathis shrugged. "Ten, maybe fifteen-thousand men?"

Feth's eyes blazed. "With *forty thousand*."

Mathis decided not to translate the information immediately, lest Hauser smile with satisfaction and alert Feth that Mathis was gaining the upper hand.

"Ah, I see. Your numbers are considerable. How many Turks are backing you up?"

"Are you so blind you can't count on your own? Ninety thousand Turks will follow us and pick up the pieces. You'll be lucky if we leave the squirrels behind."

The questioning had reached the critical point. Mathis paused and spoke in a near whisper.

"Feth, are the Turks going to stop at Győr, or will they attack Vienna?"

The Tartar smirked. "*Allah* only knows. The decision is up to the grand *vizier*."

Mathis ground his teeth in determination. He was not going to let Feth deflect his question. It was time to take a different approach.

"Feth, your people refer to Vienna as 'the Golden Apple', do they not?"

The warrior snorted.

"When does your leader promise to take his men home?" "October, perhaps."

"After you have enjoyed eating the apples from our mountains?"

Feth raised his brows at the question. "If we can stand the fruit in this wretched area."

Mathis rose to his feet, raised his voice, and switched from a questioner into an accuser. "My father killed scores of your brothers at St. Gotthard! Do you know what he says about you people? You're brave on horseback, but cowards on foot. You'd rather shoot arrows from a distance than go

281

man to man with a Christian."

Mathis' new approach shook Feth. "What . . . ?" he sputtered.

"You know what my people call the Tartars, Feth? 'Renner und Brenner.' That's right, runners and burners! You burn villages full of women and children, but flee like jackals in front of real soldiers! You may eat apples, my friend, but you will never be *man* enough to taste the *Golden Apple!*"

The Tartar strained against his ropes and lifted the chair off the ground. "Scum of Satan!" he screamed. "Make your taunts four weeks from now when we pull Vienna's walls down. I'll tie your mother in chains and screw her myself. We will see who the real men are then. We will see!"

Mathis grinned triumphantly as he translated the information to the officer, speaking loudly over Feth's rants. *I've won the tournament. The hours I spent practicing argumentation have finally proven useful.*

As a sentry threw a hammerlock around the Tartar, Mathis realized there was another piece of vital information he needed. "Calm down, Feth, if you want things to go easier for you," he said in a soothing voice. "Just tell me how many Turks are staying at Györ and how many will attack Vienna."

When the guard relaxed his grip to let Feth speak, the left side of the Tartar's cheeks trembled and drooped, the end of his mouth sagged and his speech garbled incoherently. Sweat poured down his forehead.

As Mathis leaned forward for a closer look, Hauser put a restraining hand on his chest. "Let him go, he's going into apoplexy. We have to get this to the duke right away. Good work, lad. You've proven yourself an interrogator."

The two strode to the tent of Charles, Duke of Lorraine and commander of the imperial army. Grim-faced guards met them at the entrance, barring their way. One of them asked their business, then announced in a loud voice "Captain Hauser and his assistant are here to report on the interrogation of the prisoner."

"Send them in," came the reply.

Mathis and the captain entered to face three men in pearl gray uniforms hovering over a map spread across a table. A cuirass's blackened armored plates hung on a nearby stand, ready to wear. An officer in the middle of the three had a high forehead and narrow face with an aquiline nose. His cheeks were pitted from smallpox and a frayed wig draped over the back of his neck. Mathis instinctively recognized the all-too- familiar lines creasing his face from melancholia: this was the duke.

"Your recommendation was sound, Your Excellency," Hauser said. "This young man has a talent for questioning prisoners."

The duke smiled knowingly. "Like father, like son."

Mathis gave his report of the interrogation and summarized, "If Your Excellency would indulge me, I believe the Turks intend to wage holy war, *jihad*, against our capitol. If Vienna doesn't surrender, they'll slaughter the population."

Charles' brows knit in concern. "All this time the Turks made it look like they were going to besiege the fortress at Györ, but their real objective was Vienna. The emperor must know as soon as possible, Europe is at stake."

Duke Charles ordered Mathis and a dragoon to ride as soon as possible and carry the message to Vienna. Mathis packed quickly and strode into the stable, bags and supplies bundled in his arms. "Prepare my horse," he ordered a stable boy.

The attendant jumped up repeatedly in a vain attempt to snag horse's reins dangling from a rafter. Mathis threw a saddle over a horse and knotted his leather scabbard on his sash.

The boy turned his gaze to Mathis. "Why do you have the shape of a coil etched into your sheathe, Doctor Zieglar?"

Mathis was about to brush him off when he saw the youngster's bruised cheekbone and bleeding lip. Mathis backed up a few steps, sprang forward, making a complete turn in midair, grabbed the reins from the rafter, and landed on his feet.

The boy's jaw dropped. "*Mein Gott!*"

Mathis looked him over, noting his long and sturdy legs.

He has potential.

"Do you know what a mainspring is, young man?"

"Some kind of coil inside a watch?"

"*Ja.* After you twist the mainspring, the coil unwinds and powers the watch. You can use the same motion to defend yourself, if you practice."

"How do you do that, sir?"

Mathis chuckled. "I used to take bets when I was your age. No one thought I could knock apples off the higher branches without a ladder. All I needed was a stick and a running start to put a few *pfennige* in my pocket. Later on, I learned how to turn around in mid-air. A watchmaker called me *Hauptfeder* because he said I moved like an uncoiling mainspring. As I grew older, I used the move to surprise bullies and knock them on their ass. "

"Older boys picked on you, too?"

"*Ja*. Come with me a moment." Mathis walked his horse out of the barn and stopped before a fence.

"There. Do you see that corral, boy?" "Yes, sir."

"Build a ramp and practice jumping over it twenty times a day until you can do it without the ramp. Can you do that?"

"I would do anything to help myself, sir."

"After this, learn to spin in midair as you swing a stick. Remember, the motion comes from the shoulders and the hips. When you learn to jump, twist and strike, you will never fear anyone."

"Anyone, sir?"

"Anyone. Remember, the only thing a lout respects is someone who never backs down. Never cower before a bully."

The young boy saluted Mathis as if he were an officer, not realizing he was a civilian interpreter. Mathis joined the dragoon and galloped away from the stable, his laughter over the boy's innocence rose over the pounding of the horse's hooves. But once out on the trail, Mathis' mood changed to iron determination and he urged his horse relentlessly. There were only two hours of daylight left after which he faced another day or two of travel time to Vienna, depending on the weather.

Mathis had another reason for making the most of what was left of the afternoon. He knew when he awoke, a mental fog frequently struck in the morning. Mathis described it as "the darkness that can be felt," after hearing a sermon from Exodus 10:21: "And the LORD said unto Moses, stretch out thine hand toward heaven, that there may be darkness over the land of Egypt, even darkness which may be felt." During those times, he lost his razor sharp perceptions and was distracted by every noise around him. A hot, scorching darkness clouded his thoughts.

Thank God I only have to ride and not deal with something complex. He wondered how he had made it through the university's morning lectures and what he had done to deserve this plague.

The two rode only an hour when the dragoon's stallion stumbled forward and threw the man off. Mathis reined in his horse and dismounted. He walked over to the rider, who slowly forced himself into a sitting position, clutching his left shoulder.

"Are you injured?"

The dragoon nodded. "He must have stepped into a rodent hole." He turned to his horse, who thrashed in agony, unable to stand. "You had better go on by yourself. I'll manage."

Mathis reluctantly agreed. He didn't like leaving an injured man alone, but his mission was too important to delay. Remounting, he rode until nightfall. He made camp beneath a fir tree part way up a hillside, using the remaining rays of twilight to blacken his leather riding boots before munching hardtack. "At least I will enjoy a good night's sleep," he muttered as he felt the soft bed of needles beneath his blanket.

A shaft of light from the rising sun woke him the next morning. The vision repeated itself as it did so many mornings. First, the scent of a surrounding hayloft lodged in his nostrils. He struggled to move, paralyzed by the screams of women below. He couldn't bottle the rage that boiled inside, or the scorching, dark despair that followed. Despite the cool air enveloping him, he fought to overcome his lethargy and stripped off his coat and stuffed it in his saddlebag.

Mathis fumbled through his belongings and pulled out bread and cheese for breakfast. He groggily saddled his horse and rode northwest toward Vienna, fighting to keep his eyes open. The Danube River next to the trail cast a thick dome of fog over him, limiting his vision to a few meters. The horse's hooves sank into the soft ground. He drew in the heavy air with short gasps; it was as if a blanket smothered his mouth. He had to stop a moment to keep the earth from reeling. "Push on." Mathis chanted between heavy breaths, "Vienna depends on you." He grabbed his ear and twisted until it hurt, forcing himself to concentrate. "Push on. Vienna depends on you!" He shouted again. He dug his fingernails into the reins, then urged the horse forward. "Vienna depends on you."

He lifted his drooping lids minutes later when his mount stepped faster. The trail rose higher as the ground firmed and the mist thinned. He rode for an hour until the sun burned away the overcast and revealed hills coated in green. A slight breeze wafted the scent of damp meadows into his nostrils.

Hoofbeats from behind made Mathis turn in his saddle. Two Tartars bore down, one fitting an arrow to his bow. "Damn!" he shouted, spurring his horse as he crouched as close to the animal's neck as possible. "I thought this morning would be simple."

They sped away from the river. Mathis wanted to avoid getting stuck in another patch of marshy land. He spotted a thicket to the northeast and headed for it, hoping to find cover. The Tartars fanned out, one to the left, one to the right.

An arrow sank into the back of his saddle as Mathis reached the edge of the grove. He tapped the infantry sword at his side for reassurance, but feared it would be a poor match for his enemy's shafts. Terror shot through him. "What the hell can I do?"

Mathis dashed a hundred yards into the trees, wheeled around and doubled back out of the woods the way he came. That lost his pursuers until they saw him and resumed the chase, though at a greater distance. He had to put more space between himself and them.

The Tartars gained on him just as he spotted blackberry bushes beside a stream. His horse whinnied as he circled the growth. Mathis found what he was looking for just as the Tartars closed in. *This animal path leading into the berries might bring me friends.*

His horse's nostrils flared and the animal reared as Mathis dismounted. It bolted before he could pull his coat from his saddlebag. The only protection against the bush's thorns in front of him was the shirt on his back and his brimmed hat. There was no time to hesitate. He got down on all fours and scampered into the blackberries like a hound.

Mathis pulled his hat low to protect his eyes. Spikes tore into his back. The Tartars called out to one another as they circled the bushes, trying to find him.

"Let's smoke him out!" one yelled.

This doesn't make sense, why are they going to all this trouble? He decided to appeal to their greed. "Look you two, if it's money you want, I can throw you my coin bag," he said, keeping low.

"We don't want your silver, little Zeegar," one mocked him, mispronouncing his last name. "You're worth more dead than alive."

Mathis was thunderstruck. They knew him!

"Captain Tyrek has a price on your head, Christian," the other Tartar crowed. "You won't live to see Vienna."

Someone has informed on me.

The raiders ignited the dry bush that crackled in the heat. Mathis crawled deeper into the thorns as sweat poured down his forehead from the rising temperature, but the smoke followed and choked him. He stopped after a minute, his flesh throbbing from the barbs. Salty tears stung his cheeks.

"When we catch you, you'll sprout arrows like a hedgehog sprouts quills," a tormentor called. "You'll see what happens when–"

The taunt was interrupted by a bear's ear-splitting roar. A horse whinnied in agony; the Tartars screamed. Mathis took his sword and hacked the bush away. He rose to his feet for a look.

Two bears bit into one of the Tartar's mounts, blood spurted over their fur.

Mathis saw his opportunity and cut his way out of the tangle until he reached a meadow on the far side of the fracas. The terrified noises intensified as the raiders fought for their lives and their horses.

"My guess was right." Mathis muttered, shaking like a leaf, "An upset horse and a path into a blackberry patch means bears are nearby. What an insane way to make a living! Magda is right. I must be dreaming to think I can have a family and a military career."

He said a prayer of thanks. The rush of excitement had cleared his 'darkness'. Though the immediate danger was over, his goal was farther away than ever. He had lost valuable time and his horse, could he get to Vienna in time to warn the defenders?

ABOUT THE AUTHOR

Novelist, C. Wayne Dawson, writes for The Williamson County Sun and has written for History Magazine, Focus On Georgetown, and SAFVIC Law Enforcement Newsletter.

In 2012, he founded Central Texas Authors, a collaborative literary group.

He was an Adjunct Professor of History for ten years at Mt. San Antonio College where he created the Chautauqua program. There, he enlisted scholars, government officials and activists to discuss and debate social policy before the student body and the media.

In 2009, the students of Phi Theta Kappa Honor Society honored him with the Glaux Mentor Teacher Award for bringing the Chautauqua program to Mt. SAC.

He currently lives in Georgetown, TX with his wife and two dogs.

Website:www.cwaynedawson.com
Facebook: www.facebook.com/CWayneDawson
Twitter: www.twitter.com/CWayneDawson
Email: zgeist7@gmail.com

Books by C. Wayne Dawson

Treasure of the Raven King Series:

Vienna's Last Jihad (Prequel)
The Darkness That Could Be Felt (Book I)
Caught Between Two Pagans (Book II)